THE PROTÉGÉE

THE PROTÉGÉE

ERICA RIDLEY

DELACORTE PRESS

Delacorte Press
An imprint of Random House Children's Books
A division of Penguin Random House LLC
1745 Broadway, New York, NY 10019
penguinrandomhouse.com
GetUnderlined.com

Text copyright © 2025 by Erica Ridley
Jacket art copyright © 2025 by Colin Verdi
Interior frontispiece art copyright © 2025 by Colin Verdi
Interior fleur-de-lis pattern and sewing notions art used under license by stock.adobe.com

Penguin Random House values and supports copyright. Copyright fuels creativity, encourages diverse voices, promotes free speech, and creates a vibrant culture. Thank you for buying an authorized edition of this book and for complying with copyright laws by not reproducing, scanning, or distributing any part of it in any form without permission. You are supporting writers and allowing Penguin Random House to continue to publish books for every reader. Please note that no part of this book may be used or reproduced in any manner for the purpose of training artificial intelligence technologies or systems.

Delacorte Press is a registered trademark and the colophon is a trademark of Penguin Random House LLC.

Editor: Bria Ragin
Cover Designer: Trisha Previte
Interior Designer: Cathy Bobak
Copy Editor: Colleen Fellingham
Managing Editor: Tamar Schwartz
Production Manager: Tracy Heydweiller

Library of Congress Cataloging-in-Publication Data is available upon request.
ISBN 978-0-593-89766-9 (hardcover) — ISBN 978-0-593-89796-6 (lib. bdg.) —
ISBN 978-0-593-89768-3 (ebook)

The text of this book is set in 11.3-point Warnock Pro Light.

Manufactured in the United States of America
10 9 8 7 6 5 4 3 2 1

The authorized representative in the EU for product safety and compliance is Penguin Random House Ireland, Morrison Chambers, 32 Nassau Street, Dublin D02 YH68, Ireland, https://eu-contact.penguin.ie.

Random House Children's Books supports the First Amendment and celebrates the right to read.

For Frank Stout,
who would have been so proud

who control our industries control the entire country. Every item members of the upper classes purchase depends on the continued operation of our dense, dangerous, blood-and-sweat-drenched factories, mills, and mines.

And every crumb on the chipped plates of the lower classes likewise depends on at least one family member toiling for the industrialists—and surviving long enough to bring home a meager coin.

After the last revolution here in France, it is no longer the blue of your blood or the shade of your skin that determines your worth, but rather the size of your pocketbook and the reach of your gold.

This is how Monsieur Fournier and his confederacy can control our nation, though they claim not a single noble title among them. Money determines power. The kingdom is in new hands. Hands that won't lift a finger to aid the lower classes. Not when they can be exploited to generate even more wealth for the industrialists.

Those of us at the bottom are not the only ones dismayed by this new, unimproved class system. Aristocrats, who used to perch at the top simply by being born to the right parents, can no longer waltz through life on nothing more than an exalted lineage. They find themselves scrambling to copy the very people they most despise—the flashy, pompous nouveaux riches—in order to remain relevant.

Little girls no longer dream of catching the eye of a handsome prince. What good are fleeting looks when you could wed a vault of infinite gold? It is not the viscomtes and the marquises who have the ear of President Louis-Napoléon

Bonaparte, but none other than Monsieur Fournier and his greedy cabal of soulless industrialists.

Soon, I promise myself. Soon I will earn enough as a seamstress that I can rescue my mother and sister from the Fournier textile factory. Then we need never fear hunger or danger again. My spirits rise further at the thought.

The sun is lower than it should be. It is a half-hour walk home from the dress shop, and I tarried a bit too long with Domingo. By now, the simmering pot-au-feu will be ready, and my mother and sisters annoyed with me for delaying our supper. We are rarely fortunate enough to add meat to our broth, but nonetheless it is hot, and we are hungry.

When I fly through the front door, ribbons in hand, the cramped rented rooms are dark and empty. Our two-bedroom home is hollow, an empty shell devoid of life. There's no pot on the stove, or joyful kisses of welcome. There's nothing.

"Elodie?" I call in alarm. She, at least, must be here.

At twelve years old, my baby sister is old enough to work in a factory, though she will be spared that fate, thanks to my seamstress position with Madame Violette. My new salary will be far from riches, but more than enough to ensure no one else in my family need ever spend another moment beneath that factory's cursed roof.

The front door swings open.

"Maman?" I call.

"Non, c'est moi."

I rush to hug Elodie and pause when I see her hands grip a single wilting wildflower. Elodie longs to be a parfumeur but

CHAPTER 1

Paris, France
18 September, 1850

Jagged shards of sunlight stab through my lowered eyelashes, and a needle plunges into the tip of my finger.

For a moment, I'm tempted to leave it in there. Why not? I've suffered worse.

There's no blood. Not yet. Not while the slender silver needle protrudes from my flesh, vibrating with joy at having bested me in a rare moment of inattention. Old memories are to blame again. My brain flashed to an unbidden image of the gruesome day I lost my father, and the needle saw its chance to remind me of pain.

"Keep sewing, Angélique," snaps Mademoiselle Jacqueline.

The other five girls dart their eyes at me, quick as cockroaches. They don't bother to hide their titters. They want me to hear their ridicule. To know I will never belong.

They have worked here for years. I'm almost finished with

my six-month trial in this windowless room with its hive of sewing tables in the center. Ankle-high scraps like piles of dead leaves line all four walls. We are newborn chicks in a giant bird's nest.

Baby egrets, to be exact, known for killing their siblings before they can learn to fly.

I stare at the needle again.

"Angélique," Mademoiselle Jacqueline says in warning, flipping her long pale hair over her shoulder.

She's not the owner of this luxury dress shop. That distinction goes to famed modiste Madame Violette, who is fitting clients in one of the plush dressing chambers at the front of the store, helping to turn yet another wife of an industrialist into a queen dripping with bespoke wealth. Every sign of excess is calculated to generate the maximum amount of envy from each client's peers, who will then descend upon the shop en masse, eager to glitter like diamonds too.

"Yes, Mademoiselle Jacqueline," I say dutifully. After all, she is Madame Violette's protégée—and our taskmistress. This provisional junior seamstress post is the best thing that's ever happened to me. I cannot afford to lose it.

Literally. It's this or beg for crumbs on the street.

"Well?" Mademoiselle Jacqueline prompts.

I stare at her thin blond hair, the color of an apple slice left in the sun. The strands are dry and brittle. I have a recipe for hair cream that would help, though I know from experience none of the girls in this room cares about my opinions.

The other seamstresses are watching me. Not a stitch is being sewn, but there are no harsh words for anyone else.

They have been waiting for me to err, to prove myself unworthy, since the moment I sat amongst them.

I pull the needle from my flesh. The hot silver quill sticks a little before popping free. A bubble of bright red blood blossoms to the surface, trembling as it grows. I touch the tip of my swollen finger to my tongue. The taste is salty and metallic.

For the entire six-month probationary period, I have foiled my coworkers' fervent wish to see me fail by excelling at every task, no matter how menial or time-consuming.

Madame Violette was so impressed, she instructed Mademoiselle Jacqueline to cease wasting my sewing talents on cleaning duties and allow me to work on the fine garments with the others.

The girls could not despise me more. Every day, they giggle amongst themselves and snap at me to go back to the factory, where "my kind" belongs. No one in *their* families has ever had to dirty their hands to pay the rent, much less wonder if there would be food to eat tomorrow. According to society, well-dressed young ladies like these are born better than humble girls like me—and they never let me forget it.

"Look, the poor baby injured herself," one of the girls coos, her saccharine words unable to disguise her delight.

The rest join in gleefully, mocking me. Even Mademoiselle Jacqueline smirks in appreciation at their jests.

Instead of listening, I shut off my ears—a trick I learned when I started work in the textile factory at age twelve. A shudder racks my flesh as unwanted memories bombard me. The enormous, clanging spinning machines . . . The startled yelps from other workers when the looms' automated teeth very nearly catch a finger... The sound of my father's screams when—

Madame Violette materializes in the open doorway. Panting, as though she sprinted five kilometers across a barren desert to arrive. But this is how she always looks. Rushed, winded. Rich mahogany skin, one shade lighter than my mother's. Startled brown eyes, like those of a doe hearing the crack of a hunter's rifle. Carefully ironed black hair escaping at odd angles from her coiffure. A sumptuous velvet gown bedecked with flounces in every color of the rainbow. A mad genius.

Our spines straighten. The giggles vanished when she entered. Our fingers become industrious.

Although we all work in the same room, we are far from equal. I am the youngest, at eighteen; the others are one to four years older. Half are Black, half are white. I am the only one who's a combination of both. All seven of us are French to our bones. But there, the similarities end.

Mademoiselle Jacqueline wants to show that she has us under her control. That she should rise from the role of assistant and be made a full partner.

The other five girls openly covet Mademoiselle Jacqueline's position as protégée. Its many privileges. The eye-watering salary.

Moi? I only need to survive until the end of the month. The promotion to full employee comes with a commensurate increase in wages. The glorious moment at which Madame Violette presses my new, no-longer-provisional salary into my hand.

The money I will soon earn is four times the pittance I received at the loud, stinking Fournier Fabrics factory. Which means my mother and younger sister will soon be able to quit their dangerous positions there and seek work that does not demand they risk their lives daily, even if the pay is lower. *I will provide for my family.*

Like Papa used to.

Madame Violette sweeps past each of our tables, inspecting our handiwork with a keen eye. My task is a full-torso whalebone corset, as fearsome and constricting as a serpent.

"Well done," she pronounces at last.

The relief in the room is palpable.

"Especially you, Angélique." Madame Violette holds up the hem I've just finished. "Such precise stitches, and completed so quickly."

Waves of hate roll off the other girls, battering me like a tempest tossing a sailboat.

"Merci," I murmur, ducking my head to shield my vulnerable eyes from their piercing gazes.

Madame Violette plucks a long strip of bone-white silk from my table. "What's this?"

"Left over." I gesture to one of the colorful discard piles lining the sewing room. "Shall I deposit it with the rest?"

She tilts her head. "Why don't you take it home, if you'd like."

A gasp of disbelief claws free from my throat.

If I'd like! Six *years* sweating in that god-awful textile factory, creating reams of material none of the workers will ever be able to afford in their lifetimes. A ruined finger, a dead father, yet never so much as a single precious thread was allowed out of the owner's greedy hands.

I lift the ribbon as though presenting my firstborn child to the heavens. A moonbeam, caught in my hands. The silk is soft, shiny, weightless. If I cut it carefully, there might be enough for four matching hair ribbons: one each for my mother, both of my sisters, and me.

We are exiting our final month of mourning, though the wound is as fresh as ever. It's about time a scrap of something bright and happy returned to our lives.

"Mes filles, that's enough for today. I'll see you all first thing in the morning." Madame Violette whirls to her protégée. "Jacqueline, would you help me with the comtesse?"

"Of course." As the women leave the sewing room, Mademoiselle Jacqueline tosses a triumphant look over her shoulder, smug in the knowledge that she alone is trusted in the same room as fine aristocratic ladies like the rich and fashionable Comtesse de Centre-Fleur. With her ebony tresses, smooth maple-brown skin, and enviable curves, the comtesse is a flawless model who elevates any piece she wears. I would love to fit her one day.

But no one else seems concerned with our client. As we rise to our feet, I discover all five of my bitter colleagues staring at me with glittering ratlike eyes and oversized wolfish grins.

"What—" is all I manage.

They pounce.

Ten fists fly at me at once. Not to strike me with tepid, girly blows but to snip my nicest dress with their shears. Quick as arrows, they corner me, trapping me in place as their sharp silver instruments carve holes in the best gown I've ever created.

"You're not better than us," one of the girls hisses beneath her breath.

"You're nothing more than a raggedy mop," snarls another.

"Quit now," a third whispers into my ear as she rips my thin yellow sleeve. "You'll never be worth anything."

They snap their scissors closed and place them back where they belong as if nothing of import has happened. Then they flounce from the room, cackling.

I neither cower nor sob. Simple shears will not defeat me. Those girls aren't half so dangerous as the weaving machines I conquered.

As I roll back my shoulders, a slow smile spreads over my face. Their petty insults and threats have only made me more determined than ever to prove them wrong. To make *them* quiver in fear.

To show the entire world what I'm really made of.

CHAPTER 2

Despite my coworkers' determined attempt to run me off, I emerge from the dress shop with more good cheer than I've felt in months. Perhaps even years. I hold four short but beautiful white ribbons in the palm of my hand and am now a mere fortnight away from proper wages. Money that will change the lives of everyone in my entire family for the better. No number of vindictive jabs can take such good fortune away from us.

Another blessing: When I design or sew clothing, nothing exists but my pencil or the needle. I lose myself in the flow of the fabric and the pull of the thread. Everything else vanishes. I cannot feel the pangs of hunger or hear the snide comments. I don't feel the chill of long nights when there's no more wood for the fire. There's just the stroke of my pencil dashing across the page or the hypnotizing silvery flash of the needle as it slips in and out of the cloth before me. When at last I look up from my creation, it is like awakening from the tidal pull of a recurring dream.

It's not quite dusk, so the charming boulevard is alive with people as I make my way home. All along Rue de la Paix, fancy carriages crowd the wide swath of smooth paving stones. Wealthy pedestrians stroll the sidewalks stretching beside the shop windows, deciding whether to spend today's pin money on gowns or jewels or fur coats. Items I wouldn't even be allowed to touch.

The pretty boutique at the end of the street is a luxury shoe shop equally far out of my price range, though here I do slow down. I also adjust the threadbare shawl around my shoulders to hide the damage done to my dress.

"Mademoiselle Angélique Genêt!" calls a deep, familiar voice, as smooth and intoxicating as brandy.

"Oh! Bonjour, Domingo," I murmur, as though he's caught me by surprise.

It's a little game that we play.

His tall, lanky form appears in the open doorway. He leans against the narrow doorjamb with a casualness that makes my mouth water.

Domingo Salazar is breathtakingly handsome in a dark, dangerous way. Soft black hair curling into hooded hazel eyes. Wide, firm lips that always seem caught somewhere between a smirk and a pout. A thick, jagged scar bisects one half of his face from temple to jaw.

I've no idea how he was injured. I never ask. Just as Domingo never asks why my left pinkie finger juts perpendicular from my hand, knobbing and bending in too many places.

Everyone has a past. It's what you do about the future that matters.

"Hola, guapísima," he says, his eyes hot on mine. *Hello, beautiful.*

The back of my neck heats with pleasure despite myself. I do not respond to this, or to any of his compliments. I dare not engage in flirtation. He's too difficult to read. In the five months I've known him, I can never tell if he's undressing me with his piercing gaze or if his too-perceptive hazel eyes are flaying the flesh from my bones in search of my soul beneath. Within me lies a darkness that I do not wish for him to see.

"Slow day?" I ask, careful to keep my shawl clutched tight.

He smiles, instantly melting what's left of my innards. "Scarcely. Christmas is three months away, and any self-respecting lord categorically cannot be caught dead wearing the same obnoxiously expensive boots he wore last winter."

"Ladies too, I imagine?"

He confirms with a nod. "Ladies too."

The La Croix & Sons Shoemakers sign has hung over the very door Domingo is leaning against for generations. No doubt the moment my employer's latest client finishes commissioning new gowns, she will bring her heavy purse straight over here for the perfect matching footwear.

"How about you?" I tilt my chin toward his humble leather boots. "Are those your dancing shoes?"

He staggers backward, feigning horror. "I am *the help*. I could not possibly shod my immigrant feet in French fashions. Someone might think I am putting on airs, or have pretentions, or a modicum of self-confidence."

I fluff out my wrinkled skirts and curtsey. "How I sympathize."

Domingo and I are both outcasts, if in different ways. He committed the unforgivable error of being born in Spain rather than France, whereas I made the horrific faux pas of being born poor. We are both used to being treated like a speck of dirt caught under a fingernail, destined to be flicked away and forgotten.

In fact, that's how we met. When I walked down this very block for my initial interview with Madame Violette—the only modiste in Paris who allowed me to interview at all—I happened to glance into the La Croix & Sons display window and make eye contact with Domingo.

Rather than rush off, embarrassed, I paused and smiled. He exited the shop at once to greet me. It has been our custom ever since. Despite the thousands of people who gaze into that window every single day, Domingo says I'm the first who ever noticed *him*. I feel the same way.

He's squinting at me now, the stark white scar puckering over his wrinkled frown, marring his beautiful face.

"What happened to your dress?" He abandons the doorway and strides forward, every muscle in his body suddenly as tense as a tiger's. "Are those cuts?"

"It's nothing."

I bat his hand away before he can touch me. He's never touched me. Nor I him. Until this moment, right now, as I smack his concerned finger aside. Less than a split second of contact, and I feel the electricity all the way to my toenails.

Maybe once I'm out of mourning, we might . . .

"Are you hurt?" Domingo growls, his hazel eyes flashing as though to say *just let me know who to kill.*

"I can handle them," I assure him, cursing my momentary distraction. When I swatted his hand, my shawl came loose. The ruined fabric of my faded yellow gown hangs from my shoulders and bodice. Asymmetrical holes expose the secret of my wasp waist—the ancient whalebone corset underneath. Only the very bottom of my flared skirts is untouched. "This old thing was destined for the rag bin anyway."

"That was one of my favorite dresses." He crosses his arms, displeased with my rebuff of his protection. "On one of my favorite people."

This was one of my favorite dresses too. My sartorial creations are necessarily made of the cheapest fabrics, but each one is exquisitely tailored in a design of my own making. Despite working in one of the largest, most squalid factories in Paris, my mother and sister report to duty clothed in the finest craftsmanship our savings and my fingers can provide.

Appreciative glances are common. In fact, modeling my own handiwork is how I managed to land a provisional position with Madame Violette to begin with. With this very dress.

Such resourcefulness is also why the other girls of higher station loathe me. They don't look at me and see a deft hand with a needle. They look at me and see the grasping hands of a beggar, sullying their pristine lives with my very existence.

"Shouldn't you hurry back inside?" I remind Domingo. "Monsieur La Croix will sack you if he catches you skirting your duties to chat with some urchin on the street."

Domingo shrugs. "The Messieurs La Croix . . . are not here."

My eyes widen. One of the La Croix men is *always* here. Thanks to France's almost constant state of revolution for the past few decades, the only La Croix remaining are the seventy-year-old patriarch and his eighteen-year-old grandson, Pierre. The same age as me, and one year younger than Domingo, yet heir to a cultural landmark. One he would never abandon, even for an afternoon.

"Where on earth is Pierre?" I demand, baffled.

"Can you keep a secret?"

"Better than you can imagine."

Domingo leans close and lowers his voice. "Gone, for the next three years. Conscription in the French military."

My jaw drops. I am fiercely glad Domingo is still here. "The only advantage to being an immigrant in this country is being exempt from the same fate."

His eyes twinkle. "Not the only advantage. Grand-Père La Croix is too old to manage the shop. His back and his eyes aren't what they used to be."

"*No*," I whisper in awe. "They left you in charge?"

"As far as their clients know, Monsieur La Croix is still in charge, and I am only an apprentice cobbler. I'm not to disclose that it is I, not Pierre, who designed the expensive footwear all the nouveaux riches are dying to purchase this season."

"Such hogwash," I say in disgust. "If you're owed credit, then you should have it."

He lifts his shoulders. "I don't mind working behind the scenes."

"You don't mind being constantly underestimated and overlooked?"

His eyes gleam like those of a fox. "Sometimes invisibility is the greater power."

"Oh please." I scoff and hold up my new silk ribbons. "See these beauties? They're about to brighten both my mother and sisters' day. These will make us stand out, not blend in." I give a little bounce of anticipation. "Maman, Anne, and little Elodie are going to be *so* happy."

"Go on, then," Domingo says with a flutter of his ink-black eyelashes. "Go and give your gifts while I return inside and fall back to my knees, fitting unwashed feet into fine shoes."

I make a sympathetic expression, wave goodbye, and hurry home.

Along the streets, many young boys are selling today's newspapers. I cannot afford to buy them, though I often linger close enough to scan the front page with eagerness. I hope for signs that President Louis-Napoléon Bonaparte might enact laws protecting the lower classes—or at least some safety for factory workers—but it seems he only cares about a return to the monarchy so he can stay in power longer.

Whereas some of us have never had power at all.

Oh, it is not as bad here as it is in other countries. Two years ago, France gained universal male suffrage, which my father hadn't thought would happen in his lifetime.

Although the aristocracy still exists, princes and dukes no longer rule this country. The industrialists have become our new royalty. Industrialists are more than mere businessmen— they are soulless magnates who amass their incredible wealth by exploiting vast enterprises without investing a single sou in the well-being of their workers.

First they built sprawling rural empires, and when that was no longer enough, they set their sights on Paris. The capitalists makes do with bringing a little bit of beauty home whenever she can find it.

Elodie stares up at me, her dark brown eyes wide and scared. Framed by a halo of soft, luxurious black curls, her cheeks still have some of their baby plumpness. Elodie is the only one of us sisters with a spray of freckles over her golden-brown skin. She's so innocent. I want to keep her that way for as long as possible.

"I'm hungry," she says. "Maman said I could help prepare supper."

"I'll go and fetch her. I'm sure she . . ." What? Lost track of time? Every worker in that factory counts down the seconds until they can leave, starting the very moment they arrive. Maman and Anne should *both* be home by now.

I kiss Elodie's forehead and slip from the house before she can ask questions I do not have the answers to. The same desperate feelings creep over me as the day we lost my father. Worry. Terror. Panic. All at once, I sense the truth settle into my very bones, threatening to shatter me from the inside out: Something terrible has happened.

CHAPTER 3

I run all the way to the factory, my scuffed half boots crushing brittle autumn leaves to dust beneath my worn soles as I race through the streets. Dusk has fallen. The icy wind slices through my thin, shredded dress like a thousand frozen pinpricks, but I don't care. The cold and the pain remind me that I am alive.

And as long as I draw breath, there is nothing I won't do for my family.

Unlike Madame Violette's fine apparel boutique, nestled amongst others of its ilk on the fashionable Rue de la Paix, the big brown brick textile factory is on the outskirts of the city. There, the monstrous ugliness of a sea of squat, dark buildings filled with noisy industriousness cannot mar the views from the fine homes of the city's upper-class citizens.

Until six months ago, I worked inside the worst factory's thick walls, along with my mother and sister and five hundred other desperate souls unable to find a better opportunity.

The current economic situation in France is dire. Nationwide unemployment is at an all-time high. Orphans and homeless adults fill the streets. Thousands of chiffoniers eke out an existence by sifting through discarded trash for scraps of cloth that can be resold as rags.

For many, a six-day-a-week, ten-hour-a-day post trapped inside one of the many stifling, squalid, dangerous factories would be a dream come true. For those toiling inside, it is a nightmare. One it is impossible to wake up and walk away from, because the only alternative is starvation.

I barely slow my feet in time to avoid tripping and slamming face-first into the sooty brick of the main Fournier textile building. Bent over, hands on wobbly knees, I allow myself to catch my breath for a split second before bursting through the big wooden doors into the belly of the factory.

I'll rest once I'm sure my family is safe.

A dozen sweaty faces flick toward me in unison. Some of the workers remember how I lost my father and send me sympathetic glances. Others give me the evil eye for moving on and leaving them behind.

But most of the remaining workers don't tear their focus from the machines. A moment's inattention is a quick way to lose a finger—or an arm.

I rub my own disfigured pinkie, as I often do when scared or anxious. Shortly after I gained employment here, my finger caught in a cotton-spinning mule that almost chewed my hand to pulp. My father rescued me just in time—earning him a reprimand for leaving his station. The silks my father was weaving were supposed to be more important than the bones in my body.

To say that the factory owner, Monsieur Fournier, subsequently failed to set my broken pinkie properly would be a gross understatement. He offered no medical attention whatsoever. I was told to keep working or find employment elsewhere . . . and we both knew there wasn't any. So I kept working.

With a throbbing, mangled finger, I could no longer run the looms correctly. I became a dye girl instead. Sweaty, back-breaking work with vats of thick dye and ream after ream of precious silk, which would be provided to modistes like Madame Violette. All to make gowns and trousseaus for wealthy women like the factory owner's self-centered, flamboyant wife, Madame Fournier.

But at least a dye girl need not fear losing her life.

My mother and sister, on the other hand . . .

I quickly scan the crowded factory floor and find them in the middle of the thirteenth row, running enormous growling spinning machines side by side.

At least, my sister Anne is running her machine—but not well. Her frantic gaze keeps darting to my mother's idle machine and the limp dark-brown body slumped at the base of it.

I sprint over, my heart in my throat. "Anne, what happened?"

At the sight of me, my younger sister bursts into tears, as though she has barely been keeping it together and cannot keep up pretenses for a moment longer.

"Maman," Anne whispers. "She had an accident. The loom . . . It was just like Papa."

Not *just* like Papa. Our mother is still breathing. For now.

I drop to my knees at her side. It's her arm. It looks much worse than my finger did. It will need to be amputated.

"Help!" I scream. "We need a doctor! Right away!"

No one responds. The machines around us keep whirring and chomping and weaving.

"They can't help," Anne says brokenly. "Monsieur Fournier says neither Maman nor I can leave until our work is done. If we walk out the door with a single thread unwoven, we lose our posts *and* the wages we're owed. Anyone who helps us risks the same."

"*I* will help," I tell her, my heart pounding. "It's going to be all right."

It's not all right. Maman is almost papery. Her teeth are clenched in a skeletal grimace. She is losing too much blood and is in far too much pain. Quickly, I knot together the new white hair ribbons and tie them beneath her shoulder as a tourniquet. Blood immediately soaks through the silk, turning the glossy white into sticky red.

The floor is also covered in spatters of blood. The pale yellow of my gown is now splotchy with red. No amount of vinegar will erase these stains.

I rip a large swath from my skirt and wrap the fabric around Maman's ruined arm. She swoons from the pain, thudding against the concrete floor like a doll.

"Back to work, girl!" calls Monsieur Fournier as he strides into the noisy work area from wherever he has been enjoying his afternoon plate of profiteroles with a glass of absinthe. He rarely visits the factory, but when he does . . . nothing good comes of it.

I whirl toward him. "This is unconscionable! Please don't be heartless, sir! My mother needs immediate medical attention, or she will die. Don't you remember what happened to my father?"

"He wasn't the only one we lost," murmurs an older woman behind me.

That's true. And horrific. Every month, another gory, preventable death. And yet the swarm of desperate, hungry souls eager for any work they can get grows ever larger as they line up to risk their lives at any factory that will take them.

Monsieur Fournier doesn't care about my mother or my father because he doesn't have to. We're all disposable. Easily replaced. He could make the working hours twice as long and the machines thrice as dangerous, and every man, woman, and child in here would still report for duty. They have no other choice.

Anne sobs as she tries to keep up with her machine. "I want to go home."

"Stop that," I hiss. "You're going to lose an arm too, if you don't pay attention."

"I can't stop. We cannot leave until the work is done. I'm close, but Maman—"

"I'll do hers. Mind yours."

I take my mother's seat. It's tacky with her blood. My heart pounds with fear and nervousness. I adjust the threads of silk and hesitate only briefly before throwing the machine back into motion. I have never been more terrified of an object in my life.

A machine like this one pulverized my finger. A machine like this one ripped the life from my father. A machine—this very one—might have done the same to my mother.

And here I am, tempting it with my fingers again. Fingers I need. Fingers all *four* of us need.

My nine working fingers are how we're supposed to rise out of this hellhole. We only need to survive two more weeks. Once I have a real salary, neither Maman nor Anne need ever set foot in this godforsaken factory ever again. Au revoir, Monsieur Fournier.

Two weeks.

But first, we need to get out alive tonight.

Maman lets out a little moan and struggles to sit up. "Don't, Angélique."

"Stay where you are," I scold. "We'll have you to a doctor in half an hour. Less, if I can help it."

"Step away from the machine," Maman begs. "You got out. Don't risk your freedom."

The reminder only makes my fingers shake even more. What good is my freedom if my loved ones don't have theirs?

"Would it kill Monsieur Fournier to have an ounce of empathy for the workers making him rich?" I mutter. "Hell, I'll kill him myself."

"I wish you would," Anne says, her eyes feverish.

"Walk away," Maman croaks. The two dozen careful braids of her shoulder-length black hair snake across the dirty floor like bloody tentacles. "Monsieur Fournier already stole your father. You cannot let him take more from this family."

Anne's jaw tightens. "Someone should make him pay."

"I will," I promise fervently.

Maman's voice is almost too soft to hear. "Think of your future. Think of Elodie's."

"I am. We need *you*."

The big wooden doors behind us swing open. A doctor, at last! I jerk my hands from the machine and turn to look.

Not a doctor. It is Monsieur Fournier's spoiled wife, Madame Fournier, and their equally spoiled twenty-year-old daughter, Mademoiselle Blanche. Both women are draped in outlandish silks, as though on their way to the opera—and hoping to be the stars of the show.

"Darling," Madame Fournier trills, her piercing voice drowning out even the thunder of the machines. "I hate to be kept waiting. Blanche and I have been invited to *the* fête of the month. Word must have slipped out about the increase in her dowry. No other young lady has a larger fortune!"

My teeth grind. This little speech isn't for her husband, who knows this information already, but rather is for the benefit of the exhausted peasants hunched over our looms, dreaming of being able to afford what the Fournier women spend on a single jeweled button.

"Have you thought of sharing even a fraction of your wealth with the workers slaving away in your factory?" I shout from my mother's seat.

Blanche scoffs, a high, coquettish trill like her mother's. "But then there would be less for *me*!"

"Besides," adds her mother, "quality is as quality does. You slovenly lot would never understand. We'll see you at home, darling!"

Mother and daughter flounce from the factory in a whirl of puce silks and lace.

Monsieur Fournier marches in my direction. "That's quite enough out of *you*. As I recall, you're no longer in my employ. Leave and never return, or I will throw you out with my bare hands."

"Go," Maman whispers. "Take care of Elodie."

"I can't leave." My voice breaks. "Anne will need my help to carry you, and we've got to finish—"

Monsieur Fournier jerks me up from the narrow wooden bench. He drags me backward as I kick and flounder. His grip is too tight, grinding fresh bruises between the ruined flaps of my sleeves.

"I'll do it," Anne blurts out. "I'll run both machines at once."

Maman hauls herself from the floor, swaying drunkenly from the loss of blood. "That's impossible, mon cœur. I will—"

Anne shakes her head stubbornly. "No. *I* will—"

It happens in a matter of seconds.

They reach for Maman's still-running machine at the same time. Anne's bony elbow brushes Maman's lumpy, ruined arm. Maman flinches and bites out a shriek of agony. Anne turns to face her, in horror and apology, her other skinny arm floating too close to the enormous weaving machine's hungry jaws. Maman reaches out with her good hand, but her reflexes are dulled with pain.

I struggle against Monsieur Fournier impotently as the machine mangles both of them. Gobbling insatiably.

Sickening crunches.

Sprays of blood.

Screams.

CHAPTER 4

I sway at the gravesite, my shaking hands curled into fists. Mostly into fists. My left pinkie juts out to one side in a lightning bolt of lumpy flesh. My memory flashes back to the macabre deaths of my mother and sister, recognizable one minute, with warm, soft arms capable of holding me close and squeezing me tight, only to be chewed into unidentifiable purée the next.

I'll never cleanse those nightmarish moments from my memory. No matter how hard I scrub.

At least Elodie was spared the sight.

Wind whips my long black skirts about my ankles. Tiny particles of loose soil float up into my hair, my face, my mouth. I don't spit them out.

Two men shovel dirt atop my mother's and sister's cheap wooden coffins, their resting places marked only by pieces of wood, their names carved with our dull kitchen knife. I can't afford gravestones yet. But I will.

There's a lot to do.

Elodie hangs behind me, gripping my skirt, either unable to face the graves or unable to believe Maman and Anne are dead and gone, like Papa. The only family Elodie and I have ever known have been erased from this world. The only people who cared about us, gone forever.

My heart twists in agony. Everyone my sister and I loved is dead, thanks to Monsieur Fournier and his equally greedy family. After the accident, Monsieur Fournier didn't even call for a doctor, much less stay to help. He left to join his wife and daughter at their fancy soirée as though nothing was amiss.

Because to him, nothing *was* amiss. To him, my family and I are just that: nothing. Five brave workers came to my aid once the Fourniers had gone. Women, ranging in age from older than my parents to younger than me. Every glassy pair of eyes reflected the fear of having glimpsed their own future.

If I can save these people, I will. But how? I could not save Anne and my parents. I have even less recourse to save Elodie and myself.

I stare through dry eyes as the gaping holes above the caskets fill with dirt. I've cried so much, I have no tears left. First at my father's funeral, then at the textile factory . . .

I suppose at least the three of them are now together. Maman and Anne are buried next to Papa, keeping him company.

Anger rises in me. Three members of my family killed at the same factory within a year, and wealthy Monsieur Fournier can't even be bothered to offer his condolences. Because he *isn't* sorry. Someone else has already taken their seats.

"I'm sorry, Papa," I whisper. "I didn't understand how dangerous it was until . . ."

Until I almost lost my finger.

Until we all lost you.

I shove the image of his pale, blood-soaked corpse from my mind and try to remember the good times. A childhood spent on his lap as he read me fairy tales by Charles Perrault and Madame d'Aulnoy, then later taught me to read worn leather tomes written by Black French writer Alexandre Dumas all by myself. The gentle smile on Papa's freckled face when I sewed my first crooked waistcoat for him. The awe when I fashioned one indistinguishable from those worn by lords and dandies.

The desolation in his eyes the day he told me I would have to work at the factory if we were to have any hope of keeping our home.

The sick, helpless horror in my own heart after his funeral, when Maman and I were forced to tell young Anne the same thing. Women earn half the wages of men for the same work. Without a third income, Maman and I could not afford food for us to eat. The choice was a factory—or death. And Monsieur Fournier was the only one with a free post. Because my father no longer needed it.

"Death came for us anyway," I whisper. "I'm sorry, Maman."

I miss her smiling face. Her arms hugging me upon my slightest accomplishment. Her kisses every morning. It was she who taught me to sew. To dream. To believe in a better, brighter future. It was her encouragement that ultimately led me to Madame Violette's doorstep.

If only I hadn't stopped to talk to Domingo the day they died! If only I hadn't wasted precious time by walking all the way home rather than hurrying straight to the factory from the dress shop. Perhaps I would have arrived in time to prevent the horrible accident.

Or perhaps it would have happened anyway. If not that afternoon, then the next day. Or the next.

I break free from Elodie's grip and sink to the grass in front of our sister's grave. "I'm sorry, Anne."

Her bouncy black curls pop into my mind. Big brown eyes. She was only sixteen years old, the same age at which girls like Blanche Fournier are draped in satins and silks for their grand débuts and courted by the handsomest, wealthiest gentlemen in the land. Viscomtes, bankers, industrialists.

Forever sixteen, my sweet Anne. She was never kissed by a boy. Never waltzed. Never had the chance to live a full life.

My eyes fly open. Still painfully, ferociously sandpaper dry. The graves are heaped with dirt. The workers are gone. But I'm not alone with my ghosts. My mother's last words were a plea for me to take care of my baby sister. I will do everything in my power to guarantee Elodie's safety. She will enjoy a long, healthy life and never know what it is like to be one of Monsieur Fournier's employees.

My fists clench as I struggle to stand.

I'm not sad.

I'm furious. Vengeful.

"Am I interrupting?" comes a soft male voice.

Domingo.

I've never seen him outside of our brief encounters on my

way to and from work. Now that he's here, I don't know if I should be angry at him for intruding on such a private moment of pain or if I should throw myself into his arms and sob until all the hurt has poured onto his chest.

Ultimately, I choose neither. I have to be strong. For Elodie, mon petit chou. My little cabbage.

I'm all she has left now.

Domingo lifts two matching bouquets in his thick hands.

"Is it all right if . . ."

I force a nod. "Please."

He's brought lilies. Where he found them in autumn, I cannot imagine. They're as white as bleached bones and just as fragile. Each clump is tied with a white silk ribbon identical to the ones I was going to gift Maman and Anne.

Domingo's ribbons didn't come from Madame Violette's discard pile. He had to purchase them himself, like the out-of-season lilies. I am hypnotized by their whiteness. The color seems so strange without pools of blood spreading and dripping from each thread.

He places a bouquet on each grave, then steps back to stand next to me in silence.

We stay there, not touching, not talking, as the sun rises higher and higher, baking us in place like clots of meringue. His heat is palpable. He's wearing black, as I am, and an expression that appears almost as heartsick as my own must.

It's comforting to have him here. I suddenly wish the cemetery were flooded with mourners sharing my grief. If I weren't banned from Monsieur Fournier's factory, perhaps I could also have invited the few brave coworkers who risked their jobs to help me as my mother and sister lay dying. But I have no way to contact them. Monsieur Fournier has ensured that friendly faces are denied me.

Except for sweet Elodie. And now, Domingo.

At last, he speaks. "Whatever you need, Angélique . . . Say the word, and it's done."

I shake my head without looking at him. I can't tear my haunted gaze from the graves. "Thank you. There's nothing you can do."

But there is something *I* can do.

The very last words I spoke to my sister were a promise that I would make those responsible for my family's deaths pay for their actions—and gross inaction.

Starting with the greedy factory owner Monsieur Fournier.

Avenging my family's cruel and unnecessary deaths is more than an idle dream. I unclench my fingers and bare my teeth in a terrifying smile.

Careless, affluent capitalists like Monsieur Fournier don't know what it's like to have every person they care about ripped away before their very eyes.

But he's going to find out.

CHAPTER 5

They say revenge is a dish best eaten cold. I'll savor mine any way I can.

Two weeks have passed since my colleagues ruined my dress with their shears. One week since my mother and sister's funeral.

This morning, I come to work early. Mademoiselle Jacqueline and Madame Violette are arguing in one of the dressing rooms when I slip into the shop. I've learned how to ease open the door to avoid the tinkle of the bell. After a quick trip to the sewing room, I leave the building just as silently.

I circle a dirty cobblestone alley to appear as though I am only now approaching, then kick a pile of leaves into the sewer before reemerging onto the wide thoroughfare of Rue de la Paix. The dress shop is ahead. A gust of wind picks up, flinging half-rotten leaves into the frigid air.

The other girls arrive, scurrying between elegant pedestrians like rats invading a grand ball. One of the ladies points a mocking finger in my direction.

Good. They've spotted me.

I duck my head and lower my gaze, as I've taken to doing ever since the day they attacked me. I see them gloating out of the corner of my eye. They think that they've cowed me. That they've dominated me. Broken me. That it's only a matter of time before I'm overwhelmed by my own inferiority and flee from the dress shop in tears, never to be seen again.

I do like the sound of *never to be seen again*. We'll see whose fate it describes.

As I follow the buzzing wasps into the hive, I allow myself to make the smallest of smiles. It feels foreign, as if my lips are being pulled in a strange new direction. My face hasn't shown happiness for a long time.

I will no longer accept others' cruelty as fair punishment for being poor or desperate. These girls think I am weak. They think I am helpless. They think I will not avenge the wrongs done to me and my family.

They think they are untouchable.

They are wrong.

"Mes filles," says Madame Violette, rushed and winded. "Today is critical. The comtesse will arrive later this afternoon to pick up her gowns. I want everything completed and packaged before lunch. Is that understood?"

We all nod dutifully.

Pauline pokes me in the back with a pin. I stiffen but do not otherwise react. My coworkers have parents and suitors. Their families have never experienced poverty. They haven't gone to bed hungry every night for months or sewn their Sunday best from scraps of stained cloth purloined from other people's rubbish.

They think that I do not belong here. That I sully their air with my very breath. That my mere presence lowers the value of the exquisite gowns we sew with quality materials someone like me could never afford and should not even be allowed to touch.

Most of them—Charlotte, Henrietta, Béatrice, and Pauline—are the first women in their petite bourgeoisie families to work. I think they hate me a little for this alone. As though it is somehow my fault that their desire for increased pin money has lowered them closer to my level, though our work is one of the safest, most genteel professions in the country. After all, even duchesses pick up a needle and embroider to pass the time.

Pauline claims she's here purely on a lark. She doesn't need the money and would have quit long ago if she didn't feel her talents were wasted by mere embroidery. Charlotte's grandfather is moneyed, and Henrietta has familial ties to capitalists.

Marguerite and Béatrice do come from working stock. But not like me. These girls are upscale and respected. Their fathers have so much money that their daughters' attire is made from fabrics more sumptuous than anything I've ever worn. Béatrice even brags of riding vélocipèdes with her beaux.

All five of them smirk every morning at first sight of me, shaking their heads in exaggerated pity before murmuring their insults loudly enough for me to overhear. Hoping to prick me with their words the way they stab their pincushions with their needles.

We're supposed to work as a team, but I've seen roosters get along better at cockfights.

Madame Violette gazes upon us despairingly.

I use my softest voice. "Don't worry. The items will be ready on time. What's left for us to do?"

My colleagues glower at me. I haven't spoken since the dress-slicing incident. They are not pleased with my interest in the comtesse's wardrobe.

"Not too much." Madame Violette smiles at me, earning me even filthier glares. "The sleeves of one gown, the hem of another, and the final touches on a few accessories that have been commissioned to match."

"*We'll* do it," Béatrice, the fresh-faced cherub who resembles a Botticelli painting and claims never to have worn the same dress twice, blurts out. "We understand high fashion."

"Yes," Henrietta agrees. She's the one who brags of owning a harpsichord and attending the theater in a luxury box. "There are five tasks and five of us. Angélique can mop the floors."

"That grubby ragamuffin shouldn't be touching the comtesse's finery anyway," adds Pauline, with a toss of her long snot-colored curls.

They titter.

I don't argue. I'm patient. I wait.

"Mopping would be a waste of Angélique's talent," Madame Violette says. "She can start the children's pinafores due later this week."

The girls exchange smug glances, pleased to have once again proved their superiority. Sewing pinafores isn't as degrading as scrubbing floors like Cinderella, but ordinary white cotton aprons are a far cry from the silk and satin befitting a comtesse.

Madame Violette turns to Mademoiselle Jacqueline. "Please see that everything is done to my specifications. I'll be up front with clients."

"Of course," Mademoiselle Jacqueline murmurs, her tiny, close-set eyes sparkling. The only thing she loves more than lording her position over the rest of us is an uninterrupted opportunity to regale us with stories about all the aristocratic ladies and rich industrialists' wives Jacqueline has touched and measured with her own two spindly hands.

"We would never dream of interrupting you, Madame Violette," gushes Béatrice in her toadiest voice, but her fawning obsequiousness is wasted. The modiste has already flown down the corridor.

I wouldn't blame Madame Violette for wishing to be as far away as possible from these harpies. A modiste as talented and good-hearted as she is deserves employees with those same traits. Not self-important bullies.

"Now then." Mademoiselle Jacqueline begins to circle our clump of tables. "*I* was there when the comtesse placed her order, and what she confided to *me*—"

I shut off my ears. I'm not interested in brushes with nobility. I am eager to see how the other seamstresses fare with their tasks.

We pick up our needles and shears in unison. For a long moment, not a sound can be heard above Mademoiselle Jacqueline droning on about how the comtesse appears up close, and how she smiled at Jacqueline particularly once she learned she was Madame Violette's protégée.

    Then I hear it. Pauline sets down her shears to scratch one hand with the other.

    As Pauline resumes her task, Henrietta drops her own tools into her lap in order to rub her palm—and then the back of her neck.

    Moments later, Béatrice does the same. Then Charlotte. Then Marguerite, who finishes a robust scratching session with an impatient wiggle in her chair, followed by a scrubbing of her face before picking up where she left off.

    The second stretch of industriousness is even shorter. Shears clang to tabletops. Buttons clatter and roll. Needles tumble to the floor.

    By the time the third wave hits, there is no more pretense of sewing anything. My tormentors are too busy scratching every exposed centimeter of skin. Angry red welts blossom like poppies in springtime.

    Mademoiselle Jacqueline trails off. Her audience hasn't been listening for at least a quarter hour, and now they're not even performing their tasks.

    "What the deuce has got into you girls?" she snaps.

    "I don't know," Béatrice wails.

    Charlotte bursts into tears.

    Marguerite tosses the comtesse's delicate satin sleeve to the floor and dashes from the sewing room.

    Pauline flings the silk skirt from her lap and flees after Marguerite.

    The tinkle of the bell signifies their departure.

"Sit down!" Mademoiselle Jacqueline demands. The girls do not. They cannot.

As Charlotte struggles to her feet, scratching all the while, Henrietta whirls on me.

"Why haven't *you* caught whatever this is?" she demands.

"I bathe," I reply without glancing up from my neatly hemmed pinafores. "You must all be grubby ragamuffins."

Henrietta growls in fury but is in too much pain to insult me. She darts out the sewing room door with Béatrice and Charlotte close behind her.

Good riddance.

CHAPTER 6

The room is now empty, save for Mademoiselle Jacqueline and me.

She gapes about in stupefaction. "What in the world just happened?"

I shrug and continue sewing, though of course I know the answer: *I* happened. Me, a pair of protective leather gloves, and a sack of carefully collected poison ivy leaves, which I rubbed over my tormentors' tools and benches and worktables.

"I have to tell Madame Violette," Mademoiselle Jacqueline mutters, and rushes from the room.

Quickly, I pull my gloves and a pair of soapy rags from my satchel and set about removing any sign of my intervention. If my tormentors attempt to blame me for somehow sabotaging their workstations, there will be no evidence to back up their claims.

By the time Mademoiselle Jacqueline returns, I'm in my seat.

She plucks the pinafores from my hands and retakes her

perch. "You'll have to finish the comtesse's gowns yourself, I fear."

I murmur, "I'll try my best."

But Jacqueline doesn't hear me. She's already launched back into her favorite monologue, naming and describing every rich and powerful lady she's met and measured and sewn for.

I shut off my ears again. That is, until the slimy prickle of a familiar name worms its way into my ear:

Madame Fournier.

I flinch, and my head jerks up toward Mademoiselle Jacqueline. "What did you say?"

"Madame Fournier," she repeats, delighted to have garnered my interest at last. "She and her daughter, Blanche, came in for their first consultation this very week. Madame Fournier's husband is an industrialist. He owns several lucrative textile factories. They're incredibly well-to-do. He could buy and sell aristocrats like the comtesse three times over, I daresay."

And yet cannot be bothered to pay his employees a living wage ... or even to care whether they continue living.

"Wouldn't you love to be one of them?" Mademoiselle Jacqueline says dreamily.

"Never," I say flatly. "*No one* should have that much wealth. Unless they have a heart as big as their coffers. Industrialists are the new aristocrats, and they should be tossed into the river."

"Of all the petty, jealous little—" She leaps to her feet. "The Fournier family is a thousand times better than the likes of *you*! The others were right to call you nothing more than a grubby raga—"

"Jacqueline, what is the meaning of this?" demands a shocked voice from the doorway.

My taskmistress turns in slow-motion horror, her limbs as disjointed and jerky as a marionette's. She pales to find her employer standing half a step behind her, windblown and mightily displeased.

"I don't pay you to berate my girls," Madame Violette says coldly. "Least of all Angélique, who has recently lost her parents and sister. If you cannot oversee your charges in a civil manner, perhaps I was wrong to entrust you with such a task."

"No, Madame Violette. Of course, Madame Violette. I can explain," Jacqueline babbles.

"I certainly hope so. But we shall have to discuss it later. I've the wife of an important financier arriving any moment, and I must prepare her dressing chamber."

The modiste sweeps off.

Mademoiselle Jacqueline spins toward me so quickly, I don't even see the slap coming until my face is on fire.

"If you ever make me look bad in front of Madame Violette again, you'll live to regret it." Spittle flies from Jacqueline's snarling mouth. "In fact, don't expect to be working here long if I have anything to say about it."

"Too bad you don't." I continue sewing as though neither she nor her stinging hand matter one whit. "Madame Violette told you to keep your opinions to yourself. If she knew you had gone so far as to strike one of her employees..."

Jacqueline's eyes flash. "You wouldn't dare, kitten. It's too bad you didn't die along with the rest of your family. You're gutter trash the world is better off without."

I am white-hot with fury, but I don't lash out as my overseer is clearly goading me to do. Instead, I work in silence. Soon I tie off the final stitch, collect the comtesse's newly finished clothing into a neatly folded pile, and carry the stack out to the front of the store.

Madame Violette steps out of the dressing room. "Angélique, what is this?"

"For the comtesse," I explain. "I'm done."

"That was very fast." She inspects the items. "Splendid. You are certainly a rising star."

"May I leave early?" I ask.

She sighs. "Why not? The others have, and you've already done their work for them. Pinafores can wait until tomorrow."

"Thank you." I turn toward the door.

"Wait!" She sets down the gowns and opens her purse. "It's the last day of your probation. I owe you your wages."

I hold out my clammy hand. My pulse doubles, triples. The five coins she drops into my waxy palm feel impossibly light. Two hundred francs. The equivalent of four female salaries at the textiles factory.

My stomach turns. My salary here was supposed to be Anne and Maman's ticket out of that purgatory.

"You're doing a marvelous job," Madame Violette says warmly as she closes my fingers around the francs. "You'll make a formidable protégée one day."

Pride rushes through me. She's right. I *will* make a formidable protégée. The best assistant Madame Violette has ever had. In fact, I could start today . . .

If Jacqueline weren't in the way.

CHAPTER 7

With each step along the fashionable, lively Rue de la Paix, the coins grow heavier in my palm.

This money is everything I've been working toward. What my mother and sister bet their lives on. These francs were meant to be my family's salvation.

Instead, they're discs of soulless metal.

I tighten my fist around the coins. Since I can't save Anne and my parents, I will do the next best things: funnel every hard-earned sou and spare minute into avenging their wrongful deaths, and do whatever it takes to keep sweet Elodie from suffering their same fate.

I stalk down the thoroughfare, ignoring its wide, clogged streets and multistory monoliths looming on either side. The only things I can see are my parents' and sister's faces. Screaming. Dying.

"Angélique?"

The sound of my name makes me trip over a crack in the uneven paving stones. I'm in front of La Croix & Sons shoemakers. I almost walked right past Domingo without even noticing him. A first. My glimpses of Domingo are usually much-anticipated highlights of my day.

"Hola, guapo," I say, with the soft smile reserved just for him.

For months, Domingo and I never saw or spoke to each other outside of the context of me passing by his place of work on the way home from mine. But when he showed up at the funeral with flowers for my family, something changed. I realized I'm more to him than some arbitrary girl to flirt with. He truly cares about me.

He holds up a key. "I'm locking up for lunch. Can I walk you somewhere?"

An idea pops into my head. An image. Not of my home, but of someone else's. And an errand that would unfold far more smoothly if I performed it as an ordinary young lady on a harmless stroll with her beau . . . as opposed to a vengeful banshee hell-bent on revenge.

I incline my head. "How long do you have?"

His hazel eyes glitter. "As long as you need."

I shove the coins into my pocket as he locks up the shoe shop. When he rejoins me, my palm is free to take his arm.

I cannot help but thrill at the touch. My hand trembles at the sensation of a man's supple frock coat beneath my palm. This man. My heart explodes from sudden palpitations at the unfamiliar feel of Domingo's thick muscular biceps flexing beneath the black fabric. I am driven nearly to a swoon at his proximity, his comforting heat, his earthy, manly scent.

"Where to, my lady?" he asks.

I clear my throat. "Rue du Faubourg Saint-Honoré."

If he is surprised to hear a destination in one of the wealthiest arrondissements of Paris, Domingo gives no sign. Instead, he sets out on this mission as if skulking among the rich and powerful were the most natural thing in the world.

At first, I fear how conspicuous I must look with my old boots and cheap linen. No matter how exquisitely tailored my day dress may be, it is a mere rag compared to the finery worn by the wives of the bankers and businessmen and aristocrats whose grand homes line these streets.

But I realize I needn't worry. It is not the moneyed who are out in the streets but their maids and footmen and stable boys. Domingo and I don't garner a second glance. We are as unremarkable as one blade of decaying grass from the next.

Although any of these majestic houses would dazzle the eye of persons far more well off than I, only one of them is the object of my attention. It's up ahead. Lurking between two identical white-facade abodes like a rotting tooth in an otherwise pearly row.

The Fournier family home. Our tormentors love to boast about their privileged address.

Their house is so beautiful, it hurts. It is not difficult to believe that its heavenly facade hides pure evil. Perhaps I was put on this earth to stamp it out. After what the Fourniers did to my family, I'd certainly like to try.

My mind whirs with all the ways their home could be breached. I could dress like a fine lady and sashay through the front door—if I had an appropriate gown. Perhaps I could disguise myself as a scullery maid and slip in through the servants' entrance in the back. Then there's the coal chute—inelegant and dirty, but accessible. As long as I don't slide straight into a fire.

What about windows? Good God, there are so many windows! Every one of them unlocked and cracked open to let in a trickle of cool autumn air. And perhaps to allow inside a surviving member of the family Monsieur Fournier killed with his greed and cruelty . . .

There he is right now, his head and shoulders visible in a first-floor window. Is that his study? A parlor, in which he sips absinthe and smokes cigars? It would be a shame if his liquor were replaced with poison. Or if he lit his cigar only for it to explode in his face, leaving nothing above his neck but wet clumps of flesh and a few gelatinous globs of brain.

He is not alone. A pack of like-minded men have gathered around him to drink expensive liquor by the liter and plot new ways to take advantage of lower-class Parisians. Every factory worker knows that whenever this group—the Fournier Twelve—gathers, devastation follows. Longer hours. Even more dangerous conditions. Navigating by faint candlelight instead of bright sunlight. Operating heavy machines that haven't been serviced in months because a pause of five measly minutes might take a few sous from Monsieur Fournier's bulging pockets.

Usually, these men meet in an exclusive gentleman's club called Les Chanceux on a secluded street off the Champs-Elysées. I cannot imagine what depths of evil they intend to sink to this afternoon that would require a change to somewhere more private. Then again, didn't the gossip rags say the industrialists' weekly debauchery occurs on Saturday nights? It is midweek. Perhaps one night doesn't hold enough hours to fully exploit the desperate and the hungry.

Monsieur Fournier's son is right there beside him. The heir, Odin. Named to honor a god of both war and death, and rumored to gleefully live up to that name. A nightmare with curly blond hair and dimples. Rumor has it, Odin has long been the black sheep of this family. How vile a creature must he be, that a murderer such as Monsieur Fournier would threaten to disown his own blood?

Then again, I see no sign of such dissent. The son is right there, eager to become one of them, no doubt dreaming of spun-gold factories of his own to profit from and innocent workers to trample in search of the next coin.

A flash of menace twists Odin's face, and a chill slithers down my spine. Those are the eyes of a man who would murder his own father to get what he wants.

Perhaps the heir has grown tired of waiting to inherit. I cannot dally too long planning my revenge, or the opportunity will be stolen from me, like so many others.

Three windows to the right, a bay window reveals two more familiar faces. Pampered Madame Fournier and her daughter, Blanche, model grotesque hats for each other, each one complete with taxidermied baby birds and oversized ostrich feathers. Blanche blows a kiss at her reflection in a gilt-edged hand mirror.

Disgusted, I return my gaze to Monsieur Fournier and his son. They and the other men are sipping glasses of absinthe, the favored drink of artists and poets, with its bile-green shimmer and thick anise flavoring. Monsieur Fournier probably thinks he *does* bring as much beauty into the world as any artist or poet. The textiles created at his factory are world-class. Pity he doesn't care about the humans weaving the threads that make him so rich.

I needn't enter his home, I realize. A pistol could make short work of the matter. Like shooting fish in a barrel. I'd only need a single bullet and a steady arm. I could fire off one good shot before the police or a passerby tackled me.

But where is the justice in a tactic so simple?

This demon took almost everyone I love from me. And turnabout is fair play for him and his spawn.

A bullet is too easy. Too fast. Too clean. He deserves to suffer as I have suffered, as everyone who has ever lost a limb or a loved one in his factory has suffered. People like me deserve a protector, someone who will fight for their rights.

I return my gaze to the simpering women and smile.

As the Bible says: an eye for an eye. And who am I to argue with the Good Book? I shall do unto him exactly as he has done unto me.

"Did you find what you were looking for?" Domingo asks softly. We haven't taken a step in ten minutes.

"Yes, thank you." I allow him to turn us back the way we came.

There is plenty of time to deal with evil Monsieur Fournier.

49

His fate has been sealed. But first, there are others who stand in my way. Now is the moment to plan and to *execute*. I am giddy with anticipation. Dying to begin.

There's a certain self-important, vindictive protégée who deserves my attention.

CHAPTER 8

Retribution cannot be rushed. A week later, I know what to do.

At work, I shut out the noise and ignore the flow of snide comments Mademoiselle Jacqueline sends in my direction to the delight of my colleagues—not all of whom have recovered from their itching.

At home, I labor before the oven, perfecting the art of crafting meringue from the clear mucus of egg whites, while stabbing fingers of stale bread into the runny, leftover yolks for my suppers.

By Friday, I'm ready.

I arrive at the shop at the perfect hour: Madame Violette is bustling about the dressing rooms up front, and the other girls have not yet arrived. It is only me and Jacqueline.

All week long, she has been bombarding me with relentless vitriol. My failure to respond to a single insult has only spurred her to try harder, to slice deeper, to think more cruelly. Demeaning me has become the one pastime she enjoys even more than bragging about her brushes with high society. My refusal to cry, to flinch, to quit and run away only makes the tongue-lashings harsher.

I have just the thing to sweeten her up.

"Well, if it isn't the resident guttersnipe," she begins the moment I step through the sewing room door. "Why don't you do us all a favor and stick those shears right in your—"

"Let's be friends," I say softly. "Or at least peaceable colleagues. I admire and respect you."

She's so surprised that I've spoken that she blinks at me owlishly for several seconds, processing my words in search of hidden insult and finding none.

"Please," I say in my meekest tone. "Can we cease fire?"

Her eyes narrow . . . but she's listening. She likes seeing me humble. Inferior. Begging.

As I thrust out the festively beribboned parcel, I drop to one knee before her, genuflecting. A serf to her queen. "A token of my sincerity. Please, take it. I baked them for you."

It's the ribbon that wins her over. Too long and perfect to have been filched from Madame Violette's castoffs. It's clearly been purchased for this purpose, at my expense, specifically for Jacqueline.

She can no more withstand this flattery than a moth can resist a flame.

Her long, spidery fingers snatch the parcel from my hands and pluck at the ribbon. She tucks the blood-red strip into her bodice for later. The tan linen square falls away to reveal a white porcelain plate piled high with delicious macarons, each made of meringue as light and airy as a final breath and tinted a pale watery green. The same hue as the textiles I used to dye at the factory. A blend that requires not an insignificant addition of arsenic to achieve the right coloring.

Like many other families in my neighborhood, Maman purchased the same poison to kill our rats. The percentage in these cookies might be a wee bit higher than what she used.

If our dear, delightful Jacqueline should unexpectedly fall ill and take to her bed for a few days—or better yet, a few weeks—then I will have the possibility to step into her shoes, or at least prove to Madame Violette and the others that I am every bit as capable as Jacqueline is.

And if Madame Violette wishes to name me her newest protégée sooner than planned, I will accept my new position—and its increase in salary—with haste and gratitude.

"Don't share them with anyone," I say coaxingly. "They're for you alone. In fact, you may wish to wait until you go home before diving in."

"No," she replies immediately. "They're mine. I deserve to eat them when I wish."

She pops the top macaron into her mouth and crushes it between her wide flat teeth.

Jacqueline's eyes widen, her pupils dilating. "These are *good.*"

Of course they are. Handmade. Sweets for my sweet.

As I hoped, the almond paste masks the taste of the arsenic perfectly.

"I don't want the other girls to think I'm trying to gain your favor," I fret, displaying the right amount of drama. "Perhaps you could claim . . . that the comtesse purchased them for you from an exclusive bakery as a reward for exceptional service?"

Jacqueline's eyes glitter at this mouthwatering prospect. "Yes. Of course. I would be happy to do that for you."

"Do what for her?' demands Béatrice as she and the other rats scrabble into the room.

"Correct her many mistakes," Jacqueline snaps, and shoos me into my seat as though I were a pesky fly landing too close to her. "Sit down, all of you. There's work to be done."

"Are you actually going to help this time?" Henrietta asks under her breath, tossing one of her sausage curls over her shoulder. It is the color of old teeth.

Jacqueline overhears Henrietta's question and smirks in reply. "I can't possibly help. The comtesse purchased these macarons for me in honor of my superior talent. She doesn't think much of the rest of you, but as for me . . ."

Our taskmistress makes a production of plopping the next plump green macaron onto her tongue and chewing it whole. The other girls watch with envy, salivating over each crumb licked from the flaky pink flesh of Jacqueline's chapped lips.

The morning passes in no time. It is like sitting in the front row at a play. Jacqueline is the star, swooping about and circling the room like a buzzard. Dangling a macaron from her claws before the hungry face of this girl or that, pretending to share her bounty before scooping it into her own maw instead. Lording her rank over the others with a ceaseless monologue of her fictional encounters with the comtesse and the grateful lady's increasingly unlikely fawning compliments in return.

It doesn't take long for Mademoiselle Jacqueline to start suffering stomach cramps. The other girls could not be more delighted. Not only does debilitating pain finally stifle Jacqueline's loquacious grandiosity, it is her just deserts after we have been forced to listen to her go on about how special and favored she is for the past four hours.

"It's your own fault," Pauline says happily. The only thing she loves more than flowers and her own reflection is someone else's discomfort. "If you had shared your macarons instead of gobbling them up yourself, you would not have overindulged, and your stomach would feel much better."

"She could still share," says Marguerite, her lower lip thrust out so far with petulance that it resembles the beak of the dead songbird sewn onto her bonnet. "She ate most of them, but there are still just enough cookies left. One for each of us."

"If we skip Angélique," Charlotte agrees, shooting me a biting smile. Despite her innocent, pretty brown face, her teeth flash white and sharp.

"I don't think she should share with anyone," I announce with faux loyalty to the selfish woman who smacked me and wished me as dead as my parents. "You lot are jealous of Mademoiselle Jacqueline's popularity."

Jacqueline appears pleased at this interpretation, despite the obvious stomach spasm doubling her over at her table.

"You should go home if you're feeling poorly," I tell her softly. "Rest in bed and eat all the sweets you want until you feel better."

"That's a good idea," Jacqueline gasps, wrapping what's left of the macarons in the wrinkled cloth and clutching it to her chest. "I'll see you wretches tomorrow."

She stumbles from the sewing room, chewing on a cookie.

Moments later, Madame Violette sweeps into the room like a blur of paint. "Good heavens, Jacqueline's influenza could not have come at a worse time. There's so much to do, and with five of you missing for most of the week—"

"Tell me how I can help," I say gently. "I will do as required to keep deliveries on schedule. You won't even notice Jacqueline's absence."

Madame Violette's tight shoulders relax with relief. "Thank you, Angélique. You truly are an angel. If you could finish what she started . . ."

I slide off of my rickety wooden bench and into Jacqueline's sturdy wooden chair.

The other girls start speaking over each other, furious that I have curried favor with the modiste. Livid that it *worked*, and absolutely mouth-foamingly rabid that they didn't think to do it first.

"But, Madame Violette!" they cry. "What about us?"

"Yes, yes." The harried modiste seems more stressed than reassured. "Of course you must help. Perhaps putting our heads together will ignite the missing spark."

"Missing spark?" I ask.

She slinks a glance over her shoulder toward the dressing rooms before responding. "Business is steady, but I seek meteoric success. Which means I need something big. Something *more.*"

"Can I design a dress for you?" I blurt out, leaning forward in eagerness. How I have dreamed of designing for Madame Violette! "It would be no trouble at all. I have a thousand ideas—"

The other girls shoot daggers at me.

"Oh, chérie," Madame Violette says fondly. "Once you've worked your way up the ladder and apprenticed for a while, perhaps then you will have the knowledge and skill to create a design of the caliber I need. But for the near future . . . let's leave the designing to me and to my protégée."

Ah. Precisely what I intend to do. Once I am officially the protégée, my sister and I need no longer live in fear, unsure where we'll find our next meal or whether we can keep a roof over our heads in winter. As Madame Violette's protégée, I'll be on my way to having an honest-to-goodness *career*.

As my employer dashes back to her clients, I pick up Jacqueline's abandoned project and stretch my legs beneath the magnificent table.

It feels like home already.

CHAPTER 9

When I pass the shoe shop after work, Domingo is locking the door. Right on time to escort me on a late-afternoon stroll through a privileged neighborhood in which our kind only serves as the help.

It has been less than two weeks since our first such promenade, but it is our custom now. He accompanies me in silence, hulking next to me, tall and taut. Ready to defend my honor, should the opportunity present itself.

My hand still thrills as it nestles around his upper arm. The heat from the flexing muscle beneath soaks through his linen shirt, seeps through the thick fabric of his frock coat, and bores through my eager flesh to the bone.

I no longer wish my finger weren't broken. I want to mold them all around his biceps into a pale, crooked vise he can never escape. To lock us together, two broken halves who combine to form a terrible beast the likes of which this world has never known. Unstoppable. Invincible.

Utterly and ferociously *alive*.

For now, I settle for ambling at his side. The very picture of dainty submissiveness. Mincing steps, voluminous skirts, chaste hems, tightly laced corset, demure bonnet that casts the top half of my face in shadow. These raiments are meant to keep me in my place . . . but are as ineffectual as chaining a lion with a satin ribbon.

I pause when Monsieur Fournier's home comes into view. I imagine it filling up with toxic fumes like those found in dye shops. I imagine the mattresses being replaced with ravenous machines eager to weave their masters' limbs into bloody threads the next time they slip into bed.

Monsieur Fournier stole three loved ones from me. I am owed his life in return. The beast nestled within me growls in anticipation.

Domingo's silky deep voice murmurs in my ear. "Do you want to get closer?"

He doesn't ask who lives in the house I'm always staring at. Maybe he suspects. I know what they did—and what they deserve. My dark thoughts would surprise him. I doubt he thinks me capable of acting on my true desires.

After all, I am only a girl. Stunted by poverty, by loss, by my low-class station in life. Powerless. Inconsequential.

But I am not just any girl. Never have been, from birth. I survived the cholera epidemic of 1832—my first act of defiance. Even as a sallow, helpless baby, long before I could string together a coherent sentence, I refused to die.

As a child, I did not know my purpose in life. I thought it

was to be a good daughter. A marvelous sister. My family was my North Star.

Until Monsieur Fournier extinguished their light.

"No," I tell Domingo. "I don't need to get closer."

From this distance, I can see that Madame Fournier and Blanche are doing the same thing they do every afternoon before sailing out for a fine evening on the town. They are modeling their latest extravagant purchases in the most ostentatious manner: standing beside an open window, so that their neighbors and every passerby can see their riches.

In case the large bay window alone does not afford enough of a view, they have arranged a half-circle of looking glasses behind them so as to reflect every gaudy detail out onto the street. Madame and Mademoiselle Fournier choose each luxurious purchase not because the fragile fabrics and extravagant hats are useful or beautiful but because they're exclusive and expensive. I've peered into enough shop windows on Rue de la Paix to recognize the styles as belonging to designers who can charge more for a single feather than I will earn in my lifetime.

The fine Fournier ladies acquire more than they can ever wear in order to lord their privilege over others. The current items haven't been in their possession for more than an hour, and already they're dreaming of their next flashy purchase to parade about.

I can't wait to provide it for them.

"Have I told you that you look lovely today?" Domingo asks.

"You tell me every day, mon loup."

Not that words are necessary. The desire in his eyes is palpable. I can feel him smoldering at me through the shoe shop window, through each thick stone wall, through half a street of boutiques and cafés. I can feel him staring at me even in my dreams. The intensity of his unwavering attention whispers along my flesh, summoning goose bumps with a force twice as powerful as gravity.

It is all I can do not to fall into the black hole of his gaze and disappear forever.

I spin us away from the Fournier family. "Take me home, please."

"At once."

Domingo knows where I live. Foolish, perhaps, for a young woman who resides alone with her baby sister. No other family, no servants. Tempting a stray admirer whose interest in me crackles in the air like electricity.

Maybe I like the danger. The risk. The possibilities.

In the natural world, some male creatures leap onto females unawares, taking them whenever and however they wish. In the wild, some of the females are coquettes. In heat, indiscriminate. Or perhaps discerning, selecting only the best of the best for a mate, after the males compete to the death.

Consider the praying mantis. When she is done with her lover, she bites the head off her paramour and eats his still-quivering body for strength. Lord knows I will need some for what is yet to come.

We smell my neighborhood as soon as we turn onto my

street. Gone are the fresh breezes and flowering trees of the Fourniers' Rue du Faubourg Saint-Honoré.

My street is grim. Dark, gray, crumbling, dirty, neglected.

Not nearly as bad as the hôtels garnis where underpaid workers from the countryside rent tiny rooms in windowless quarters, with barely enough room for a lumpy cot and a pot to piss in.

If anything, my family's humble apartment is too much house for a teenage girl and her twelve-year-old sister. It would be cheaper for us to leave, though I do not dream of it. I cannot bear to abandon the walls that held such joyful memories. Nor can I rent out my parents' bedchamber and allow a stranger's filthy head to nestle where my mother and father once slept.

It's bad enough to lie awake every night, gazing at the thin mattress opposite mine, where soft, cuddly Anne slept every single day of her life. Now it is only Elodie and me, gripping each other's hand tight as we stare up through the heavy darkness at the growing cracks in the ceiling. Our home's unrelenting emptiness drains us. The silence crushes. The cold where our lost family's warmth once was hardens my heart and stokes the fire of revenge.

"I'll see you tomorrow," I tell Domingo.

I don't invite him inside. I never have. He is an attractive distraction I can only afford in small doses.

"If you should need me for anything . . . ," he says softly.

"I won't."

My words are too harsh, so I gentle them with a smile. I

may not need him, but the wanting simmers beneath my skin every time I see his face or think his name. He can smell it on me, the same way I can on him.

Instead of taking my words at face value and walking away, as he has done on every occasion until now, Domingo lowers his parted lips slowly toward mine. His magnetic gaze turns liquid.

I duck out of reach at the last possible second.

"Be careful, torero," I warn.

He straightens, undaunted, though his forehead lines in confusion. "Do you mean tesoro? *Torero* means 'bullfighter.' *Mi tesoro* is a lovers' endearment that means 'my treasure.'"

"I meant torero."

Our roles could not be clearer. He is the attractive gentleman in sophisticated garb wielding a mighty spear. I am the confused bull, unsure why I'm in this ring, why I've been singled out, and why everyone wants my blood. But I'm dead certain what I intend to do about it.

Don't poke the bull unless you're prepared for the consequences.

Domingo takes this as chastisement, and his expression twists with self-reproach. "Of course. Here I am flirting with you while you are still in mourning."

I nod. "This is not the time."

His gaze has not ceased devouring me. "Will there be a time?"

I cradle his face. "Who can say what the future holds?"

A wicked smile blooms over his scarred face. My heart flutters.

He touches his lips to my palm. "I can be patient, mi tesoro. I'll be ready when you're ready."

I can be patient, too. Domingo is a fine catch, but I cannot think about romance. Not yet.

First I need an eye for an eye.

CHAPTER 10

For my plan to come to fruition, several puzzle pieces must fall into place. Three days later, I sweep into the house and enfold Elodie in a relieved hug, kissing her cheeks and forehead until she giggles and pushes me away. It is good to hear her laugh.

We prepare supper side by side, then dine together, sharing stories of our day. I tell her about the fabulous gowns I've been sewing. My current project is a sky-blue evening gown with a daring décolletage and short lacy sleeves that accentuate the curve of the shoulders. The bell-shaped skirt is full of sumptuous ruffles, like the layers of a beautiful cake. Only the tips of dancing slippers will peek out.

Elodie tells me about the fine house with the open window where she can overhear a governess instructing children her age. She has been lurking outside that window, rain or shine, for years. As soon as I have Mademoiselle Jacqueline's post—and wages—I vow to procure my baby sister a tutor of her own.

After supper, when Elodie curls up with the worn family volume of old fairy tales, I slip back out into the twilight.

My evening plans are only beginning.

A brisk twenty-minute walk is all it takes to reach Jacqueline's lodging house. I followed her home from work the day before I baked her cookies. She never once glanced over her shoulder.

Her upbringing was far more privileged than mine. She never learned what it is like to fear what creeps in the shadows.

Jacqueline lives in a respectable boardinghouse. The sort with comfortable rooms rented to reputable young ladies. A better quality of girl than me. The kind that earns more than my entire family did, even when my father was still alive. The type of girl who dreams of marrying for money and puts on airs because she once sewed undergarments for a comtesse.

I slow my pace as I approach the boardinghouse. Rushing is dangerous. There are few people in the street after dusk, but nonetheless, it is best to appear nonchalant. One more young lady strolling home after a long day of monologuing at six seamstresses. Perhaps smacking the newest, grieving one, who should know her place and not attempt to climb past her station.

A flower girl lurks a few meters from the door, next to a large wooden wagon filled with broken stems and loose petals. If I had to guess, I'd say she isn't a professional flower girl but a scavenger who plucks fallen blooms from the pavement and weeds from the roadside. Nothing at all like the beautiful lilies Domingo brought to my family's graves.

I am the only thing keeping my sister Elodie from this same fate—or worse.

The flower girl asks half-heartedly if I would like a posy for a sou and isn't surprised in the least when I shake my head.

She *is* shocked when I hand her the sou anyway.

There are twenty sous in a franc. As Madame Violette's junior seamstress, I earn six francs a day. Which calculates to a sou for every five minutes of labor. This girl looks like she'd be lucky to earn five sous in a week.

"Oh, thank you, madame!" she gushes.

Madame! *Me!*

At eighteen, I am barely four years her senior. But to her eyes, my perfectly tailored, ancient day dress likely seems a ball gown fit for a princess.

"De rien," I assure her, then step around her wagon to try the door to the boardinghouse.

It is unlocked, as it was the day I followed Jacqueline to her door. She never glanced over her shoulder.

Tonight I am on my own as I scurry deep into the corridor and slither up the stairs. Here, I *do* hurry. If the other residents see me, they will recognize that I'm not one of them. I must be swift.

But when I reach the second floor, there is a plump older woman outside Jacqueline's door. A housekeeper, perhaps. She wears a disgruntled expression and jingles a large brass ring of keys.

Merde. If Jacqueline is feeling well enough to ruin this poor woman's day, then my cookies did not work after all. My stomach sinks. Instead of giving me a week or two to prove myself, as I'd hoped, Jacqueline will be back to bully me bright and early tomorrow morning.

Before the housekeeper can disappear, I hurry over. "Were you speaking to Jacqueline?"

"I wish I were. She's late with her rent. Probably why she isn't answering her door." The woman sends me a suspicious glare. "Who are you?"

Not a housekeeper, then. The landlady. This might work to my advantage. Especially if the macarons *did* upset Jacqueline's stomach and she's currently kneeling over a chamber pot, unable to refute the story I'm about to spin.

"I'm Jacqueline's cousin Marie," I answer with wide-eyed innocence. "I'm to let her know that we're due on the morning train to Lille to visit our sick grandmother. Perhaps Jacqueline is ill too. Can you let me in to check on her?"

"No. It is against policy to allow—"

A scream sounds abovestairs, followed by a loud thump.

The landlady makes a disgusted expression. "Has there ever been a clumsier tenant? If you'll excuse me, I must—"

"Oh, of course," I say quickly, pulling a handful of coins from my pocket. "How much did you say Jacqueline's rent was? I'll make sure she pays me back after you let me in."

"I told you—"

"Madame Bernard!" calls a frantic voice from somewhere upstairs. More heavy items thunk. "Come quick! She's really done it this time!"

The landlady snatches the coins from my palm, unlocks Jacqueline's door with a long brass key, and races up the stairs.

I waste no time entering the room, closing the door tight behind me.

"Jacqueline?" I call softly, my voice tentative and quavering. Not at all the way Jacqueline's confident cousin Marie is supposed to sound. Berating myself for my nervousness, I force myself to speak louder. "Jacqueline? Are you in here?"

No answer. Perhaps the cookies made her sicker than expected, and she's vomiting too hard to hear me call.

I edge deeper into the apartment. It appears to consist of two rooms: a small parlor, in which I am currently standing, and a single door leading to a bedchamber.

The parlor appears untouched. Narrow sofa, tea table for two, unlit fireplace. The hat Jacqueline usually wears is on the table, but there's no sign of Jacqueline herself—or the plate of poisoned macarons.

I cross to the bedchamber. The door is ajar. It sticks as I push it open, creaking as though the very hinges dread to show me what lies on the other side.

It's Jacqueline, lying face-up in the center of her bed.

Dead.

My stomach bottoms out, and for several anguished moments, *I* am the one making extended use of the chamber pot.

When at last there is no more acid left in my gut, I wipe my mouth with the back of my hand and stare again at the corpse atop the bed.

I killed her. By accident, of course, but that doesn't change the outcome. If anyone learns of this, I will spend the rest of my soon-to-be-very-short life in jail, awaiting the heavy blade of a guillotine to separate my head from my body.

And Elodie will have to fend for herself. Even if she takes a full-time post at a factory like Monsieur Fournier's, a twelve-year-old girl cannot earn enough to pay for food and winter clothes and rent. At best, she will end up on the streets. At worst, dead within a year . . .

Unless I make certain no one learns of Jacqueline's demise.

Hands trembling and stomach still shaky, I dart forward to collect the empty porcelain plate from her pillow. I knock the crumbs into the parlor's icy fireplace, then set the plate on the tea table. There, that looks normal enough.

Now what? I wring my hands, momentarily distracted by the gorgeous moonlight streaming through her sparkling bed-chamber window. Because of the expensive door-and-window tax levied by the government, lodgings for the poor contain only one entrance and no windows whatsoever. Oui, fresh air is free, and even *that* is denied to the poor.

Jacqueline is—*was* lucky enough to have a window in both rooms. I ease open the bedchamber window and stick my head outside. The narrow cobblestone alleyway is no rolling vista but rather a precipice of broken concrete overlooking a cesspool stinking of stale urine.

It's perfect.

As the bedchamber fills with cool air, I wrap Jacqueline in her blankets, rolling and trussing her like a fat sausage. There's no rope with which to bind the edges, but a small basket on her dressing table provides a cornucopia of ribbons made of silk—which happens to be the strongest textile in the world.

With a few false starts, I knot several thick strands together and tie off the ends of the blanket. I also discover a traveling trunk, which I quickly stuff to the brim with garments from Jacqueline's wardrobe.

How much time has passed since I discovered her body? Ten minutes? Fifteen? I don't own a pocket watch, but I do know I can't waste another moment. Whatever drama is unfolding upstairs won't keep the landlady busy forever.

I stick my head back outside and shiver. Night has fallen.

So will Jacqueline.

It takes some maneuvering to heft my heavy woolen sausage up the wall and over the wooden sill. At first she teeters, her corpse stiff, as if she were carved from ivory. Then she disappears over the brink, landing in a pool of shallow muck with a soft, wet thump.

My stomach heaves at the sound. Did anyone else hear the body fall?

My breath is shallow as I wait in fear, counting the seconds. Nothing moves but scurrying rats. The tenants in the building opposite aren't rich enough to have windows. And the night is too cold for anyone in their right mind to let in the chill and stench from the alley.

No one has heard anything.

Excellent. Next, I must dispose of all evidence. If there's no corpse, then there's no crime to investigate. No reason to fear for my baby sister's future.

After tidying the rooms to appear as though Jacqueline left to visit a sick grandmother, I snatch up the overstuffed traveling trunk and scamper down the stairs as fast as my feet can carry me. When I burst through the front door, the flower girl is still there, admiring the sou in her pale, scrawny palm.

"This valise is full of fine clothes," I tell her. "It's yours if you let me borrow your wagon for an hour. Starting right now."

Her eyes widen. "That entire trunk would be mine?"

"Your wagon," I repeat urgently. "Right now. Oui ou non?"

She looks happy enough to swoon. "For that much finery, I'll help you do whatever you need to do."

"I can manage. Wait for me three streets down, with your new trunk of clothes. I'll return your wagon as soon as I can."

She reaches for the tall valise with greedy hands.

I scoop up the worn wooden handle of the wagon and head toward the alleyway. The night is young. The inky black sky, starless.

The perfect time to dump trash into the Seine.

CHAPTER 11

Days go by. No one knocks on my door to accuse me of murder or to drag me to the gallows for my crimes. I left too much to chance, risking my freedom, but I got lucky. I'll have to be smarter, more careful, if I'm to eventually repay Monsieur Fournier for everything he's done.

For a novice, I was magnificent. Power rushes through my veins for the first time in—well, *ever*. Revenge is sweet. I can't change the past, but I can certainly retaliate for it.

After breakfasting on bread and water, I kiss my sister goodbye and send her on her merry way to eavesdrop on her morning lessons. I have done this every day for years.

But today as I head to work, there's an unprecedented spring in my step. I'm afraid to glance over my shoulders, lest I spy a parade of woodland creatures dancing and chirping merrily behind me. The world is so bright, I must squint to behold it.

When I pass La Croix & Sons, Domingo is on his knees, fitting an obviously aristocratic lord with new dancing shoes.

Domingo's handsome face jerks toward the front window the very second I trip into view. His hazel eyes drink me in.

Despite the presence of a client who far outranks him socially, Domingo abandons the aristocrat's dancing slipper to give me a cheerful wave.

"Torero," I call out in rebuke. My bullfighter. My temptation.

"Mi tesoro," he responds, adding a shameless wink before returning to his business.

My sunny mood only brightens. It's as though the day is made of crystal, all sharp edges and transparent facets, each one reflecting the sun until my eyes dazzle and blur from the ceaseless assault.

In the modiste's shop, the air is stifling. It seems Madame Violette's celebrated protégée hasn't shown up for work for the fifth day in a row. And without a single word to explain her absence.

Madame Violette is visibly annoyed, but loyalty prompts her to mutter, "She must be very sick. Perhaps I should check in on her."

"I'll go," I offer without hesitation.

My shears-wielding colleagues will have none of it. Under their breath, they berate me with increasingly inventive insults, until Pauline seals the matter with a loud "We've been there for tea. You don't even know where she lives. *We* shall go."

Perfect.

I mold my face into a properly humbled expression as they traipse from the sewing room in triumph . . . leaving me alone with our resident goddess, Madame Violette. It is strange to see her standing still instead of rushing about.

"How can I help you?" I ask. Behold, an eager assistant.

She sighs. "My list is ten kilometers long."

I crack my knuckles in anticipation. "Let's start with the first item."

She smiles at me. "You're right. We cannot be idle. I am glad to have you around, Angélique."

I beam at her. See? I'll be a phenomenal protégée.

We're knee to knee across the same worktable, laughing over one of Madame Violette's ribald stories as we work, when the girls ooze back into the room.

They are none too pleased to realize I have spent the past hour in such a casual manner. It's all Marguerite can do not to yank me out of my seat.

"Well?" Madame Violette prompts. "What did Jacqueline say?"

"We knocked forever," Béatrice says with vexation. "She never answered. We thought she was asleep, but she's no longer there!"

"The door was unlocked," Charlotte explains. "Most of her clothes are gone."

Henrietta nods. "The landlady told us Mademoiselle Jacqueline went to visit family in Lille."

"Lille!" Pauline exclaims. "That's over two hundred kilometers away! She must not be planning to return for weeks."

"She won't be returning *here* at all." Madame Violette's face expresses something between disappointment and indignation. "After everything I've invested in that child! I need someone *reliable* to be my right-hand girl."

At this, six spines snap to attention at once, our vertebrae aligning as noisily as popping-corn. I am far from the only one present who seeks to take Jacqueline's place.

Despite my attempt to slide seamlessly into that role, Madame Violette divides Jacqueline's work amongst the six of us equally. I am disappointed, though not surprised. I am confident in my talent and work ethic but not delusional. The other girls are also competent in their skills, or Madame Violette would not employ them. They've also worked here longer.

If I'm to have any hope of being chosen to take Jacqueline's place, I may need a miracle. Or non-divine intervention.

I will do whatever it takes to provide for Elodie and to avenge our family's deaths at the hands of Monsieur Fournier. Who perhaps even now is idly observing some other parent or child lose their life to his looms.

My heart thuds. I know precisely how to exact my revenge on that conscienceless industrialist and his ilk . . . but it will require a subtle hand. There'll be no marching into their houses, swinging a knife. I'm going to make them come to *me*. Tangle themselves in my web.

Like their machines did to my family.

"Angélique," Madame Violette says suddenly.

My head snaps up from my needle and thread. "Yes, madame?"

"Would you still like to design a dress for me?"

Victory rushes through me, sharp and sweet. I can barely

keep hold of my needle. Every bone feels like it has shattered into fireworks.

"Yes, of course," I babble. "At once. You'll have it within the week. Anything you want."

With the way the other girls are glaring at me, I know that new holes in my dress are the least of my concerns.

"All of you," Madame Violette continues, and my elation diminishes. "Rather than search elsewhere for a replacement for Jacqueline, I shall choose one of you."

The expressions on my colleagues' faces are no longer murderous. They are somewhere between delight and panic. We all want the post. And we all know that each of us will do whatever it takes to be the one chosen.

"To be eligible, you must design a gown that impresses me," Madame Violette continues. "Meanwhile, your work for my clients must not suffer. Each entry must be completed on your own time. Understood?"

Six heads bob as though invisible shears have severed our spines.

"And don't rush," Madame Violette warns. "I'm not looking for good. I'm looking for genius. And genius takes time. You have one month."

One month. I glance at the calendar on the wall. Entries will be due on Monday, the twenty-fifth of November.

Leaving me thirty short days to display talent so inspired, it blows away the competition. My hands shake with excitement.

I *need* this role. The privileges of the new position will grant me access to the upper classes in a way I'd never be able to achieve otherwise. Becoming protégée will allow me to exact the perfect revenge on Monsieur Fournier and heartless, exploitative industrialists like him.

I must be chosen. Everything depends upon it.

The bell tinkles at the front of the store. Madame Violette rises to her feet. "That'll be the banker's wife, here for her fitting. Carry on, girls."

The moment the modiste blows down the corridor, my five tormentors whirl around to face me.

"Don't think for a moment that you'll win this competition, mud lark," Henrietta spits.

I shrug and continue my work. "Anything could happen."

"You'll quit and walk away this very second if you know what's good for you," says Béatrice.

I bite off a thread and start another. "I feel pretty good right here."

Charlotte says with incredulity, "Angélique *does* think she'll be the next protégée."

"The orphan?" Pauline picks up her shears and snaps them savagely. "Over my dead body!"

"And mine!" Marguerite adds.

"And mine!" the rest echo.

I guess we'll see.

CHAPTER 12

When the first knock comes, I am not expecting it. I've spent so many sleepless nights terrified that I was seen dumping Jacqueline's corpse in the river that every creak and every footstep and every murmur sounds like the impending doom of armed policemen arriving to drag me off to prison ahead of my public execution.

At the second thunderous knock, I jump out of my skin. Elodie is watching me from the rickety dining table, so I cannot ignore the harsh fist that bangs again and again against our thin front door.

I answer the summons with trepidation. I must act as though everything is normal, but life will be very far from normal when my baby sister witnesses me getting carted away to the nearest guillotine.

The man on the other side of the door is so familiar that I don't even register danger at first. He might be armed, but he's not a policeman. He's our landlord, Monsieur Leroy.

And he's here to collect our rent.

"Uhh . . . ," I stammer eloquently.

Monsieur Leroy holds out his hand. It is encased in an impeccable black leather glove, with nary a scratch or worn edge. His gloves are so expensive and perfect, one could almost believe he buys a new pair before knocking on each door, throwing the old pair away after its surface is sullied by the brush of his tenants' fingertips depositing coins in his palm.

Coins I don't have.

"Your *rent*, girl," he snaps. "I haven't all day."

I shift my weight. "The thing is—"

"The thing is," he interrupts, his blue eyes harsh and unfeeling, "you were short on last month's rent—"

"Our sister and mother died! There were funeral expenses to pay, and Monsieur Fournier refused to relinquish their remaining wages, saying our mother and sister failed to provide sufficient notice they'd be terminating their employment, when he's the one who—"

"I didn't come here for excuses, pet. I came for your rent. If you don't pay me in full for this month and the last—with interest—by the end of the day, then you will have to find alternate housing. This city has too many families happy to pay for lodgings for me to waste my time listening to sob stories."

"Pay him," Elodie hisses, jabbing her elbow into my ribs. "You got your raise, didn't you?"

Monsieur Leroy's eyebrows shoot up. He gives a little bounce to his empty palm. "Hand it over."

I would, except . . . I already did. To *Jacqueline's* landlord, so she'd let me into her apartment. At the time, I'd believed

Jacqueline to be alive and well on the other side of the door, and perfectly capable of paying me back for my impulsive good deed.

As it turned out, however . . .

"Please don't kick us out. I do have some of the money."

I fumble for my coin purse. When I dump the meager contents into his palm, Monsieur Leroy stares at each falling sou as if clumps of bird droppings were accumulating in his hand.

He closes his fist around the coins, jangles the contents as though he can sum up their value by the sound the hard copper makes against the supple softness of his leather glove. He pulls out his own coin purse—a heavy monstrosity almost large enough to hold a severed head—and deposits my offerings inside.

"Thank you, monsieur," I gush in relief. "Next month, I swear to you, at dawn I'll be outside your door with every cent I owe you—"

"Tomorrow at dawn, you will be living on the street," he interrupts. "You have until sundown to settle your account."

"B-but—" I sputter. "You *can't* evict us! You just took every sou we possess—"

"Sundown," he repeats. "Or I shall remove you from these premises. All your physical belongings will be confiscated as payment for past due rent."

"B-b-but—" is all I can manage.

Monsieur Leroy spins on one pristine, shiny black boot and stalks off without waiting for further response.

Elodie rounds on me before I even have time to close the door.

"Why did you do that?" she shouts. "Why didn't you pay him?"

"I *can't*," I blurt out. "I don't have the money anymore."

"Why the devil not? Were you robbed?"

"No, I . . ." Er, yes. I should definitely have claimed to have been robbed. The look Elodie is giving me now is filled with enough disgust to curdle fresh cream.

She crosses her arms and glares at me. "What did you buy that was more important than keeping our home?"

"Rien," I mutter.

I have nothing at all to show for my efforts—yet. But there *is* a new vacancy at my workplace. An apprentice position worth double the salary even the best-paid junior seamstress could hope to earn. Life-changing money.

But that doesn't help us today.

"I can't believe you." Elodie's face is waxen, her voice a whisper. "As if losing our entire family wasn't enough, now we're going to lose our home as well."

"*No*," I say firmly. "I swear that won't happen."

"We have until sundown," she reminds me. "And we have no money. That gives us five hours before we're forced to live on the streets. Unless you have a miracle up your sleeve."

Alas, all I have up my sleeves are goose bumps and clammy flesh.

My mind whirs. What are our choices? Even if Monsieur Leroy were to grant us an entire week to come up with the money, there are no open posts to be had in this godforsaken city. And even if there were, wages aren't paid until after thirty days are up, not before.

If we had a single coin to our name, we could try gambling—if we were men . . . and allowed into such clubs.

The flower girl springs to mind, but that too is a fantasy. Even if Elodie and I collected every stray weed in Paris, we wouldn't earn enough to cover our overdue rent by dusk.

"Angélique, this is serious! Stop woolgathering and start coming up with solutions. If we don't pay our rent in a few short hours, Monsieur Leroy will toss us into the gutter with nothing more than the clothes on our backs—"

"That's it!" I hug her in relief.

She jerks out of my arms in fury. "That sounds like a good idea to you?"

"Not the gutter. The clothes." I race for our parents' bedchamber and motion for her to follow. I wish I still had the flower girl's wagon. "If we work fast and sell every item we can, we'll make the money before sundown."

She stares at me with horror. "Sell the last traces of Maman and Papa?"

"Elodie." I grab her hands. They're ice cold and trembling. "If we don't do this, we'll be out on the streets without any trace of Maman and Papa *or* the home we were forced to leave behind. There's no choice to make. Some things come down to survival."

Her big brown eyes well with tears—and disgust. She knows I'm right and hates me for it. I have never disappointed her more.

"Tie the neck closed on Maman's nightgown," I command, pointing at the old piece of blue linen. "We'll use it as a sack to cart the clothes to a resale shop."

"The nightgown is dirty," Elodie says stubbornly.

"That doesn't matter—"

"It *does* matter," she bursts out, grabbing the wrinkled nightgown from our mother's unmade bed and pressing the worn fabric to her face. "It still smells like Maman. How can we get rid of something that still smells like Maman?"

I stare at her without words, torn between the practical necessity of acquiring rent money by any means available . . . and the childish desire to snatch the dirty nightgown from my baby sister's hands and press it to my face instead. How I long to breathe in my mother's scent one last time!

"Tie the neck," I repeat, choking out each word.

Elodie hears the break in my voice, and the telltale crack almost breaks *her*. Incontrovertible proof that I care as much as she does, but there are no other options. Either we sell every stitch we can in the next few hours, or we'll join thousands of others on the streets.

With tears streaming down her cheeks, she ties the neck of the nightgown closed. She flips the thin dress around, opening the bottom in silent acquiescence to our fate.

"This won't happen again," I tell her as I toss in our father's old stockings. "Once I earn the protégée position with Madame Violette, you won't need to worry—"

"I wasn't supposed to worry *this* time," Elodie snaps. "You said paying the rent would be easy once your position ceased being probationary and you earned a full junior seamstress salary."

"Cabbage—"

"Do you know how I know this will never happen again?" She shakes the open hems of our mother's upside-down nightgown. "Because once we sell every trace of our loved ones, they'll be gone forever. It can't happen again because we won't have anything left to take away."

"We won't sell everything," I mutter. "We'll keep the best of Anne's clothes so you'll have something to grow into. It'll be cheaper than having to buy new material next year."

She drops the nightgown. "You want to sell every trace of Anne, too?"

"No." I scoop up the fallen dress and shove our parents' underthings atop their old stockings. "I don't *want* to do any of the disagreeable things I've had to do recently. But providing for your shelter, food, and safety is my number one priority. If that means letting go of precious memories . . ."

"Where was your number one priority when you spent your wages on nothing at all?"

"Elodie, I am doing the best that I can! I swear that I have done more and tried harder than you can possibly imagine. I will keep doing so for as long as it takes. Right now, I need you to try too. The only way we have a prayer of a chance of keeping this roof over our heads is by working together."

She wipes away tears and snot with the back of her arm, then takes the nightgown from me and silently holds it open.

"I'm sorry," I tell her as our father's work pants disappear into the makeshift sack.

"I'm sorry," I say as I add a trio of threadbare shirts to the growing pile.

"I'm sorry," I repeat as I—

She jerks the nightgown away. I'm left holding a pair of charcoal-black trousers.

"Those are his church trousers," she whispers.

"Elodie—"

"Papa married Maman in those trousers. They're his very favorite trousers. He wore them to each of our christenings."

"Elodie—"

"How can we do this?" She digs through the remaining clothes, pulling out item after item. "This is the apron Maman wore when she cooked the meals we ate together every night as a family. This is the tailcoat *you* sewed Papa, which he said was finer than anything any king had ever worn. This is the shawl Maman wore at our last family picnic, when we were all still alive and here with each other."

"Stop it." My throat is so clogged with tears, the words come out garbled. "I remember all those things too."

That's *why* I will take my revenge. My family didn't have much, but we were happy with what we did have: each other. Now it's just me and Elodie.

Monsieur Fournier killed our innocence, killed our parents, and killed our sister. I will never forgive him for that. *Never.*

"We're not ridding the house of every trace of them," I tell Elodie. "We can save anything that cannot be sold. That's good, isn't it? Anything valuable only to us can stay."

She shakes her head. "It's not enough. Why should strangers get to keep the best parts of what our family left behind?

These things are all we have left. Angélique, please. I cannot bring myself to part with—"

"The truth is, I feel the same way."

"One item," I choke out. "We can save one thing each of Maman and Papa that has true monetary value and could be sold."

Elodie sags in relief, then tenses with renewed anxiety.

You might think this task would be easy when you come from a family where the detritus of life is scattered everywhere throughout your home. But for us, there is nothing extra. Nothing around merely because it's pretty. Nothing not being used in five different ways with ten more planned.

My fingers grasp one of the anthologies by Alexandre Dumas that Papa used to read with me. The leather cover is worn with love, the embossed title faded. The much-handled pages are sprinkled with bent corners, but nonetheless, books like this are collectors' items worth good money.

I shouldn't save it. I have every story memorized. But each page is a cherished memory of my father reading aloud to us before bedtime. Tales like *The Three Musketeers, The Count of Monte Cristo,* and its predecessor, *Georges,* featuring a mixed-race hero just like Alexandre Dumas himself—and me. And Elodie. These stories brought us joy in the past. With luck, perhaps they can continue to do so in the future.

"One thing each," repeats Elodie. "The book is yours. This is mine."

She holds a simple sketch. Though the ornamental frame is of fine quality, the illustration itself would not be worth the cost of its paper if we attempted to hawk the drawing on the Pont Neuf next to all the other street vendors. Many of them are talented artists, whereas this picture was sketched by an untrained hand.

Our mother's hand. This is her interpretation of the sea. She was the only one of us who had seen it.

Elodie and I love this image. Our eyes can detect the curve of the shore, the waves of the ocean, the undulating grains of sand. This isn't any old sea. It is *our* sea. Where we will go one day, together as a family. Where we will finally experience peace and happiness again.

The expensive frame is worth twice as much as Papa's book. These two items alone would go a fair way toward a month's rent. But we deserve nice things too, and they are ours now. Pieces of a past we cannot bear to leave behind. Promises of a better future.

We place the beloved items on the worn couch in our small salon, then return to our parents' bedroom to collect the final remnants of their too-short lives. Neither of us can bear to do what must be done.

"Story time?" I ask Elodie.

She gives a short, brave nod. "Story time."

Stories live forever. In this way, so shall our parents.

I snatch a waistcoat from the wardrobe and hold it up. "This is what Papa wore the day Anne sang her solo in the church choir. He said she had a voice like an angel. The entire congregation agreed. If she'd lived, Anne might one day have performed—" I shove the waistcoat into the sack, unable to go on.

Elodie pulls a folded day dress from the wardrobe and

shakes it out carefully. "This is the dress Maman would wear when she took long walks with us along the Seine on summer evenings. When she'd point at the dirty brown water and tell us all about the endless blue of the North Sea, and how we'd go there one day as a family."

I hold open the nightgown.

She folds the dress with reverence and places it inside.

My turn. I reach for our father's top hat. "This is the hat Anne wore when she pretended to be grown. We told her ladies wore bonnets, so she said who wants to be a lady? Gentlemen get to race horses astride and celebrate their victories like so. . . ." I place the hat on my head, then wave it wildly, making comical snooty expressions the way Anne used to do.

Elodie snorts a laugh through her tears.

It takes us over an hour, but each beloved item of clothing receives a proper eulogy before disappearing inside the sack. We share treasured memory after treasured memory of the countless times we felt cherished and supported and valued by the family we loved more than anything.

The family that we'll never have again.

Memories of a promised future that died along with them.

Every last contribution our hardworking, book-loving father and talented soprano sister and skilled seamstress mother could have made to the world, had Monsieur Fournier not stolen their chance to live up to their potential, snatched away with their last breaths.

Though I manage to pay our rent before sundown with a surplus left over, my chest is hollow. Victory comes at too high a cost.

I learned from a young age that life is full of carelessness and cruelty. Monsieur Fournier did not single out my family. He and all the other greedy industrialists treat their hard workers with the same disinterested callousness. Replacing each disposable human with a vexed sigh, as though the real tragedy was the time it took out of his day to order the rest of us to clean the blood from the machines so that someone new could risk their lives running it.

For the first eighteen years of my life, I took the constant inhumane treatment in silent submission. Believing that this is how the world works. We aren't the people in control. This is our lot in life. The rich and powerful put us in our place, and we have no choice but to stay there.

To the devil with that nonsense.

I'll be a docile lamb no longer. I am the wolf. Revenge will be mine, no matter what sacrifices it may require.

I *will* mete justice for my family. By stopping men like Monsieur Fournier, I'll save countless others from the same fate. My baby sister will one day never have to cry another tear again.

I swear this on my soul.

CHAPTER 13

Poisoning Jacqueline was an act of rage and hurt and grief. I tried to be a perfect employee, and for that she struck me and wished me dead. Still, I didn't mean for her to *die*. Just to feel badly, for once. I must have put too much arsenic in the macarons. Now it is I who feels dreadful.

It does not lift my spirits to see my coworkers in bubbly moods, brandishing selections from their sketchbooks and bragging that they will be the one to win Madame Violette's protégée contest.

Is one of them right? Frankly, my mother drew better than Béatrice. She boasts of never wearing the same dress twice, which proves her wealth but not her ability to design clothing. Her sewing, while technically competent, is uninspired and flat.

Pauline is somewhat more skilled; Henrietta, actually talented. But Charlotte and Marguerite are the real dangers. They've sketched designs it hadn't even *occurred* to me to create. Ones that are imaginative, bold, daring.

Worse still, even if those two were as dull as Béatrice, lack of skill might not matter. For all I know, the competition is in name only. An excuse to give a promotion to a pet. They've worked here longer than me, put in their time. They feel they are owed the increase in status and salary. Perhaps Madame Violette agrees.

The girls glance my way and laugh.

"Forget it," Pauline says with a smirk. "You don't stand a chance, orphan."

"Don't bother trying to win," Charlotte says, smug. "You'll waste your time."

"Like you waste ours," Béatrice adds. "We don't need you here."

"Or anywhere," Henrietta adds, her eyes hard. She loves to wish me out of existence most often.

Their jibes do not ruffle me. I am determined to win this competition.

Whatever it takes.

After work, I walk to La Croix & Sons Shoemakers for my afternoon promenade with Domingo. Although I'm staring straight ahead, my eyes are unfocused and sightless. My brain is too full of strategies to become protégée for me to process my bustling surroundings.

Though my competitors take every bit as much delight in tormenting me as Jacqueline did, I am not the sort of person who could murder in cold blood. But if I could disqualify one or two of them, or distract them long enough for Madame Violette to notice my talent and realize I'm the one she should pick . . .

What choice do I have?

No other modiste in the city was willing to give me a chance, even on a probationary basis. Not with unemployment this high. Without Madame Violette, I am destitute. I cannot even return to being a lowly dye girl. After my unwelcome outburst when Maman and Anne were killed, Monsieur Fournier barred me from his factory—and blackballed me from the industry for good measure.

Without me able to provide any income, it would be up to my sister to brave the machines or toxic chemicals. I can't let it come to that. I vowed before God and my dying mother that I would do anything for my family.

I will keep that promise.

"Lost in thought again?" comes my favorite silky male voice.

I blink to find myself staring right at Domingo. Not only at his handsome face, with its dashing jagged white scar and his intense, dark-lashed hazel eyes, but also at the single red rose he holds in his hand. A grin spreads across my face.

He presents the flower. "I saw this and thought of you."

"Because of its thorns?" I tease.

He doesn't deny the comparison. "Prickly and beautiful. Apparently, I have a weakness for things that are dangerously pretty."

My cheeks heat as I accept the rose. "I'm not certain a girl with a shabby dress and scuffed boots deserves a flower so fine."

"You deserve everything you desire," he says softly. "And as for scuffed boots . . . may I be so bold as to touch your feet?"

My eyebrows shoot up and my skin tingles. "In gratitude for this perfect rose, I shall grant your wish."

"Then I should've asked for a second chance at that kiss." Domingo tosses me a roguish look over his shoulder and disappears back into the shop. He emerges a moment later with a small, bushy-bristled brush and a tin of tar-black shoe polish.

Before I can say a word, he kneels before me, right there on the sidewalk in front of hundreds of elegant shoppers. A few well-coiffed pedestrians send curious looks at the boy on his knees, but Domingo pays them no mind. One hundred percent of his attention is focused on my boots.

On me.

I hold the rose in my hand, mindful of the thorns. He brushes the scuffed leather gently, tenderly. Each stroke sends shivers up my legs and spine and down my arms. It's as if he's petting my entire body. By the time he's done, I am both speechless and breathless.

He springs upright and takes a half step backward to inspect his handiwork. "What do you think?"

"Absolutely gorgeous," I pronounce. I'm staring at him, not the boots.

A smile flashes across Domingo's face as he pivots to return the brush and shoe polish to where they belong.

This time when he emerges, his hands are empty. He gives me his arm. "Are we off to Rue du Faubourg Saint-Honoré again?"

"No, not today."

I don't need to squint up from the shadows at wealthy Monsieur Fournier's grand residence anymore. I know what he and his confederates are like, and I know where to find them. More importantly, I'll have a covert way of paying them back for their crimes—as soon as I earn the protégée position.

With the rose in my hand and the freshly shined black boots on my feet, I'd rather think about the boy who brings me joy, not the man who causes me pain.

"Can we walk by your house today?" I ask Domingo.

His eyes widen in surprise, but he acquiesces without hesitation. "Of course, mi tesoro. It's only fair, isn't it? I've known where you live for weeks. Although you never invite me in."

"And I won't be entering *your* lair unchaperoned, either. I am a lady, after all," I tell him primly.

This is a feint, and we both know it. Only the privileged need chaperones. Girls like me are free to besmirch our virtue whenever and however we please.

As though to prove the point, I clutch his warm, strong arm a little tighter than is proper. We step away from Rue de la Paix and set out for a different area of the city.

Although I dare not tell him so, I am dying to kiss Domingo. I dream about what the experience might feel like. The scent of his skin. How his lips would taste against mine.

And if I am that obsessed without ever having indulged in the smallest, briefest peck, then I certainly cannot cross that line. I'd risk derailing all my plans with a distraction that neither I nor Elodie can afford.

As much as a romance with Domingo tempts me, I cannot contemplate a family of my own until I've taken care of the one I have. Once Anne and my parents are avenged, and my sweet cabbage of a sister has a safe and secure future, then and only then will I allow myself to be courted.

In the 10th arrondissement, we turn down a residential street I've never visited before. Not fancy, like the rich 8th arrondissement, but also not dirty and run-down like the street in the 13th arrondissement where I grew up.

Every fortunate family here has access to an uncracked, sparkling-clean window. Each building has three stories of smooth beige stones, not a single one of which is crumbling or defaced with paint or rancid substances. I take a deep breath. The air is so clean, I can smell the rose in my fist.

"This one on the corner," Domingo says, and points. "My window is on the ground floor, so not much of a view."

Not much of a view! Elodie and I have no window at all. Domingo gets to see this spectacular street when he wakes up in the morning? There are gas streetlamps everywhere, and a profusion of ivy vines clings to the buildings. In spring and summer, flowering plants must spill forth like waterfalls from the wide hanging baskets of his neighbors' windows.

I gape in awe. "You live *here*?"

"It's not much. My apartment is only one room, but . . . yes, I live here." His obvious self-consciousness vanishes when he realizes how much I love his street. "You're welcome to come over any time you like."

I narrow my eyes. "For a croissant, or a debauching?"

He flutters his eyelashes at me innocently. "Which answer earns me a 'yes'?"

"Either one," I mutter to myself, with a last, longing gaze at his pretty street. To him, I say, "You can walk me home to my fine mansion now."

He leads us toward my arrondissement at once, although

he hesitates before speaking. "My humble immigrant background means I have no social status in Paris, but it doesn't mean I'm poor."

I flash him an annoyed eye. "Like me, you mean?"

"No," he says quickly. "I'm not trying to make you feel bad. The opposite. What I mean is, I have nothing much to spend my money on. Monsieur La Croix pays me well, and I have no need for expenses like carriages and extravagant evening wear. So if there's ever anything *you* desire . . . it would be my honor to acquire it for you."

I lift my chin. "I don't need anything."

His eyes are infuriatingly kind. "Angélique . . ."

Oh, very well. We both know he's right: I have absolutely nothing. No parents, no middle sister, very little food on the table, and the all-too-real possibility of losing our decrepit apartment if I don't earn enough to pay the modest rent.

But I *can't* ask Domingo for bread and alms, like a street beggar. He would give it to me without question, and I would hate myself even more than I already do for failing to protect Anne and Maman.

"No, thank you. I'll figure things out on my own," I say firmly.

I will provide for my baby sister. I promised my dying mother that I would.

As soon as the protégée position is mine, I will give my brilliant sister the tutor of her dreams, clothes to fawn over, and food to feed her until she is fashionably roly-poly. And maybe even have enough left over to save up to live on a street like this someday.

"I'd buy you the moon, if you asked me for it," Domingo says quietly, his intense gaze unwavering.

"I don't want the moon, mi torero. I'm happy with your friendship."

A twist at the corner of his mouth. "My friendship, and nothing more?"

I let him see the matching hunger in my own gaze. "For now."

CHAPTER 14

When Domingo and I arrive at my street, I'm thinking about kissing him so hard I'll feel it down to my toes. We both need to be patient, though. Family has to come first. So I send him off with a proper curtsey and a smile.

I throw open the front door and call out for Elodie. The governess lessons she eavesdrops on are over by midafternoon, so she should be home by now.

On cue, she skates out of our bedchamber in her stocking feet. I should scold her—our wooden floors are far from smooth, and liable to rip holes in stockings we can ill afford to replace—but her eyes light up at the sight of the rose in my hand, and I cannot bear to ruin a rare moment of happiness by nagging at her.

"It's *so* beautiful," she gushes, plucking the sharp stem from me in order to shove her nose into the cherry-red bloom. She breathes in deeply. "I've never seen such a perfect rose. The scent is intoxicating."

"Well, you can smell it later." I rescue the flower. "I'm taking you out for a special treat."

Her eyes widen. We *never* have special treats. Our family scarcely has enough money for the bare necessities. But I am determined to be chosen as Madame Violette's next protégée. Once we have the extra hundred francs a month, life will be much better. Today, I want to show Elodie a small taste of what I'm working toward.

She claps her hands. "Where are we going?"

"You'll find out when we get there. Now go and put on your shoes." I turn her toward the jumbled pair of abandoned half boots in the corner and place Domingo's rose in the chipped vase on the small dining table.

The vase is not empty—Elodie has found another wildflower, which is hunched and sickly drooping next to Domingo's exquisite rose with its abundance of red petals and strong, thick stem.

"That other flower is chicory. I'll take it out of the vase when we get back home," Elodie promises. "It's time for my next experiment anyway."

Elodie and her perfumes. Twelve years old and a self-made prodigy. She gifts her creations to members of our family every birthday and Christmas. I swear Elodie's concoctions are every bit as exquisite as the perfumes sold in fancy stores. If she'd had access to a real tutor from a young age, who knows what she would be capable of becoming?

I cannot alter the past, but I can ensure Elodie has every opportunity in the future.

"Come on, then," I say, locking the door before we go.

It's still autumn, and the sun won't set for another hour. You could argue, with all our gas-lit streetlamps, that the sunshine never does go away here in the City of Light.

I cannot afford both a treat for my sister and the omnibus fare to ride across town in comfort, so we set out on foot.

Elodie doesn't complain. She's never ridden in a carriage, so she doesn't know what she's missing. As soon as I receive my new protégée salary . . .

"*Please* tell me where we're going?" she wheedles, batting her eyelashes at me impishly.

I wag my finger at her. "You'll find out soon enough."

She doesn't actually care. Elodie is too overjoyed at the prospect of a pleasant surprise. She frolics beside me like a fawn in the woods. I must take care to protect her from predators.

"Is the surprise . . . the beach?" she asks.

She knows it is not. But this is a game we have played since she was very small. Although we have never seen the ocean, we dream of it the way caterpillars dream of sprouting wings and flying. In other words, it seems impossible, yet simultaneously feels like something we were born to do.

"Of course we're going to the beach," I tell her. "We are going to take a train all the way there."

Elodie claps her hands. We are one hundred and seventy kilometers away from the closest shore.

She grabs my arm and leans her head against me. "How many days will we spend at the ocean?"

"As many as you want," I tell her. "We'll stay until you get sick of it."

"I'll never get sick of it!"

"Then I guess we'll have to live there forever, in a cottage on the shore."

"We'll be able to smell the water from the front door?"

"From every corner of the cottage. We won't just smell the salt in the air. There will be windows in every room, and we'll keep them open all day and all night, so that the warm sunlight and the cool ocean breeze fill the house like a summery perfume."

"And when we go outside, the waves won't be too big?"

"The waves will be perfect. We'll help each other learn to swim, and when we tire of that, we'll float on our backs beneath the sun and let the cool water rock us gently like two little ducklings."

She lets out a soft sigh filled with so much longing, it nearly breaks my heart.

"Can we really go someday, Angélique?" she asks in a small, wistful voice.

"We really will, I promise. Once I'm Madame Violette's official protégée, I'll be able to afford to travel. We'll be relaxing on the beach before you know it."

"Next year," she whispers.

Next year is what we always say. Since before Elodie was born, and it was Maman and Papa and me dreaming of a better life. Then Anne along with us. Then Elodie. And now only the two of us.

I mean every word about the protégée position. It's going to change our lives in ways Elodie cannot even imagine.

"You won't have to wait a year," I tell her. "We'll visit the ocean this coming spring."

She stares at me as though she's never heard of springtime in her life.

"Spring?" she repeats with incomprehension.

"Soon, cabbage. This coming May. A few months from now. You, me, and the sea. A sister holiday."

Her eyes are wide as gold pieces. "It's truly going to happen?"

"Really and truly."

She throws her arms around me and hugs me so hard, it's impossible to walk. I try to move anyway, stiffening my legs and clomping forward with her smaller boots atop mine. The other pedestrians on the busy street cast us disapproving glances and step out of our path.

I laugh and hug my sister back, grateful that I have her in my life.

Before long, we are on le Boulevard des Italiens, surrounded by rows of luxurious shops and restaurants. "All right, cabbage, we're almost there. Be ready."

Elodie surveys the area in wonder. "Can we *afford* anything on this street? It's as fancy as where you work, on Rue de la Paix."

I shrug. "Maybe the surprise is that we are going to beg for our supper."

She swats my arm. "You would never. You won't even consider letting me apply to any of the factories."

"You shall *not* spend a single second risking your life at an unsafe machine," I vow fiercely. "Everything I am fighting for is so that you can have a better—"

"I know, I know." She holds up her palms in surrender. "You've always taken care of . . ." *Anne and me.*

Elodie doesn't finish her sentence. Her voice fades instead. But I know exactly what she means. My own throat grows tight at the reminder.

I stop her before we cross the next intersection and point left down Rue Laffitte. "Look, there!"

She gasps and clasps her hands to her chest. "It's Sacré-Cœur!"

Elodie has seen the iconic white basilica hundreds of times, but she appreciates beautiful things. This vantage point offers a stunning view of the domed white towers reaching up into the pink-and-orange-streaked sky.

We gaze in silence for a long moment as the sun sinks below the horizon, taking its brilliant colors along with it.

Elodie throws her arms around my torso and hugs me. "Merci, Angélique."

"That wasn't your surprise, my little cabbage," I tease her. "Unless you're tired of walking?"

She drops her arms from me at once, shaking her head wildly. "I'll walk wherever you want to go!"

"Five hundred meters," I tell her. She falls into step beside me. I point out famous landmarks as we pass. "The restaurant on the corner there is Café Anglais, where aristocrats and businessmen dine on multicourse meals."

Elodie's eyes widen. I'm not actually certain of the number of courses served at one meal—someone like me would be turned away from the door even if I had enough money—but Parisian caricaturists oftentimes depict factory owners like

Monsieur Fournier and his wife surrounded by countless silver trays heaped with delicacies I've never tasted.

"Et là"—I point as we walk—"that's the aptly named Café Riche."

A family so refined that they could have been outfitted by Madame Violette herself strolls out of the café as we watch, seemingly very satisfied indeed. When they see us staring, they wrinkle their noses and turn their backs to us.

This family is the reverse of ours. The mother white, the father Black. Three boys instead of girls. Rich instead of poor. Healthy and happy. Alive. I try not to be jealous but fail miserably. I need to distract Elodie from making the same bleak comparison.

"See right over there, cabbage? That restaurant is called La Maison Dorée. It's full of paintings and mirrors, and is known for its gold balconies and balustrades." I'm not certain if the railings are made of gold or merely gilded, but either way, they're finer than anything Elodie and I have touched.

She stops walking then sighs with longing. "Oh, Angélique. Can you imagine?"

Elodie can stand transfixed before something beautiful for hours, so I am forced to tug her across the next intersection by the hand in order to break the spell.

"And look here," I tell her with satisfaction, "c'est le Café Tortoni."

Her mouth falls open and she licks her lips. "The best ice cream in all of Paris?"

I grin at her. We may be poor, but Elodie *does* know what ice cream is. Whenever one of us girls had a birthday, our parents would take us out for ices. Or rather, *an* ice. There was only ever enough money for the birthday girl, and even then, from the cheapest street vendor Maman and Papa could find.

Café Tortoni is nothing like that. The most fashionable people in Paris dine here for their famous ice cream. And today, I will buy a scoop for my baby sister. She deserves the very best, at least once in her life.

Elodie hugs me. "Merci beaucoup, Angélique. This is the best birthday present ever."

I blink, suddenly feeling far less smug about my generosity. She's right. Her birthday is coming up fast. Elodie will be thirteen years old before I know it. With my new post, and the double tragedy of losing Anne and Maman, I lost track of time.

"It's not your birthday present," I tell her. "The fourteenth of December is six weeks away. This year, you'll have cake for your birthday."

She wiggles in place. "Any piece I want from the bakery?"

"An entire cake of your choice, mon petit chou. The whole thing, just for you."

"*And* I get ice cream today?" she says dubiously.

Laughing, I drag her to one of the few vacant outdoor tables. It hasn't been cleared of the previous customers' waste yet, which is probably why no one else has taken these seats. Elodie and I don't mind waiting.

"What fancy flavor are you going to get?" I ask, trying to ignore the tidal wave of disparaging glances from well-dressed patrons.

Elodie bounces and claps her hands. "Truffle. No—saffron. What about you?"

My stomach growls in eager anticipation.

"None," I tell her. "I'm not hungry. But you can have a scoop of both flavors, if you like."

With a squeal, she wraps her arms around me and lays her head on my shoulder. "You're the best biggest sister in the whole world."

That's a private joke the three of us used to have, Elodie and Anne and me. I was the best eldest sister, Anne the best middle sister, and Elodie the best youngest sister.

Now there's no longer a need to clarify. We've become each other's *only* sister.

But I kiss her forehead and play the game. "Anything for the best baby sister in the world."

CHAPTER 15

The long hours at work fly, now that it has turned into a battleground. All six of us girls, competing for the role of protégée. I size them up the next day when they're not paying attention.

Béatrice, the daredevil daughter of a wealthy butcher. She doesn't *have* to work, but she chooses to, in order to fund her fashion obsession. She very recently commissioned a special riding dress. Not for a horse, but for her cousin's vélocipède, a two-wheeled contraption that only the rich and reckless dare to ride.

Her sketches are dreadful, as usual, but I can find no fault in how she wields a needle. If she tried harder, she might actually provide some competition.

Henrietta's father is a foreman at the national railway and therefore not quite as rich as Béatrice's, though Henrietta is every bit as advantaged. Her mother owns mink coats and lets Henrietta wear a fur muff on special occasions in the wintertime. Henrietta likely wishes she were wearing it right now, if only to gloat.

She certainly brags enough about her designs for the competition. I've seen a few, and they're . . . better than expected. She's unlikely to take Paris by storm, but I would trust her to dress a young lady for her debut or fashion a decent wedding trousseau.

Marguerite is the daughter of a successful taxidermist. Her prized possession is a straw bonnet with a tiny stuffed songbird sewn to the brim. She says she trapped the bird herself and suffocated it with her bare hands so that her father could douse the corpse in chemicals to make it last forever.

Her designs might also last forever. Of the competition, Marguerite is hands down the most talented. Her challenge won't be coming up with an idea capable of winning, but rather, choosing from dozens of winning ideas. A chilling thought.

Boy-mad Pauline claims she can ensnare the heart of any man alive with a single beam of her dimpled smile. Her ample curves, smooth brown skin, and eye-catching twists of shiny black hair don't hurt her chances, either.

With the boys, anyway. The odds of Pauline winning the protégée position are . . . less likely. Her best designs seem to be cobbled together from glimpses of other people's work. She can re-create any fashion plate illustration with her eyes closed, but when it comes to innovating her own pattern, her needle stops.

Lastly, there's Charlotte, a rich dairy farmer's granddaughter, who has never known a hungry night. She loves to tell us about her leisurely breakfasts of fine cheeses and ice creams. The others say she must be constipated. I think they're jealous. I know I am.

Not only is she well rested and curvaceous, Charlotte is second only to Marguerite when it comes to designing. If the right inspiration were to strike, perhaps Charlotte would shine brighter than us all.

I can't let that happen.

As our workday closes, Charlotte is last in line for the door, so I catch her elbow before she leaves.

"What do you want, Angélique?" she snarls.

Charlotte is actually the nicest of the lot. Like the others, she never has a kind word for me, but at least Charlotte calls me by name, rather than "orphan" or "guttersnipe."

And let's be honest: If Elodie and I had a dairy farmer for a grandfather, we would be eating fine cheeses and ice cream for breakfast too, no matter how constipated it made us.

"I'd like to ask a favor," I say in a rush.

"No." Her lip curls. "Whatever it is, I don't owe you a thing."

"It's for the competition. I need a live model in order to tailor my contribution—"

She splutters in disbelief. "You want me to help you try to *beat* me?"

"If you're the better designer, I won't win no matter what I sew," I point out. "And in appreciation for your sacrifice, no matter who wins the contest, I'll let you keep the items. You'll look even more glamorous than the aristocrats."

She snorts. "As if I would want to wear anything that you created."

True. She would rather cut off her own nose than do a kindness for me. Or for any of the other girls. The cattiness in our little sewing room is thick as gravy. Which gives me an idea . . .

I shrug, as if nonchalant. "Perhaps I should ask Béatrice. Her proportions aren't as ideal as yours, and her face is a bit pasty for my taste, but with the right design and fit, she could outshine us all. In fact, such a transformation alone makes her a much better choice of model than—"

"Show me the design." Charlotte's black eyes glint. She'd say yes to anything if it means being better than Béatrice.

"Oh, no, never mind. There's no sense wasting your time, when there's a better—"

"I said I'll do it," she snaps. "Leave Béatrice to her own amateurish designs. Besides, a change from plain to pretty is far less appealing than elevating beautiful to stunning."

Absolutely breathtaking modesty. Appealing to Charlotte's vanity was clearly the right choice.

"Very well." I shake my finger at her. "But no copying. You'll see what I make as I create it. Each piece specifically crafted to highlight your best characteristics."

"And I'll be the prettiest of us all," she finishes.

"You already are," I assure her. "Especially with your gorgeous black curls and beautiful dark brown skin. Your beauty will be celestial. Béatrice *wishes* she could be half the magnificent goddess that you will be."

A pleased smile twitches at Charlotte's lips. She likes the sound of "magnificent goddess."

"What exactly will I have to do?" she asks.

"Stay half an hour after work, two days a week. The first pieces are a corset and a nightgown. I'll even let you take them home with you as soon as I'm finished."

My process includes dyeing the nightgown in a variant of the special mixture I learned to make at Monsieur Fournier's factory. Not the lifeless pale mint of his factory-produced silks but a rich, vibrant green resulting from a higher concentration of ingredients. His watered-down proportions to cut corners won't do, so I had to visit chemists far outside the city to find a price I could afford. To achieve the results I'm hoping for, my version of the dye contains a bit more arsenic than we used in the factory. Not enough poison to kill her . . . but enough to weaken Charlotte and keep her from winning the contest.

"All right," she says. "I'll do it. But first you have to tell Madame Violette and the others I get to keep every item I model for you. That way there's no going back on your word."

"It's a deal," I promise. "We start tomorrow?"

She nods. "Tomorrow. Now if you'll excuse me, some of us have lives to get back to."

I step aside and let her flounce out the door, buoyant in her certainty that she got the best of me.

Charlotte boards a passing omnibus. I cannot turn away. How dizzying it must be to spend your salary on nothing but treats for yourself! At least, it would be dizzying for me. Charlotte doesn't even notice her good fortune.

I thoroughly cherish every bit of luck that trickles toward me, and practically skip down Rue de la Paix toward La Croix & Sons.

Ten meters from the door, who should step into my path but my baby sister?

"Elodie!" I exclaim. "What are you doing here?"

"I couldn't wait," she blurts out. "I wanted to thank you for being such a marvelous sister. For the ice cream, and for spending time with me, and for taking care of me—"

"Bien sûr, it is my pleasure. I will always take care of you, my little cabbage. I love you." I pull her into my arms and breathe in the scent of her hair. She smells like a bouquet of flowers.

Elodie presses a small bottle into my hand. It's the chipped eau de cologne Papa bought for Maman on their ten-year wedding anniversary. The perfume ran out long ago, but the empty bottle remained on Maman's bedside table until eight-year-old Elodie informed us all that she was going to be a great parfumeur one day. Maman gave her the bottle and told her never to give up her dreams. Elodie has slept with that tiny glass bottle beneath her pillow every night since.

And now it's in my hand. Heavier than it should be . . .

"What's this?" I ask.

"A gift." Elodie's big brown eyes shine with pride. "A present from me to you. Try it on. It's rose water!"

I blink. "Rose . . . water?"

I know what rose water is, of course. It's one of the cheapest, most widely available non-perfumes on the market, made by steeping rose petals in hot water until they lose their color. But where could Elodie have procured a rose? Unless . . . she used . . .

"Was this made from the rose that *I* brought home?" I

demand, shaking the bottle in my fist. "Did you *boil* the first flower a boy ever bought me?"

"Wh-what?" Elodie's smile wobbles, then falls completely. "I thought . . . I thought the rose was for me."

"Why would you think that?" I snap, frustrated that she's destroyed the one beautiful thing I owned.

"I-I'm always the one bringing home flowers . . . to brighten your day," she stammers. "I thought that this time, it might have occurred to *you* to . . ."

She trails off.

No. It did not occur to me. I didn't even realize that the reason an endless stream of flowers wilts on our small table before disappearing into another of her experiments is because she thinks the presence of something pretty would cheer *me* up.

All along, she's been trying to take care of me, like I've been trying to take care of her.

I feel like such a shrew. "Elodie . . ."

She snatches the bottle from my hand. "I wanted you to be able to enjoy the rose all winter long, not for a few scant days until the petals fell. I'm tired of being useless. Just a mouth to feed. I wanted to do something nice for you, and making things out of flowers is all I know how to do."

"You're not useless, or a mouth to feed. You're my sister—"

"—who ought to have a job," she finishes. "You're taking on too much. Instead of you staying after hours to work on additional projects, if I could provide an income of my own—"

"For the last time, Elodie, there is no way in hell I will allow you to set foot inside a dangerous factory. How you could even *want* to work for someone like Monsieur Fournier after his machines killed our—"

"Not there! As an apprentice parfumeur."

"Elodie . . ."

The chances of anyone hiring a twelve-year-old to be an apprentice parfumeur are so low that they're almost nonexistent. As brilliant as she is, Elodie is an uneducated little girl. With over half the population of Paris unable to find work, there are plenty of skilled adults willing to lower themselves to apprentice positions, if any were available.

But that isn't what Elodie needs me to say. She is a child, and she wants the fairy tale. It's the big sister's job to give it to her.

"You started to work on your twelfth birthday," she reminds me.

I hold up my disfigured pinkie. "A gift I will always cherish."

"Parfumeuries aren't dangerous," she bursts out, her voice shaking. "I will take every precaution—"

"Cabbage, if you find an apprentice position at a parfumeur's shop, of course I will support you."

She eyes me suspiciously, then drops her mournful gaze to the rejected rose water in her hand. Before I can reach for it, she shoves the perfume bottle out of sight into her pocket.

"Angélique?" comes a soft voice, rich like chocolate.

Domingo.

Has he been watching us from his shop window? Waiting for us to stop arguing long enough that he could come and greet my sister? Would he even recognize her from that emotional day at the cemetery?

"The one and only Mademoiselle Elodie Genêt. A pleasure to meet again." Domingo sweeps into a deep bow.

Elodie's cheeks flush. It seems like she's not sure whether to burst into confetti or melt into the pavement.

"Don't get any designs on Domingo," I tease her. "He brings *me* flowers."

Her eyes dull. "So you're the boy?"

Domingo appears amused. "I suppose?"

"You owe Angélique a new rose," Elodie says. "I ruined the one you bought her."

I shake my head. "It wasn't your fault. How could you know where it came from if I failed to tell you? And I do love your gift. I was merely caught by surprise—"

Domingo waves both of us into silence. "I will buy a dozen such roses for each of you. It is no problem." He turns to Elodie and whispers, "And you're free to ruin yours however you like."

She giggles, then ducks her head so that her glossy black curls hide her face from view.

"How *does* one ruin a rose, by the way?" Domingo asks.

Elodie slinks a mortified look at me.

I hold up my good hand. "If you expect to be taken seriously as an apprentice, you'd better be able to convince my friends of your skill."

Domingo raises his brows. "Do all Angélique's friends give her flowers?"

"She doesn't have any other friends," Elodie puts in.

I *did* have friends, back at the factory. Five female friends. But this is not what Domingo is referring to, and we both know it.

"We talked about this," I admonish him. "I'm not ready for anything more."

He grins unrepentantly. "And I'll keep trying to change your mind."

"I'm a parfumeur," Elodie blurts out.

Domingo blinks. "You . . . are?"

She takes the eau de cologne bottle from her pocket and hands it to him. "I made this for Angélique."

He pulls out the stopper and takes a sniff. "Rose water. From my rose?"

She nods.

"It does smell nice." He hands back the bottle.

"I will do better once I have more equipment," Elodie mutters without meeting his eyes.

"You intend to become an apprentice?"

"Not any old apprentice." Her head jerks up so fast, the curls bounce away from her face. I know the name she's going to invoke before she even says it. "I want to apprentice Pierre-François-Pascal Guerlain."

She says his name the way some people say *Napoléon Bonaparte* or *the Pope*. As if this parfumeur were an emperor and a god all at once.

"Lo siento—I . . . don't know who that is," Domingo admits.

"Only the most celebrated parfumeur in France," I inform him. "Elodie has been obsessed since she was a toddler."

"His parfumeurie, La Maison Guerlain, has a boutique right here on Rue de la Paix." Elodie bounces on her toes. "If I apprentice for him, the three of us will work practically right next to each other. We can take our lunches together!"

That's my baby sister: kindhearted, forgiving, and sunny to a fault.

"Well," I say, "Rue de la Paix was the first street in Paris to have gaslight. Why not also be the first street in Paris to boast soon-to-be celebrity parfumeur... Mademoiselle Elodie Genêt?"

"And soon-to-be world-famous designer Madame Angélique Genêt," she adds.

I laugh. "'Madame' is for married women. Don't you mean Mademoiselle Angélique?"

Elodie gives Domingo a playful grin. "*Is* that what I mean?"

"That is up to Angélique," he tells her. "I'm still trying to earn the chance to court her."

Now my cheeks are on fire.

"All right, you two," I grumble. "That's enough."

But I don't mind their teasing. It makes me feel hopeful. Like Elodie and I might have a bigger, loving family again one day.

Maybe I'll let Domingo have that chance sooner than he thinks. Revenge needn't be such a lonely endeavor.

CHAPTER 16

On Sundays, I don't have to work. Neither does the governess Elodie eavesdrops on. This Sunday, we spend the lazy morning in our usual routine: breakfasting together, then washing and arranging each other's hair into braided chignons. Except it is not the same routine, not without Anne and Maman. Our fingers are clumsy in comparison, and we finish our tasks with too much time to spare.

Once we look the best we can, Elodie and I sit cross-legged on our sole rectangle of worn, mold-colored carpet. We play countless rounds of mouche with playing cards so old, they're soft as silk.

After sharing a lunch of bread and soup, we curl up against each other on the threadbare sofa to read aloud from Alexandre Dumas. Before long, we tire of *The Count of Monte Cristo* and gaze upon our mother's framed sketch of the North Sea in its place of honor on our wall. Our talk turns to our plans to see the ocean for ourselves one day.

Eventually, Elodie excuses herself to work on her perfume

experiments. Usually, I spend the afternoons designing dresses in my little sketchbook, but today the competition with my co-workers reminds me of every advantage they have that Elodie and I do not. Parents, plenty of food, free time to spend frolicking with useless toys. I cannot get Béatrice's smug claims of having ridden an actual vélocipède out of my head.

The dangerous two-wheeled contraptions are expensive and unpredictable, so we rarely see one on the streets. The wealthy, who promenade in the prettiest parks in the afternoons to show off their horseflesh and their finery, are the ones who race their vélocipèdes in public areas for all to admire.

Béatrice says she mixes with aristocrats and haute bourgeoisie in the Jardin des Tuileries on Sundays. Always decked out in the latest fashions, and never rewearing the same gown. Now that I think of it, I'm not certain it's possible to ride a vélocipède while corseted and bustled and draped in long skirts down to one's ankles.

The idea of catching her in a lie intrigues me and cannot be resisted. I stuff my sketchbook and pencil into my reticule, a mitten-sized cloth pouch I can hang from my wrist by its drawstring, then head out toward the public park. Despite my freshly arranged hair and painstakingly sewn dress, amongst the upper classes I'll come off as a housemaid at best.

For once, I don't mind the invisibility. I want to find Béatrice without her noticing I'm here.

The Jardin des Tuileries is an Italian Renaissance–style garden, built by Queen Catherine de Medici three hundred years ago for royal use. One hundred years later, it was opened to the public... except for beggars, soldiers, and undesirables. Meaning people like me. The vast garden has only bloomed bigger and brighter in the decades since and is now open to everyone. I slip in unnoticed.

Despite the vast acres and countless walking paths, it doesn't take long to find Béatrice. She is indeed dressed like a popinjay, in a shocking confection of bright red and yellow and blue. She is also talking so loudly, her voice carries throughout half the park. Boasting incessantly, exactly as she does in the sewing room. It is a wonder any of her beaux can stand her. Or perhaps the flock of young men surrounding her are brothers and cousins, with no choice but to chaperone one of their blood?

I spy the vélocipèdes, and my breath catches. There are two of them, both being ridden by young gentlemen. There is no way to propel the vehicle, nowhere to place your feet while it is in motion. You either balance on its little leather seat and take off at a run until you can lift your shoes and coast to your destination, or you start at the top of a hill and let gravity do with you as it pleases.

Once you get started, there is no way to stop, other than slamming your feet down on the ground—which often has the effect of tossing rider and vélocipède in opposite directions. Staying on is an art akin to riding a bull.

"Please," I hear Béatrice whine in a false, grating soprano. "Let me have a turn."

"Vélocipèdes are for men, cousin," replies the disinterested gentleman to her left. "Théo and I are next."

Ha! I knew it! These are not her beaux, and she has never ridden a vélocipède. She's probably worn that dress many times too, and does not throw them out every night as she likes to claim.

The boys on the two-wheeled contraptions fly toward the bottom of the hill like two flashes of lightning. One of the lads tries to stop with his boots and ends up bucked off the leather seat. The other boy barrels straight into a bush and lands with a clatter.

They both spring up, smiling.

It looks incredibly dangerous, and incredibly fun. Careful to stay out of sight, I climb the hill and station myself behind the trees so that I can watch the next duo take on the sloped stone path from the very beginning.

I'm in place for less than a minute when the two lads appear, vélocipèdes in tow.

Béatrice is right behind them, still begging for a turn.

I sink to the grass between the tree roots and pull the brim of my bonnet low. No one even glances my way.

The one called Théo leans his vélocipède against the very tree I remain hidden behind, so that he can better argue with Béatrice.

"You *have* to let me try," she wheedles. "Papa said so."

"Papa may let you have everything you want, but I don't have to," Théo says stubbornly. Her brother.

"Oh, let your sister try," says the cousin. "If she crashes into a bush and gets leaves in her hair, she'll never want to do it again."

"Fine," Théo grumbles, and gives a long-suffering sigh. "But only this once."

Béatrice squeals and shouts down to her cousins at the bottom of the hill that her turn is next. They are too busy talking amongst themselves to acknowledge her presence, so she juts her lower lip into a sulky pout.

"Now, listen close," says Théo. "I'll be watching from up here, but I won't be able to help you. Move the handles to steer the front wheel. When you get to that section of pavement stones there—" He grabs her elbow and points down the path.

No one is paying me any attention.

Impulsively, I scoop up a fist-sized rock and bring it down violently against the bolt securing the front wheel.

The entire vélocipède shudders at the impact, rattling against the bark of the tree. Startled, I drop the rock and duck back into my hiding place just as the others turn around to glance at the vélocipède.

"What was that?" asks Béatrice.

"The wind," Théo answers in disgust. "If you're going to be missish . . ."

"I'm not afraid of anything!" Béatrice protests.

"Then let's go," says the cousin, arranging himself on his vélocipède.

Théo retrieves his vehicle from beside my tree and positions it parallel to the other vélocipède. "Try not to crash into Louis."

"I won't," Béatrice huffs, then hikes her skirts up to her knees so that she can mount her brother's vélocipède.

Despite my tantrum with the rock, all appears to be well. She'll probably even win the race.

Théo counts down from five. Then Béatrice and Louis are off, flying down the slick stone hill. The ribbon tied beneath Béatrice's chin comes untied, and she erupts in peals of laughter as her bonnet sails off behind her. With every meter they descend, the vélocipèdes roll faster and faster.

They are almost to the bottom of the hill when it happens.

The bolt I hit works loose and tumbles free. Béatrice's front wheel dislodges from the handlebars, pitching her forward—straight into the path of Louis's vélocipède.

He has no time to stop. No *way* to stop.

His perfectly attached front wheel rolls directly over Béatrice's splayed legs, followed immediately by his rear wheel.

The loud cracks of splintering bones ricochet through the park like cannon fire.

Not made for riding over human bodies, Louis's vélocipède pitches him from his perch and falls to one side.

After a short flight, Louis lands squarely atop Béatrice's chest.

I cannot hear the crack of her ribs, but her screams stop as abruptly as they began. The sudden silence is deafening. Her family races over to her in horror. Louis launches himself off his cousin, reaching for her motionless wrist to check her pulse.

"She's alive!" he shouts to the others.

I sag against the tree in relief at the news. Thank God I didn't kill her. I'm not a *monster*. One accidental murder doesn't make me a killer at heart.

But . . . now there *is* one less rival to worry about in the protégée contest. Creating a gown worthy of Madame Violette will be tedious, backbreaking work, and from her cries of agony, Béatrice will not be able to stand, much less sew.

The competition is down to five.

CHAPTER 17

Monday evening, Elodie arrives home in a fury. She refuses to speak to me, stomps into our bedchamber, and slams the door behind her.

On Tuesday evening, fury has splintered into panic, causing her to raid Anne's old clothes in search of something "older" and "more professional" that might make fashionable perfume masters take a twelve-year-old seriously. It hurts me to see what's left of Anne's clothes strewn about, when we can never have our sister back again. But Elodie is desperate. She claims if she had prettier bottles, a better library of essential oils, and something called a Faraday burner, she would be gainfully employed.

By Wednesday evening, she's not speaking at all. My sister has instead lapsed into a morose, nonverbal fugue in which nothing exists but the dark fog of crushed dreams and continual rejection.

Thursday morning, Elodie blocks the door when I try to leave for work. She bursts into tears when I ask her gently to step aside.

"Everyone wants me to step aside!" Tears streak down her cheeks. "They laugh in my face or shoo me away with a rolled-up newspaper as though I'm an irksome fly to squash."

"Elodie," I say, my voice as soft and kind as possible.

I do not have words of encouragement. I knew from the start that no parfumeur in his right mind would hire a child with no real experience when there are grown men seeking work who have practiced chemistry for decades.

Make no mistake: I believe in my sister. She *will* get there someday. But today is not that day. Perhaps not even tomorrow. And *I* have real work to attend to, in order to feed, clothe, and house us both.

"I have to go to work, cabbage."

"No!" She throws her arms about my neck, clinging to me the way she used to do when she was two and three and four years old. Her tears drip into my bodice. My neck is wet with her snot.

"Elodie. Please be reasonable. One of us has to earn money."

"I'm *trying*!"

"Yes, I know. But until you find an apprenticeship, the only working person is me. You must let me go. I am trying to secure an important promotion. We cannot risk me losing my position altogether."

"Stay home," she pleads. "Just for today. They won't sack you. Not with your colleague out sick."

Sick, maimed, whatever. Not reporting to duty.

"That's not the point, cabbage. There's much to be done. If the other girls are punctual and must perform my tasks for me, how do you think that makes me look to Madame Violette?"

"Then stay with me for half the day," Elodie haggles, still clinging and sniffling. I haven't seen her in a state like this since the night I was forced to tell her about the tragedy at the factory. "An hour, Angélique. *Please.* Spend thirty minutes with me. Fifteen."

I peel her arms from me, and she slumps to the floor like I've cut the strings to a marionette.

"Get back up, mon petit chou. Don't let the world win. You're not beaten yet."

"I asked everyone," she says hollowly. "Even the charlatans whose 'eaux de cologne' are little more than river water. I'm useless."

"You can help *me*," I remind her for the fifth day in a row. "I'm barely sleeping as it is, between working extra hours and designing my contest dress. You have an excellent stitch when you take your time and concentrate. When I get home from work, I could cut the pieces while you—"

"I don't want to do your job. I want my own!" The tears start anew.

I haul her to her feet like a rag doll stuffed with sand. "Get ahold of yourself. The best lesson you can learn is that crying doesn't solve anything. Action does. If you can't find work today, keep learning and improving. In the meantime, if we leave right now and you walk with me, I'll detour through Les Halles and buy you a plum at the market."

Her eyes widen, and the tears stop. Elodie wants to believe she's grown, but she is still of an age where a sugary-sweet treat is enough to distract her from her darkest hours.

There is no time to change clothes, so we shrug into our

coats and set out with my bodice and décolletage still crusty with her snot and tears. I scrub at myself with a handkerchief as we walk, leaving the skin flushed and angry but at least free from sisterly residue.

The Halles market has operated in the same hectares of the 1st arrondissement since the eleventh century. It is as dense and bustling as ever. Monsieur Baltard, the official architect of Paris, is rumored to be planning a steel-and-glass structure to house the sprawling market, but for now we are left to defend ourselves against shouting vendors, jostling elbows, and the chill of the open air.

It's November, so plums are still in season for a few weeks longer. I buy Elodie two, even though I can ill afford to splurge right now.

"Be good," I tell her. "Go learn from your governess and enjoy your plums."

She's not listening, more concerned with ingesting every drop of nectar.

With a roll of my eyes, I hurry on to Rue de la Paix. Today I am in such a rush that all I can do is offer Domingo a distracted wave in the general direction of the La Croix & Sons shop window as I sprint down the street, dodging pedestrians as I run.

I'm late, of course. Madame Violette doesn't notice—she's with a client in one of the dressing rooms. But the other girls spear me with their eyes, unsure whether to be offended at my tardiness or pleased at having fresh material with which to judge me lacking.

"Did you finally wake up, ma princesse?" asks Marguerite, the dead songbird on her bonnet bobbing as she sews.

Henrietta tosses one of her blond sausage curls over her shoulder. "*Some* of us deserve our posts and arrive to work on time. You should go back to the factory."

"It's where you belong," Marguerite agrees.

"My family *died* there!" I blurt out, tears pricking my eyes. I hate myself for letting them get to me. "Every year, those factories kill dozens of workers and permanently injure hundreds more. Don't you care?"

Henrietta shrugs. "As the saying goes, you can't make an omelette without breaking a few eggs."

I'm so furious, I can't even see straight. Or maybe that's because of the tears I'm desperately trying to blink away. If my coworkers spot my weakness, they'll eat me alive.

Pauline smirks. "Speaking of broken eggs, we have Béatrice to thank for making the contest a little easier."

Charlotte's tone is amused. "None of us are shedding tears over losing a competitor. . . ."

"She was never going to win," Marguerite snaps. "Neither will either of you."

Henrietta's hard eyes swing toward me. "Why stop with Béatrice? Care to make another omelette for us, orphan?"

She mimes crushing an egg in her fist. The shells are my bones, and the slimy yolk sliding between her fingers is the last of my lifeblood.

I don't give her the satisfaction of reacting, but inside, my mind is whirling. If the police *were* to sense foul play in Béatrice's accident, I might not be the primary suspect after all.

I might even be a future victim.

CHAPTER 18

For the entire week, I am tense and jumpy. The days pass in a blur as I ignore my colleagues' insults while trying my best to become the perfect protégée for Madame Violette. By the time I leave the dress shop on Saturday evening, all I want to do is wrap my hair, fall into bed, and remain oblivious to the outside world until Monday morning.

Perhaps because of this abstraction, when Domingo asks if I will spend Sunday afternoon with him, the hurried word that flies out of my mouth is *oui*.

When morning comes, I fear that Elodie will not forgive me for spending a few of my rare free hours with someone else. However, she is lost in an obsession of her own, striving to create a cologne so superlative, every parfumeur in Paris will fall to their knees, begging her to join them.

And so we share our little table, Elodie with her flasks and I with my sketchbook. By the time we break for lunch, neither of us is certain we're any closer to our goal.

After scrubbing our dishes, I kiss her cheek. "I'll be home to cook supper."

"Hug Domingo for me," she answers.

The thought is far more tempting than I'd like. He is tall and solid, with wide shoulders and a natural warmth. I've no doubt that if I were to let his arms envelop me, I'd never wish to leave his embrace.

Before exiting our home, I pat a hidden pocket in my skirt to ensure I have everything I'll need. Fine ladies carry fancy purses, but when you can't afford to replace one, you do not risk losing or being robbed of such a flashy object.

Unencumbered by heavy coins, I hurry toward the border between the 3rd and the 11th arrondissements. Autumn is fraying into winter, and yet the streets are still crowded with pedestrians enjoying the clear, brisk day.

Although I am early to our rendezvous, Domingo is already waiting exactly where he said he'd be. His eyes light at the sight of me, warming my skin more thoroughly than the sun ever could.

A normal Parisian greeting consists of two air kisses. The barest touch of each pair of cheeks. It is fast, breezy, casual.

Today, Domingo's greeting is nothing like that. The boulevard is too noisy to hear his slow intake of breath at my proximity, but I can *feel* him inhaling my skin. Savoring my aroma—the rose water Elodie made—as if I am not flesh and blood but rather the embodiment of scent and pleasure.

I keep an appropriate distance between us. Or at least, I attempt to. Somewhere between reaching out and actually touching him, my fingers forget to push him away and instead splay against the lapels of his gray frock coat. The wool should be scratchy, repellant, but my fingers luxuriate in the comforting heat emanating from his chest.

For a moment, I think I feel his heartbeat, rapid and shaky. Then I realize there are too many layers between his heart and my palms. It is my own pulse that skitters through my veins.

I jerk my hands back to my sides and fumble to find my pockets. Here, at least, I am on safe ground. I withdraw a folded scrap from the hidden folds. "This is for you."

He takes it from me, opening the small white handkerchief to reveal a lively blue border of men's shoes in all shapes and sizes, painstakingly embroidered. "You made this?"

I shrug, then nod.

It is the least I could do for all his kindnesses. His friendship, his presence at my family's funeral. Not that I was thinking about any of those things as I carefully sewed each stitch. I was wondering what it might be like to be more than friends. To be the sort of carefree girl who entertained a suitor. To have a romance. To share a kiss.

"It's nothing," I mutter instead. "A leftover scrap, and extra thread I needed to get rid of."

Domingo's eyes take on a new intensity. He doesn't believe my lie. If anything, he's now considering how much this gift must have cost me. Elodie and I do not own spare scraps of perfect white cloth. The thread in that embroidery could have hemmed our clothes and darned our stockings all winter long.

But I gave it to Domingo instead.

"Thank you." He offers his arm. "Shall we stroll down le Boulevard du Crime?"

I smile and curve my hand around the warm wool. "Those villains had best beware of *me.*"

Though the street name on the rectangular plaque reads *le Boulevard du Temple,* Parisians have been referring to it as le Boulevard du Crime since before my birth. The nickname arose from the proliferation of crime melodramas in the many theaters lining this street.

Twenty thousand people stroll these dense four hundred meters every day to watch the street entertainers. We clap at the circus performances and strive to catch glimpses of the rich and fashionable alighting from their carriages in front of the most exclusive theaters.

The elite do not hurry into their private lodges to ready themselves for the show. They *are* the show. Before the curtain rises, it is the aristocrats and the industrialists who capture the eyes of the audience.

I imagine that once the wealthy are settled inside, nestled beneath the light of a dozen chandeliers, they preen like birds in cages at the admiring gazes of the petite bourgeoisie and merchant classes—fellow Parisians well-heeled enough to attend performances but not wealthy enough to purchase private boxes in view of the entire theatre.

Half of what I know about fashion I learned from magazines and illustrated fashion plates. The other half I gleaned right here, on le Boulevard du Crime, gaping at duchesses and bankers' wives and capitalists like Monsieur and Madame Fournier.

I can admire their fine looks without forgiving their conscienceless behavior. Their beauty is a flimsy mask for the rot it covers.

Sculpted black hair and a sunshine-yellow gown trimmed in tangerine catch my eye, and I jump out of my skin.

"What is it?" Domingo asks in alarm.

My brain bubbles out of my ears like water boiling over the rim of a pot. You don't point at your betters. You glance out of the corner of your eye with your face averted and your shoulders bent to avoid attention.

But I cannot help myself. I point and I bounce, and I grab Domingo's arm with an involuntary wiggle. "Look! That's the comtesse, Madame de Centre-Fleur, alighting before the Théâtre de la Gaîté!"

His forehead lines. "And?"

"And she's wearing the gown I sewed for her!" Giddy excitement rushes through me. It is all I can do not to erupt in hysterical giggles. After years of visiting the most elite areas of Paris to gaze at high fashion, this time *I* am the one who created it.

"Congratulations," Domingo says with a smile. "This is cause for celebration."

I cannot move an inch. I am utterly transfixed by the sight of the comtesse in her new gown born out of Madame Violette's dress shop from my painstaking hard work.

The panels are hemmed perfectly to highlight our client's plump curves. The sunny yellow showcases Madame de Centre-Fleur's smooth brown skin. Orange accents draw the eye to the heart-shaped bodice and the wide bell of the skirt. She is positively glowing.

I've no doubt I am too.

That is, until the next carriage pulls up and vomits out its passengers: Madame Fournier and her daughter, Blanche. Patting their blond ringlets, which some unappreciated servant molded with curling tongs. Smirking at each other and striking poses. Without a care in the world for the lives lost in their factories so that they can primp and strut, convinced of their superiority.

I want to run up and smack them. Shove their pasty manicured hands into the machines that murdered my parents. Make them share a portion of the suffering they and their dangerous factories have caused for generations. Not only the Fourniers, but everyone like them.

Something in my face alarms Domingo. Possibly murderous rage.

"Are you all right?" he asks with concern, taking my hands in his.

I force my gaze toward him and struggle to slow my breaths. "Tell me something calming. Make up a story about the sea."

The corners of his eyes crinkle. "I don't have to make up a story. I am from Cádiz, at the south of Spain. At some spots on a clear day, you can gaze out over the ocean and see Africa."

My mouth drops open. "Really?"

He nods. "The best view is from Tarifa. The water is as blue as you've ever seen. The land on the other side rises in hills of purple, like smudges from a brush dipped in watercolors. The sun makes the ocean sparkle as though it is made of jewels rather than drops of water."

I grip his hands. "And you spent time there?"

"As a boy, yes, as much as I could. Cádiz has beautiful white sand beaches, stretching for many kilometers. You don't need money or even special clothing to enjoy the bright sun and the warm waves of salt water lapping against your bare skin."

I can picture it. The reality is undoubtedly even more magical.

"Why would you leave that behind?" I ask.

The sparkle leaves his eyes, and his face hardens. "France is not the only place where the elite view the poor as objects to be used and discarded. My family moved to Barcelona in search of a better life. A much bigger city, still with beaches, but also bustling with industry and nightlife and aristocrats."

"You found a better life?"

"We found *other* people with better lives," he replies dryly. "The move cost us every peseta we owned. We became servants to a wealthy family in exchange for food and shelter. The hope was to save money while living in luxury."

I touch my poorly healed hand to the scar on his cheek. "Things didn't go according to plan?"

"There was no luxury for us, of course. My parents likely understood what sort of lives we would have to lead, but I was too young to see beyond the beauty of the palace, even as we slept in the cramped servants' quarters. None of us suspected we would soon be separated."

My mouth drops. "They tore your family apart?"

"It was supposed to be temporary. The master of the house needed my father in Madrid, at one of their other mansions. The mistress of the house demanded my mother accompany her on a trip God-knows-where."

I frown. "You don't know where your mother went?"

"There were whispers that they sailed to the Philippines. But I never saw her again," he replies hollowly. "Either of them."

My heart fills with horror.

"I remained with the heir, Gonzalo. He was only a few years older than me. As a future count, Gonzalo was fascinated by higher nobility. According to local gossip, the Spanish royal princes used their illegitimate cousin Francisco as proxy for their punishments, forcing him to endure the sting of a whip that should have struck royal backsides instead. Gonzalo could not wait to mimic them."

My insides heave. "Your employer didn't prevent his son from . . ."

Domingo shrugs. "I don't know if he knew or frankly cared that Gonzalo would act out on purpose, then strike me in 'penance.' I took the abuse for as long as I could."

"Why?"

"To leave my post would mean never finding my parents again. I always hoped they would return. They were all I had left."

I nod. I understand this to my marrow. "What happened?"

"Eventually, he struck me so hard I almost didn't wake up. I regained consciousness a week later with a ladder of uneven stitches across my swollen face. It took another week for me to remember what had happened."

"What did you do then?"

"Shattered his nose with my fist and escaped out the window with only the clothes on my back."

I nod again. That's the least that monster was owed.

"Because his family was noble, I could not stay in Spain. Not with the looming risk of being imprisoned for assault. Luckily, Barcelona is not far from the French border. It took weeks, but I eventually made it here. Months passed before my French was comprehensible. Years went by before I felt safe. And then I met you."

I tilt my head as I stare up at him. "Do I make you feel safe or unsafe?"

He presses my crooked hand back to his scarred cheek. "You terrify me. I feel like a little boy again. Gazing in wonder at a palace of beauty and hoping that this time, my dreams will come true."

I hope both our dreams come true. No. More than hope—my vengeance will ensure it. And then I will place my hand in Domingo's and take the biggest leap of all.

The risk of loving someone again.

CHAPTER 19

On Monday, Pauline sneaks an admiring look at herself in a hand mirror pulled from her beaded purse, then tilts the glass toward me and gives an exaggerated shudder. "Did you *sleep* in those hideous old rags?"

Charlotte merely sighs without bothering to glance in my direction. From the stiffness of her spine and the unique flare at her hips, I can tell she's wearing the new corset I created for her. Good. I hope its secret ingredient keeps her awake at night.

At lunchtime, my colleagues dash out the door en masse, chattering to each other about promenades in parks with boys and late evenings at expensive theaters. The girls are horrid to me but surprisingly decent to each other. I suppose bigoted birds of a feather flock in self-important swarms together.

I stay behind to see if Madame Violette needs help. I wish her other employees were more thoughtful. I can't help but feel Madame Violette would be the jewel of Paris by now if only my coworkers weren't holding her back. They're too busy gossiping and sniping at me to see what a phenomenal career Madame Violette could be growing, if she were supported by the best.

"It's hard without Jacqueline," my employer admits. "I was half hoping she'd return and beg forgiveness. I'd dock her wages for leaving without notice, but I'd let her have her post back."

I am appalled that she might not have honored her word.

"But . . . the protégée contest!"

"Yes, yes, the competition. Less than a fortnight until you must all present your creations. I do hope one of you is worthy of the position."

My stomach does somersaults. She'd said one of us *would* win, not that one of us *might* win. I need this post. Madame Violette *has* to choose me. She must.

"Tell me what you need," I stammer. "I'll do it. I don't need lunch breaks. I can come in earlier and stay later."

"What I need is a miracle," she says. "I'm fortunate enough to have a fair number of loyal clients. But I want to be the number one modiste in Paris. I daresay I already *am* the best this city has to offer. But its citizens haven't quite realized it yet."

I think furiously, determined to be the one to come up with a solution. "A woman has to stand out to get ahead."

She raises her brows. "Are you suggesting my work does not speak for itself?"

"I'm suggesting the rich aren't bright enough to read between the lines. You have to *tell* them what they should want."

She scoffs. "Post an announcement in the newspaper, is that it? 'Attention, s'il vous plaît. Madame Violette is the best in the land, and the richest among you should pay thrice her current fees for the privilege of working with her.'"

The bell over the door tinkles, and two well-known wives of bankers stride in, their noses wrinkling under their lacy parasols.

"Not the newspaper," I murmur to Madame Violette. "I told you: Their reading comprehension is a fright. You have to tell them to their faces. Watch this."

"Angélique! Don't you dare—" She tries to grab my good hand, but I am too slippery.

And I *do* dare. I am fearless.

"Oh, you poor dears," I tell these ostentatious peacocks in my best bored-butler voice. "I do hope you haven't wasted time by entering our establishment without an appointment."

Madame Violette makes a choking noise behind me.

The wrinkles in the wives' noses disappear, and they exchange startled looks of alarm.

"I'm certain I sent my maid to schedule one a fortnight ago," one of them fibs. "Did that lazy wretch not complete her task as assigned?"

I pull out my sketchbook and squint at a blank page as if consulting the day's agenda. "Names?"

They both gasp audibly at the indignity of not being recognized at first sight.

Of course, I know who they are. Mesdames Pageau and Olivier are frequent objects of caricaturists' scorn, as well as prominent attendees of the opera, sharing a private box with a public view so that those crowded in the gallery can gaze up at them with awe and envy.

They are exactly like heartless, selfish Monsieur Fournier and his family.

I tap my pencil against the sketchbook. "If you don't have an appointment, I really must ask you not to distract Madame Violette from her important work. Our next opening to evaluate potential new clients isn't until three o'clock in the afternoon, four weeks from Thursday. If you'd like to come back then, I'll need to write down—"

"Je suis Madame Pageau," blurts out the much more extravagantly bejeweled one, desperate not to be cast aside. "I definitely made an appointment for my bosom friend Madame Olivier and me. We were sent by . . . Who recommended this establishment to us, Bernice? Was it the duchesse?"

"Yes, during a soirée at the president's palace," Madame Olivier lies without hesitation. "We are *so* friendly with Napoléon III and his set."

"Hmm." I make a production of consulting our busy schedule. "There *is* something written here, but I can't quite make it out."

"It's us, of course," Madame Pageau assures me, waving away my little notebook. "I was thinking of commissioning a day dress for my debutante daughter, but if there's also a new style more fitting for mature women such as Bernice and me . . ."

I twist to glance over my shoulder at Madame Violette and stage-whisper, "Can we trust them with the news? It wasn't to be unveiled until next year."

At first, poor Madame Violette has no earthly idea what I'm talking about but then catches on to my game with aplomb.

She gives a dismissive sniff and murmurs, "Are you certain these two have the bearing and the presence to pull it off?"

"Show us," Madame Olivier pleads. "We'll buy it."

With as much reluctance as I can muster, I slide on a pair of ivory gloves and pull a square of silk from my pocket. It is a scrap from home, left over from the dress I've been designing. It has been dyed a jade so deep, the fathomless green takes the breath away.

Or maybe that's the arsenic. Hence the gloves.

Mesdames Pageau and Olivier nearly fall over each other in rapture. "I have never seen a green so brilliant! It is impossible! How was it done? Even queens and princesses have not worn such a vivid color! We *must* have it."

I name an astronomical sum.

Their eyes widen, and their mouths fall open.

"Per square meter," I add. "Paid in advance. The cost of labor is extra. Half in advance, half on delivery."

"B-but," stammers Madame Olivier, "that number is ten times the price of the most expensive silk in Paris."

"And this"—I hold up the square by one corner—"is the most exclusive color in the *world*. No one else has access to this shade of green. You will be the envy of your peers and royalty alike."

"May I inspect the color in the light?" asks Madame Pageau.

"But of course." With a smile, I place the square in her ungloved palm.

She cradles the jade silk as she walks to the window, and she and Madame Olivier pass the scrap back and forth while talking over each other in excited whispers.

"We'll take it," Madame Pageau announces. "An evening gown for each of us, as well as for our daughters."

She starts to hand the square of silk to Madame Violette, but I intercept the poisonous sample in time and stuff it back into my pocket. I flip to a new blank page in my sketchbook.

"I suppose we could squeeze you in for a first fitting on . . . Wednesday next, at five p.m.?"

Usually, we're winding down the workday by then, but since I don't actually have access to Madame Violette's real schedule, I cannot guess a time during regular business hours without risking encroaching on an existing appointment.

"Perfect." The ladies beam at each other, then skip from the shop like schoolgirls.

"How did you *do* that?" Madame Violette asks in wonder.

"It's a trick I used to use on my middle sister. When she would get stubborn, I would merely suggest she ought to do the opposite of whatever I really wanted her to—"

"Not your sales technique. That *green*. I've never seen its like! And those prices! How will we ever afford—"

"Ah." I grin at her. "This is a sneak peek at my competition garment, and a color I perfected myself."

Madame Violette's mouth falls open. I can practically hear the gears of her brain spinning.

"The color is *only* for your competition garment?" she asks slyly.

I had intended to use the dye as part of my revenge on the Fourniers for murdering my family. But they are only part of the problem. Other brutal industrialists exactly like them destroy dreams and ruin lives every single day in order to fatten their own pockets. If they all wish to pay for a chance to suffer, then perhaps I should let destiny unfold as it will.

I smile at Madame Violette. "Purchase whatever materials you normally do, and I will dye them for you. The ingredients barely cost more than the norm. My secret recipe stays with me, of course, but you are welcome to use it on an exclusive basis if you like. And only for the families of rich industrialists."

"If I'd like! Did you *see* those ladies' faces? We truly will have a queue of queens and princesses stretching outside the door by noon tomorrow."

Royalty who *could* enact laws to prevent the ill-treatment of workers . . . if they cared—or even thought—about the poor.

"Then . . . you aren't displeased with my interference?" I ask shyly.

Madame Violette gazes at me with open astonishment and respect. As though I've already won the protégée position. As if I were almost her equal.

She throws her arm about my shoulders and gives a happy squeeze. "Ma chère Angélique, hiring you might be the best decision I've ever made."

Warmth infuses me at the compliment. I desperately hope the sentiment is still true when it comes time to choose a new protégée.

"If there's ever anything else I can do for you, please let me know," I say in a rush. "I can come in early, or stay late into the night, or—"

"Chérie, I've no wish to intrude on your . . . social life." Madame Violette's voice trails off as she takes in my appearance.

She sees me almost every day, but it is as if this is the first time she's truly *seen* me and understood what my plainness means.

After my vindictive coworkers' destruction of my best gown, I have only three appropriate dresses to cycle through. They are spotlessly clean and meticulously sewn, both by my own hand. The time and care spent on those two tasks is enough to ensure I don't look like a vagrant or beggar.

But Madame Violette is a modiste. At first glance, I might distract her attention with an innovative design and scrupulous needlework. But closer inspection reveals the cheapness of the fabric. The gossamer thinness of the cloth, from being scrubbed so often and for so many years. The slight shadow of the seams, because the creases haven't been as bleached by the sun as the panels exposed to the air and weather.

Her lips purse.

My muscles tense out of habit. I have heard every cutting comment imaginable. Not just from my colleagues in the sewing room. They *wish* their insults were half as inventive as the invectives tossed at me and my family by strangers in the street. Especially on the rare occasions when we dare to venture to places where only our "betters" are meant to tread.

But Madame Violette's expression is not cruel. It is . . . pitying.

Shame floods my neck and face. I duck my head, rather than face those compassionate dark brown eyes.

"You seemed rather pleased to take home a white ribbon a few weeks back," she says, as though she means something else entirely.

I was more than pleased. I'd felt blessed, and believed my

mother and sisters would too. I hadn't known my good fortune was about to turn into the worst day of our lives.

I say none of this, though. I stare down at my folded hands instead, squeezing them tight to keep from running away. I can shrug off the comments from my fellow seamstresses. And I'm used to the spite of strangers. But after my best efforts to prove myself, I cannot bear for Madame Violette to also deem me unworthy.

"Come." She spins on an expensive heel and strides confidently toward the rear of the dress shop.

I scramble to follow close behind.

At the end of the corridor, she points to the first of three closed doors. "That is where deliveries of fabrics and ornamental embellishments are made. Only I and my future protégée will have keys. Don't even touch the door."

I nod obediently, though my throat tightens at the implication that I won't be the next protégée.

She points to the door opposite. "That is an empty pantry. I hoped to turn it into a second sewing room and hire more employees, but it's not big enough to hold more than two small tables. For the moment, it's wasted space."

I nod again, although I have no idea why she's telling me this.

"And here . . ." She grasps the handle of the narrow door at the end of the corridor. "We have the graveyard."

She opens the door and motions for me to step inside.

It is a wonderland. I turn in a small circle—that's all the space there is—as my eyes widen and my jaw drops in shock.

I'd thought the leftover bit of ribbon was a marvel? This

is an entire closet piled floor to ceiling with leftover *everything*. Squares of silk and muslin and cotton the length of my arm. Single buttons, in every color and shape imaginable. Ribbons . . . mon Dieu, *so* many ribbons. There's more than enough spare material here to sew a patchwork quilt big enough to blanket the Royal Palace gardens.

"This is where Jacqueline deposited the scraps from the sewing room at the end of every week," she explains.

Ah, of course. The discard pile I plucked my white ribbon from seemed a veritable mountain to me, but it could not have contained the accumulated detritus of a dress shop in continuous operation for decades.

"Can you keep a secret?" she asks.

"To the grave," I promise.

Madame Violette smiles at me. "I thought so. If you believe yourself a designer capable of using this rubbish to make something worth wearing, help yourself."

Yearning, sharp and sweet, cleaves me in two. There is nothing I want more than to make myself a new gown. A design so clever, it will shut up my colleagues for good. A silhouette so pretty, Domingo will never have eyes for anyone else.

Almost nothing I want more.

"Would it be all right if I make a dress for my sister instead of me?" I venture.

Madame Violette gazes at me, then rummages on an overstuffed shelf before retrieving a rumpled swath of burlap.

It isn't exactly what I had in mind for Elodie, but if I line the scratchy material with something soft, and decorate the coarse cloth with—

"Here." Madame Violette shoves the burlap toward me. "You may take home two sackfuls of anything you see here, to use as you please."

I . . . *can*? For a heartbeat, I am incapable of making anything other than happy choking noises.

"Merci beaucoup, madame," I blurt out, repeating my thanks over and over and over. "I don't know how to repay you. Oh! The empty room! It's more than big enough for a few vats. Could I turn it into a dye station for creating our exclusive signature green?"

Those greedy wives want something no one else has . . . and I'll be glad to give it to them.

"That is a brilliant idea, Angélique. Before you go home tonight, write down the items you'll need, and I'll have them delivered tomorrow." Madame Violette ducks out of the crowded closet, leaving me alone in Aladdin's cave.

I turn in a much slower circle, my head still spinning at all the sumptuous materials surrounding me. This cave holds more than mere treasure. This is the wellspring of a transformation.

For eighteen years, I have been the spiky brown caterpillar, slinking through a world too big.

At long last, I will emerge a butterfly.

CHAPTER 20

The rest of the week passes in a whirlwind, days spent mixing arsenic-laced green dye and nights vacillating between my sketchbook and my shears.

I learned the art of dye-making at the Fournier textiles factory. Although the arsenic makes the color last longer, Monsieur Fournier was as cheap with that ingredient as he was when it came to paying his employees. His silks came out a tepid, watery green that faded with use and disappeared with soap.

My little chemist, Elodie, was the one who suggested experimenting with the proportions. Green is a notoriously difficult color to achieve. If a little bit of arsenic helped it stick, then wouldn't more arsenic—and more dye—be even better?

The answer was yes, obviously. Since Madame Violette's clients are covering the cost, I can use as much dye and as much poison as I please.

As for the proportions... For those who do not amass their wealth at the expense of others, I use only as much arsenic as necessary to set the dye. For the selfish aristocrats, the greedy industrialists' wives happy to risk their employees' lives, I give the garments a second wash with as much extra arsenic as the fabric can soak in. The resulting vivid green is unparalleled, meaning the self-absorbed upper-class would never wish to wear anything else. Lording their wealth and privilege over their peers is top priority.

For those who spend their days idling with a glass of wine rather than sweating over a vat of dye, the effects will creep up slowly.

While ingesting a high enough dose would cause certain death within a few days, long-term exposure is more insidious. First, there's numbness. Abdominal pain. Diarrhea. Symptoms easily attributed to influenza or poorly cooked seafood. Then come dark patches on thickening skin. Lesions and ulcers. Internal organ damage. Invisible suffering that could last months or years before an inevitable painful demise.

There is a reason none of Monsieur Fournier's dye girls lasts more than a few years.

I am smarter, however. Safer. Arsenic has been the poison of choice for centuries because its symptoms are often indistinguishable from those of cholera. I learned quickly to use long leather gloves and to wrap cloth around my nose and mouth when leaning over the vat. Madame Violette's room has a small window, which I keep open. And I never, ever let the dye or its ingredients touch my skin. I won't let the chemicals kill me. I'll wield their beauty like a weapon.

Of course, the silk with secondary effects isn't for everyone. This is my special batch, made only for specific members of the upper class who are heartless and have proven themselves to care more about the dead animals that form their fur coats than living employees.

Once Madame Violette allows me to design for the masses, I will provide ordinary citizens with the most brilliant colors I can, without any risk of harm to their persons. They've already suffered enough. It's time for the pampered to have a turn.

When I am not at the dress shop, I am at home crafting my new wardrobe from Madame Violette's leftovers. I design thinking not only of myself but also of my intended future audience. A member of the working class might be able to save up enough money to purchase a cheap but fashionable gown—designed by me—but the poorest among us must resort to doing exactly as I am now: the best we can, with the scraps available.

I am fortunate. While there wasn't a complete square meter of any single fabric, much less a swath long enough from which to fashion an entire gown, there are more than enough strips and corners of the same materials and colors to create a complete ensemble with some very clever cuts and seams.

After creating an outfit for Elodie to impress parfumeurs, I devise separate skirts and bodices for myself, so that they can be interchanged to give the impression of a far grander wardrobe than I actually possess.

Many modern women wear up to half a dozen petticoats beneath their skirts, in order to maintain that full bell shape. I have never owned more than two at a time . . . until now. I piece together clashing scraps without fear, prioritizing sensation and warmth over pattern and color. Softness for the layer next to my legs, stiffness for the outermost. Thin layers for summer, thick for winter. All in the riotous colors of the rainbow.

The outer layers are chosen with great care. Bold stripes out of necessity but cut to look intentional. Puffy sleeves perhaps a shade darker or lighter than the bodice, which in turn contains other monochromatic elements. Piping and striping and lace and silk and satin, combined in such a way that my skirts and bodices are nothing so boring as "pink" or "blue" but rather "warm hues of the sunrise" or "moonlight sparkling over the violet ocean."

How I love designing! Fashion has long been my passion, my outlet, and my safe space. Nothing can hurt me while I am sketching or creating. All that exists are my imagination, my pencil, and my thread. It is alchemy. But instead of turning tin into gold, I'm converting leftovers into high fashion.

The results are stunning, if I do say so myself. Elodie is pleased with the items I made for her, though she has more of a nose for perfume than an eye for fashion. She thinks her new frocks look *nice* but cannot appreciate the details only another dressmaker would notice.

The true test shall be my coworkers.

On the last day of the week, I waltz into work wearing a particularly eye-catching combination of black and white. It is as difficult to maintain inky black dye as it is to keep white bleached bright, which means these two colors are rarely found together in the same item.

I do not have such limitations. Thanks to clever little hidden fastenings and judicious use of invisible threads that can be snipped for washing and easily resewn after drying, today's day dress features billowing sleeves of black-and-white striped silk, a soft black satin bodice, and a picture-perfect frothy white bell skirt with vertical darts of sooty black peeking between the pleats.

No one looks like this. But when they see me, they wish they did. Admiring gazes followed me all the way to work this morning, and I reveled in their appreciation.

My colleagues' jaws drop to the sewing room floor. By choosing to eschew color, I stand out all the more. A swan stretching her wings in a field of tulips.

They squint and sneer and peer closer despite themselves. They want to hate my daring new appearance, but they cannot. They covet my dress. So they despise me instead.

I could not smile wider if I tried.

"Who made that for you?" demands Marguerite, the dead songbird on her head bobbing. "Was it Madame Violette?"

There could be no higher compliment.

"Wasted on her," mutters Pauline. "*I* should be wearing it."

"You!" protests Henrietta. "More like me. I know just the fur muff...."

I float to my table and take my seat as they bicker amongst themselves and shoot barbed comments my way. Let them. My gown is my armor. Their words cannot pierce it. I wonder if they noticed that for a few moments, even their insults were tinged with respect. No more *orphan* and *guttersnipe*. My colleagues are so flustered, they're disparaging me like an equal, rather than someone lesser.

"Wait," Marguerite says slowly. Fearfully. "Did *you* design that?"

The others nearly break their necks to watch my reaction.

I needn't even respond. The answer is in every asymmetrical cut and every hidden stitch.

"No," Pauline gurgles. She sounds like she's swallowing bile.

Henrietta's expression is aghast, all thought of fur muffs forgotten.

The dear girls are realizing I'm every bit as dangerous a competitor for the protégée position as they are. The evidence is right here before their eyes.

It's proof to me, too. Maybe they've worked here longer. Maybe a few of them are as talented in their own right. But they lack my primary, unequivocal advantage: desperation.

"Don't even fantasize about it," says Marguerite, her eyes cold. "You won't win. We'll see to it."

I shrug and smooth my skirts. "Do your worst."

"I will," she snaps.

"We all will," adds Henrietta.

Pauline crosses her arms and sniffs. "You have no idea what I'm capable of."

I smile and pick up my needle. "I guess we'll see."

By the time I leave the dress shop, night is swallowing the last dregs of the sun. Between Jacqueline's and Béatrice's discontinued employment and my unplanned additional role helping to secure rich new clients, I'm busier than ever. There's no time to rest. Only about a week remains until we present our designs for Madame Violette's protégée competition, which means there's plenty more work waiting for me when I get home.

When I reach La Croix & Sons, it is time for Domingo to

lock up. Not temporarily, with an "I'll return soon" sign, but for the night. The hour is late, and the store is closed.

Nonetheless, he takes a long gaze at my new creation before kneeling at my feet to shine my boots.

Domingo smiles up at me as he works. "Buenas tardes, guapísima."

I return his smile, keeping one protective hand on the burlap satchel over my shoulder. "Bonsoir, mon beau chevalier."

"A knight in shining armor, am I?"

"Bien sûr, straight out of a fairy tale." I would love to tackle him to the broken pavement and kiss him right here on this busy street.

My daydreams are consumed with thoughts of kissing him. Morning, noon, night. But I cannot permit a major distraction. Flirtation is one thing. A full-blown courtship is quite another. I don't give myself more than three hours of sleep at night, let alone allow myself to have something more with Domingo.

But I do want a true romance with him. As soon as possible. And I need Domingo to know he has a piece of my heart, even if I cannot yet give him all of my time.

"I made something new for you," I blurt out.

His head jerks up from my boots. "Another handkerchief?"

"Not this time." I reach into my freshly sewn burlap satchel and pull out the garment I designed just for him.

Although every thread and bit of cloth comes from Madame Violette's scrap closet, the result is far from quilted rubbish for a rag doll. The shimmering waistcoat is made of thick vertical stripes of jewel-toned silk. Instead of an ordinary printed pattern, the striking panels give the waistcoat a depth and richness most aristocrats couldn't hope to match.

Domingo leaps to his feet to accept his gift, his eyes raking me in as though I am a goddess walking the earth. "Angélique! This is incredible."

"Better than the last gift," I admit, my neck flushing.

He frowns in confusion. "Are you jesting? I never go anywhere without your embroidered handkerchief. Nothing in this world could look finer poking smartly from the breast pocket of this waistcoat."

I blink. "You use the handkerchief I gave you?"

"I would marry the handkerchief you gave me." He pulls the square of linen from his trouser pocket and gives the embroidered cloth several dramatic, impassioned kisses.

"You look foolish," I inform him, but it is a lie, and we both know it. I'm the one grinning like a fool as he holds the waistcoat and handkerchief to his chest and twirls like a stage actor about to bow before his adoring public. "All right, that's enough. It's getting late."

Domingo swiftly returns the shoe polish to the store and locks up tight. With his new gift safely tucked away in a leather satchel, he offers me an arm.

Because it is late and hours of work still await me, we no longer have the freedom to promenade aimlessly through Paris. He must walk me straight home. Nonetheless, despite the limited time in Domingo's company, I savor these moments of closeness. The warmth of his body, his comforting scent, how easy it is to stroll at his side, our steps in perfect rhythm.

"How is Señorita Elodie?" he asks.

"Distraught, as usual," I reply with a frustrated sigh. "Every morning, a new scheme to make the master parfumeurs take notice and hire her. Every night, more tears when all her latest efforts have come to naught."

He's silent for a long moment before saying hesitantly, "Is the problem . . . money? You know that I have more than I need. I'm happy to give you—"

"No," I say firmly. "No charity. I can handle my own affairs."

"I know you can. Of course you can. If you won't accept a gift, then perhaps a small loan would allow you to—"

"Stop. I have to do this on my own. I promised my mother."

Domingo does stop. Literally. Physically. He grabs my shoulders right there in the middle of the sidewalk, stares me straight in the eyes, and says, "Are you *certain* that 'refuse all gifts or offers of aid' is what your mother meant when she asked you to take care of your sister?"

That probably isn't what Maman meant. But it's how I *feel*. I was supposed to save all three of them, and I failed two. I cannot fail Elodie.

"Maman did it on her own," I mutter. This is only partly true. Papa did the lion's share, until Monsieur Fournier killed him.

Domingo's big hands don't let go of my thin shoulders, but his voice gentles. "No, she didn't. Your mother had *you* to help her. And now you have me."

The backs of my eyelids sting. I miss my mother. And I despise feeling like a failure. Like I'm eternally almost-but-not-quite good enough. Worst of all, I hate the constant worry over not being able to guarantee I can provide Elodie with the better life I've promised her.

Because of the money I spent on Jacqueline's rent in order to dispose of her body, I didn't have enough left over for our rent and we were forced to sell my parents' old clothes in order to cover the difference. As much as I hated to give up anything Maman and Papa had touched, or worn, or loved, Elodie and I now have enough cushion to cover two more months.

Or one month's rent and a restocked pantry.

Which is another way of saying we're one emergency away from sliding right back to having no rent money whatsoever.

"All right," I say at last.

A comical mixture of shock, relief, and joy wrestle for control of Domingo's handsome features. "You'll accept a loan?"

"A gift. But not money, and not for me. If you want to help, then help my sister. I want to be there for her, but I won't have any free time until after the contest. Elodie says if she had better bottles and oils, and some sort of special equipment, she could improve on her own and have a much better chance of landing the apprenticeship of her dreams. I don't remember the name—"

"Done." He drops my shoulders and links my arm through his. "I'll have her write me a list, and she'll have her new tools tomorrow, or as soon as I can arrange delivery."

I hug him, trying not to disappear into his lapels forever. "Thank you. I mean it."

"Anything for mi tesoro," he replies gallantly.

"Is there something I can do for you?" I ask, forcing myself to pull away.

He touches my cheek. "I'm perfectly fine. The latest riding boots I designed are flying off the shelves. I couldn't be happier or prouder."

"Wouldn't you be un petit peu happier and prouder if the customers knew you were the one who designed them? It is an utter travesty that old man La Croix claims your talents as his own, without giving credit where it's due."

Domingo shrugs. "That's life. I don't mind."

"*I* mind. It's not fair. I wouldn't accept such a slight, and neither should you."

He slants me an exasperated look. "There's nothing I can do about it. I can't risk angering Monsieur La Croix with an uppity attitude. You know as well as I do that if I lose this job, there won't be another one."

That's true, but still unacceptable. I don't think our "betters" are actually better than us. Especially the ones who siphon our talent and steal our lives. They're simply richer. Sophisticated pirates in top hats and feather bonnets.

"At least leave your mark," I beg Domingo. "That's what I'm trying to do."

"And how do you propose I achieve that?"

Good question. My brain works furiously.

"How about including a secret symbol?" I suggest. "Say, an unobtrusive little flourish on every shoe you design to function as a signature. When you become famous in your own right one day, you can reveal the man behind the symbol. Then all of Paris will flock to you rather than La Croix and Sons."

Domingo tilts his head, considering this idea, then nods. "From now on, we leave our mark on society, no matter what?"

"No matter what." I smile widely in anticipation. "We're unstoppable. The world hasn't seen anything yet."

CHAPTER 21

Nine days until the competition deadline. I can hardly sleep.

My contribution is coming along swimmingly. I spend an hour with Charlotte every afternoon after work, pinning her into the sumptuous, venomous confection.

She loves it. After she saw my white and black ensemble, she came to me with the idea to model for me daily instead of twice a week. I refuse to let her take my creation home, though I did "lend" her a specially dyed, stunning green petticoat to match her nightgown.

Her work has suffered. She is listless, achy, clumsy. If Jacqueline were here, she would snap at her and slap her face. I suggest that perhaps Charlotte should get more fresh air—that the contest might be weighing on her.

Everything is going to plan. The changes are happening so gradually, it doesn't occur to Charlotte that her lethargy could be related to the green color. After all, who in their right mind would suspect their clothing to have been dyed with poison?

Another influenza going around is a much more reasonable explanation.

Meanwhile, the rest of us must mend Charlotte's uneven hems and trim her crooked cuts while she picks at the open wounds festering along her skin. The other girls are so disgusted, they rarely allow her to wield needles and shears anymore. Pauline has even been whispering that Charlotte ought to be fired for her many mistakes and general lack of contribution. The other girls smirk and say the unsightly scabs are the real reason Charlotte should stay home—this dress shop is a place of beauty, not ugliness.

Charlotte registers none of this. She barely has the energy to stand there like a living doll and allow my gloved hands to pin ever more layers of green silks and satins onto her body. She stays only because of my unending compliments and the delusion that the others remain jealous of her.

We're almost done now. At least . . . with this aspect. Once the competition is over and I've won, I'll need no longer bother with Charlotte. Her after-work fittings will be the least of my duties.

By day, I must sew my portion, as well as perform bleary-eyed Charlotte's tasks, while the other three help cover for missing Jacqueline and injured Béatrice. When Madame Violette calls, I rush to help her with an ever-increasing flow of new clients.

And of course, the most taxing, tiresome task of all: I have become a dye girl again.

This time, I don't mind. I revel in it. The spoiled wives of colonizing aristocrats and factory profiteers will soon be wearing a very special shade of green. Ladies' magazines are already calling my deep jade recipe la couleur de la saison, highlighting my green on their fashion plates. The imaginary waiting list I invented a week ago is now very, very real.

And not a single name on it will go home empty-handed.

"Angélique!" It's Madame Violette again. "The banker's wife will arrive at any moment."

"I'll be right there," I call back, hurrying to finish the batch of silks I'm dyeing.

The girls send me dirty looks as I pass the sewing room, but I ignore them. They don't see the fumes, and the sweat, and the sleepless nights. They just see that I am quickly becoming Madame Violette's favorite.

And they despise me even more for it, if that's possible.

"By the way," Madame Violette murmurs as soon as we're alone, "the garments you've created out of remnants are truly impressive."

My heart sings and my face flushes with pleasure. "Th-thank you."

She smiles at me. "Consider this your official permission to raid the scrap closet whenever you'd like."

It is hard to wipe the smile from my face in order to project a suitably unimpressed, snobbish aura for the banker's wife. She is one of the wealthiest women in Paris. I make sure to pronounce her name wrong, as though I've never heard of her. I also pretend to struggle to find her in the appointment book.

By the time I allow her into a dressing room with Madame Violette, the banker's wife is ready to throttle me—and desperate to go home draped in absolutely anything Madame Violette wishes to sell her.

After the banker's wife leaves, Madame Violette turns to me, beaming. "Well done, Angélique."

"You know what else we could do?" I ask before my courage deserts me.

"I am all ears."

"High fashion needn't only be for the wealthy. The lower classes—"

Madame Violette's attention dulls, and I can tell she has lost interest.

I push on. This might be my only opportunity to promote my idea. "All right, high fashion is exclusive and expensive, and therefore inherently for the wealthy, who have the resources to pay any price. But everyone deserves to dress their best, non? Everyone wants to feel beautiful. To *be* beautiful. If we created simpler versions, tailored specifically for—"

"At the moment, I haven't time for such fancies," Madame Violette cuts in.

"At the moment?" I repeat. "Meaning you'll consider it in the future?"

I can already envision the difference more accessible fashion would make. Pastels, whites, jewel tones—and not a drop of arsenic among them. To lower costs, we could reuse the same pattern dozens or even hundreds of times. Add extra-wide hems so that the lower classes could take in or let out the seams at home, without needing to pay extra for tailoring or a custom design.

Who cares if the fanciest place they'll ever see is the

rear pew at church, rather than some grand ballroom? Why shouldn't their day dress and wedding dress and night dress have form as well as function?

"Oh, Angélique. I've enough going on right now," Madame Violette says noncommittally. "We'll see how things look once I've selected a protégée to help me."

Yes. We shall see, shan't we.

I accept my dismissal, but not defeat. While the new batch of silks are steeping in their special tea, I head back into the sewing room to resume progress on my piles of waiting items.

Henrietta snarls. "Here comes Madame Violette's little pet."

"Don't look so smug, guttersnipe," says Pauline. There is no sign of her irresistible dimples now. "It's not over until the contest has a winner."

"I wouldn't worry about her, girls," says Marguerite, the dead bird on her bonnet bobbing in time with her words. "She's been so busy sucking up to Madame Violette, Angélique hasn't had time to sew a dress for the competition."

This is patently untrue, and the colleague at her side knows it—but Charlotte doesn't say a word. I'm not even certain she's following the conversation. She's staring at a jumble of un-hemmed stockings with a sewing needle facing the wrong way in her limp hand.

"Well, as long as our pauvre petite understands that she's not going to win," says Pauline. "Her wardrobe may have improved, but it's still cobbled together from scraps. No amount of toadying can replace actual talent. *I'm* the one with design skills."

"I'm every bit as talented as you are," protests Henrietta,

flinging her dirty-blond sausage curls over her shoulders in indignation.

"You're close, anyway." Pauline kicks off her heeled slippers in order to scratch the arch of one brown foot with the yellow toenails of the other. "You and the other girls *deserve* to be here with me. Angélique doesn't deserve to breathe the same air as us."

How tempting it is to set a match to her highly flammable lace trim.

"You're right," says Henrietta. "Angélique's pathetic attempt at a daring new look is . . ."

She can't even come up with an insult. They both stare at me with open envy, coveting my latest creation and hating themselves for not thinking of it first.

I've chosen a base of white and black again, but this time with scarlet accents to balance the modesty of the high-necked black bodice. My long white sleeves flare at the elbows, gathering in bell-shaped ruffles at my wrists. Tiny cloth-covered buttons trail from my throat to my pelvis, where a fringe of wavy black silk encircles my hips. The bold skirt with its interlacing white and black ruffles flows to the floor like water from a fountain, its lines graceful and soothing. A crimson underlayer peeks flirtatiously from beneath whenever I take a step—or fold myself into my chair, as I am doing now.

They glare at me, furious that I've created a work of art they cannot find fault with.

I bow my head and set about sewing my own projects without a single word to defend myself.

"Don't put on airs," Pauline says at last. "Your dress means nothing. A rotting burlap sack would be an improvement over the rubbish you used to wear."

She smirks, confident she's won the battle yet again. But this is war, and I'm the one with a winning strategy.

I bump my heavy shears with my elbow, knocking them to the floor with a loud clang. They land inches from Pauline's bare feet.

"Ugh," she groans. "Could you possibly be any clumsier?"

"Sorry," I mutter, scrambling out of my chair to crouch down to the floor.

I do retrieve the fallen shears, but I don't return to my seat. Not yet. First, I pick up one of Pauline's expensive slippers, which she always removes for comfort. I jab one of the silver blades of my shears along the seam between the two-inch heel and the sole of the shoe, damaging the connection.

Spraining her ankle on the way home this evening won't be nearly as dramatic as Béatrice's vélocipède accident, but as long as Pauline can't walk to work, she can't win the contest. It'll have to be enough. She's not nearly as good a designer as Marguerite anyway.

I nudge the vandalized shoe back where I found it and retake my seat and my duties.

There are only a couple of hours left in the workday, and they go by quickly. When it's time to leave, everyone but Charlotte springs up to go home. I'm not certain Charlotte has moved all afternoon.

Pauline sashays from the room without a single wobble. I can scarcely believe my bad luck. Without the slightest disruption to her stride, she chatters with Marguerite and

Henrietta all the way to the front door. Through the main dress shop window, I watch them waltz across the wide, busy street without hesitation.

I *knew* I didn't do enough to that heel! Maybe tomorrow I'll get another chance. If I'd only thought to jab the shears—

Pauline's hip juts to the right, and she windmills her arms for balance. The shoe has come apart. There in the middle of the crowded street.

While flailing, she knocks the hat off a passing ruffian, and he reflexively pushes her away. She sprawls on her back.

Right in the path of an oncoming omnibus.

There is no time for the driver to react. The horses rear, and their heavy hooves clomp down on top of her. Henrietta and Marguerite stare in shock and horror. All the other pedestrians are screaming, as are the panicked passengers inside the omnibus.

Pauline doesn't so much as twitch. She can't. Not anymore.

Pauline is dead.

CHAPTER 22

Five more days until Madame Violette judges our designs for the competition and finally chooses a protégée. Only Henrietta, Marguerite, and myself remain. Charlotte still wanders to and from work, but she requires ten hours to accomplish what she used to do in thirty minutes.

We're not doing the fittings anymore. It's been three days, and she hasn't even thought to ask me about modeling or whatever happened to the dress I was making. She can barely look after herself. She's come to work twice still wearing her sleep bonnet and today has accidentally worn the green nightgown I gave her instead of her petticoat.

The other girls spend all week tattling to Madame Violette that Charlotte has been coming to work drunk. Madame Violette has ordered her home several times to "sleep it off," but Charlotte always mumbles that she's trying to win the protégée position and refuses to rise from her chair.

By the time boils begin to appear on her skin, it's clear—to me, at least—that an excess of wine is not what ails Charlotte.

Instead of sympathy from the others, she receives nothing more than vitriol.

"You're a disgrace to us all," Henrietta informs her with a sniff. "You've always been an inferior designer, even before you started showing up resembling a rotting corpse. Why are you still here?"

Charlotte is tenacious, I'll give her that. She may have forgotten how to sew, but she clutches her poisoned green silk as though it were a security blanket. All she seems to remember is that it gives her beauty.

Meanwhile, I must contend with Marguerite and Henrietta. This close to the end of the competition, the girls snipe at each other as much as they snipe at me. All day, Henrietta has been waving around her ticket for tonight's performance of *L'Aventurière* and bragging about her fur muff, driving us mad.

For her part, Henrietta is trying to exert superiority however she can. She knows she was never the best designer amongst us . . . until the others started dropping out of the race. Marguerite is still an unparalleled force to be reckoned with, but since Henrietta doesn't even count me as a person, to her, Marguerite is the sole competitor left to beat.

Charlotte would have been the other major challenger if the poison weren't addling her brain. It would be a shame to waste such a creative mind in perpetuity. I await the end of the contest, when I can retract the poisoned clothing and allow her faculties to return.

After the contest is over, Charlotte will be angry with me when I insist she give me the items back—but she'll be her usual self soon enough. Once I'm Madame Violette's protégée, perhaps Charlotte will agree to be my next-in-command.

Marguerite would absolutely die of jealousy.

At the moment, however, they're not speaking about the contest. The topic has turned to more salacious gossip.

"Terrible about what happened to Pauline," Marguerite says to Henrietta in a gleeful voice that indicates our co-worker's untimely death was a gift from God. Aside from how she's going to win the contest, Marguerite's favorite topics are animal taxidermy and other people's tragedies. "Did you hear Béatrice won't be attending Pauline's funeral?"

As usual, Henrietta isn't listening.

"Émile Augier is *such* a respected playwright," Henrietta gushes, as if we were discussing a play at le Boulevard du Crime and not the very real, recent death of our colleague. "Did you know la Comédie Français refused to produce *La Ciguë* a few years ago, and Augier was forced to move the production to the Théâtre de l'Odéon? Fools. His script was one of the biggest successes of the year."

Marguerite glares at her icily. "As I was saying, Béatrice won't be attending our dear Pauline's funeral because—"

"Did I mention I'll be wearing a fur muff tonight?" Henrietta interjects for the hundredth time. "My uncle is the one who invited us to the theater. He's an important industrialist, you know. Part of Monsieur Fournier's sacred circle."

Sacred? Va te faire foutre. The Fournier Twelve are disciples of nothing but greed. An infamous cabal of power-hungry men who control the majority of the city's most profitable—

and deadliest—factories. They value gold more than human life and are worshipped for their excesses.

I didn't know that Henrietta is related to monsters like the one who killed my parents and sister.

She plucks at one of her pus-colored curls. "You'll all miss the show of the season. Critics have been saying what a brilliant and clever comedy *L'Aventurière* is since the night of the first performance. *I* will be watching from a private box."

"'Brilliant' and 'clever' mean the same thing, you utter dinde," growls Marguerite. "And nobody cares about your play or your box."

"Doors open at seven," Henrietta continues blithely. "I'll have to leave work early today in order to dress my hair appropriately. My mother is lending me her best fur muff for the occasion. It's not truly cold enough for a fur muff yet, but good quality mink looks so dashing." Henrietta stretches out her bare hands and places them on top of each other, as though pretending to be wearing the mythical fur muff even now.

Marguerite is practically frothing at the mouth. Even half-comatose Charlotte cringes with irritation every time Henrietta squawks *fur muff, fur muff, fur muff.* Or perhaps she winces because her entire body is now dotted with scabs and boils from the arsenic dye rubbing against her bare skin.

"In fact," says Henrietta, "the mink that my mother's fur muff is made from—"

Marguerite slaps her hands down onto her workstation, causing all its pins and needles to jump six inches into the air. "Béatrice isn't going to Pauline's funeral because Béatrice will never walk again!"

This, at last, shuts Henrietta up.

Marguerite's eyes shine triumphantly, having proven herself more interesting than someone else's secondhand fur muff.

"Confined to a bed for months and months," she says in satisfaction. "And then the rest of her life strapped to a wheelchair, if she's lucky."

I tamp down a twinge of guilt.

Henrietta continues admiring her hands. "Not as lucky as—"

Marguerite explodes. "If you dare to say she's not as lucky as you, with your theater ticket and your fur muff, so help me, Henrietta, I swear that I'll strangle you with my bare—"

"Angélique!" calls Madame Violette. "Make haste!"

I scurry from the room, unsure how many of my coworkers will still be breathing when I return. Then again, if they throttle each other, they'll save me a bit of effort.

The rest of the day vanishes in a whirlwind of activity. Between frequent interruptions to help Madame Violette deal with customers at the front of the store, I finish my projects as well as Charlotte's as efficiently as I can.

I'm returning to the sewing room from yet another customer interaction when I pass Henrietta in the corridor.

She wiggles the backs of her perfect fingers at me and crows, "Tonight, these hands will spend hours in the luxury of a fur muff! I wager you wish *you* had some way to hide the ugly monstrosity of your hand."

Can I stab her with knitting needles? One through each eye? Or at least break her beautiful fingers until all ten of them mirror my ruined pinkie?

"You're not going to wear the fur muff during the performance," I tell her impatiently.

She smirks. "You're obviously jealous that I—"

"It's gauche to wear outdoor garments indoors. And it'll be hot inside the theater, with eight hundred other sweaty bodies pressed together. If you wear the muff, you'll be trying too hard not to melt to pay any attention to the spectacle below, and *then* what will you brag about tomorrow?"

Her lower lip wobbles. It's a good point, and she's devastated to hear it. She'll be conspicuous in the wrong way if she wears that stupid rodent pelt through two acts and an intermission.

"You're just jealous," she says again, and flounces from the dress shop.

I don't even have time to roll my eyes at her petulant departure. There's too much to do, and Charlotte is barely responsive. This time, Madame Violette successfully sends her home to rest—with the admonition not to return unless she's in optimal working condition. Which leaves me to carry both our weight.

By the time I complete my work and Charlotte's, I'm exhausted.

When Domingo walks me home that evening, I barely have the energy to talk. Instead, I content myself with holding tight to his arm.

At supper, Elodie doesn't register my silence. Most of our small table is full of the bottles and beakers Domingo gifted her, and she bubbles enthusiastically about how these things are going to change her life.

My studious sister is so involved in her nightly experiments, she doesn't even notice when I slip from the house at a quarter to ten.

My heart beats faster as I approach the Odéon. Henrietta's play will be ending soon. I've never seen a show or entered a theater. I'm not completely certain what I intend to do, but I pray an answer will come to me.

Deep in my heart, I beg my mother to send me a sign. There is no response. Either the dead cannot answer the living, or I am already on the right path.

The Odéon is a grand four-story beige stone building with beautiful arches and a soaring facade lined with eight enormous columns. Everything is so large, I feel like an insignificant beetle scurrying across its pristine marble floor.

A frowning box office guard stops me inside the entrance. I don't even pretend to be fashionable enough to afford a ticket to a place like this.

Instead, I pull a folded square of blank drawing paper from my pocket. An idea has begun to form. The protégée position *will* be mine. Neither Elodie nor I will have to work at a horrid factory ever again. I will also be one step closer to repaying the Fourniers for their cruelty.

"Oh, thank heavens," I tell the guard, practically collapsing against him in feigned relief. "I thought I was too late to catch her. My mistress is inside, and she simply must receive this missive at once. It is of the utmost urgency."

The guard's frown clears. Normally footmen deliver urgent messages, not handmaidens, but any employee can be assigned any task. Now that the theater guard's brain has classified me as the servant of someone important, he sees me as harmless. Nothing more than wallpaper. I could dance across the stage with my faux letter in hand, and the upper classes would not pay my existence any mind.

"Who is your mistress?" he asks.

"Madame . . ." Oh God, what was the factory owner's last name? Henrietta only told us a thousand times. "Laurent."

As soon as I invent the lie, anxiety sets in. What if her uncle isn't married, and there *is* no Madame Laurent? What if—

The guard nods, already distracted by something over my shoulder. "Private box. Third floor, second doorway, stage right. Be quick. The play will end any minute, and you might lose your mistress in the crowd."

"Thank you so much." I head for the sweeping spiral stairs covered in luxurious carpet.

The guard catches my elbow and points toward a small plain door in the opposite direction. "Use the stagehands' passageway so that you don't disturb the audience."

Hidden servants' access. Of course.

I turn from the beautiful wide stairway and take the narrow concrete passage instead. It's dark and smells of dust and old paint.

The theater guests are still in their seats and therefore would not notice even a flock of sheep bleating up their precious carpeted stairs, but logic doesn't matter. French businessmen and aristocrats have their place in society, and I have mine: here in the stench and the shadows, surrounded by sharp edges.

When I emerge on the third floor, I find a stone to prop open the door. I'll only be a minute.

As I step out onto the fine carpet at last, a jolt of satisfaction runs through me. I don't mind creeping through the darkness to achieve my goals. Paradise awaits me on the other side.

By my count, Henrietta's private box is only a few feet away from me. I slink over, peeking a single eye around the box's open doorway to spy on the backs of the six fashionable heads inside.

I spot Henrietta as the actors onstage take their bows. The theater erupts with cheers and applause.

Henrietta leaps to her feet, the infernal fur muff in her hand. I duck back around the corner and press my spine flush to the clean, silk-draped wall before she has a chance to see me.

"I'll meet you all on the pavement outside!" she sings out merrily. "I'll be standing beside the main doors wearing my fur muff!"

Henrietta flies from the private box like a bat out of hell, determined to be the first out-of-doors so that all the other theatergoers can admire her on their way to their carriages. She is too focused on sliding the rodent pelt onto her hands to notice me step out of the shadows and jab a sharp elbow into her side.

Thrown off-balance by the force of my blow, she stumbles sideways into the opposite wall.

Or would have, if there was a wall there.

Instead, her unbalanced limbs sail through the propped-open doorway of the stagehands' exit. Where she immediately encounters four flights of sharp concrete stairs.

The fur muff trapping her hands together prevents her from being able to grab the banister and break her fall. She tumbles down to the first landing head over heels, coming to rest in an ungainly heap with a thud and a whimper.

I'm still standing on the carpet, out of sight. My breath is shallow, and my heart is beating far too rapidly.

Henrietta has no idea what happened to her, and I'd like to keep it that way. I reach out my foot to knock loose the stone propping open the door, to hide her body from view. Only seconds have passed, but already the audience is starting to leave their seats and fill the hallways.

"Angélique, is that you?" croaks Henrietta. "I saw you there! Did you *push* me, you jealous orphan? I'm going to tell everyone that you—"

Merde. I cannot risk it.

I slip into the employee passage and close the door behind us. With only the exterior moonlight from a high, narrow window, the scene in the stairwell resembles a smudged charcoal sketch.

"Help!" she screams. "Anyone! I'm down he—"

I'm at her side before she can finish the word. Her fallen fur muff is now lying on the chipped concrete beside her obviously broken leg. I'm sure it hurts, but she'll live.

We can't have that.

I clamp my hand over her mouth to silence her screaming, but it's hard to hold still with her bucking beneath me.

She bites my hand hard enough to pierce the skin. I yelp in surprise, jerking back out of instinct. It's all the opening she needs to slash her arm toward my face. I tilt my head to avoid a direct blow, but her clawed fingernails scrape across my head, sending rivulets of blood into my hair.

Frantic, I scoop up the animal pelt and shove the muff into her screaming mouth until the fur reaches the back of her throat. Now all that escapes from her mouth are muffled whimpers. She flails her arms uselessly, her eyes bulging out of her face as her lungs are depleted of oxygen.

Seconds later, it's done. Her face is slack, her body limp.

I'm breathing heavily, my blood pumping, my shaking body having reacted more out of defense and fear than premeditation. Cold settles along my skin as reality seeps in.

I leave the muff pressed against Henrietta's open mouth for a few minutes more, to make sure she isn't merely unconscious and still a threat.

When I'm certain I'm crouched in the stairwell with a corpse, I remove the mink muff from her throat. The damp fur will soon dry. After cleaning my blood from her nails and lips, I shove Henrietta's hands inside the brown pelt, which I place on her stomach. The final touch is a quickly jotted note from a "secret admirer," asking Henrietta to meet him at their usual spot after the performance.

I brush the stray mink hairs from my skirts and pat a handkerchief against my hair. The head wound is superficial. The bleeding has stopped. No one will suspect a thing.

As soon as my breathing returns to normal, I make my leisurely descent back to the lobby. There's no need to rush. My work here is done.

A dreadful accident, by all appearances. Was the poor girl too excited to watch where she was going . . . or was her secret admirer more sinister than romantic? The public will be too entranced by the salacious scandal to consider any other possibilities.

"Did you find your mistress?" asks the guard as I exit.

I smile. "Yes, thank you. Message delivered."

CHAPTER 23

Two days remain until the protégée contest has a winner—and there's just one competitor left to speak of. Charlotte is present only in body, if she shows up at all. Béatrice can't leave her bed. Pauline and Henrietta are dead. Marguerite and I race to the finish.

As it perhaps would have been all along. Marguerite is a phenomenal designer. If she offered to design a piece for me, I would be no different from Charlotte in my eagerness to wrap myself in its beauty.

Earlier, Madame Violette muttered that of us girls, she thanks God that it is Marguerite and I who are not prone to accidents or addicted to the bottle. She says we are her angels.

She is wrong. *I* should be her only angel. Choosing Marguerite is a mistake I cannot allow her to make.

I am surprised she suspects nothing, though that is perhaps not entirely true. Madame Violette suspects all the wrong things. She believes in old magic. She is convinced she is cursed. That some jealous modiste has cast a spell or prayed to the devil to keep her from succeeding. That this string of unfortunate coincidences is happening to *her*, not to her unlucky employees.

Her self-centered naivety is a godsend. Madame Violette's myopic view of herself as a persecuted heroine makes her all the more trusting of those she perceives as being on her side. She counts on me now more than ever.

I am glad my dress has been done for a week. There is no more time to work on my own projects. Not when two pairs of hands must do what it previously took six seamstresses to accomplish.

With luck, Marguerite might not be as far along as I am and won't have had enough time to finish her contribution.

But only a fool relies on luck.

After Elodie commandeers the post-supper kitchen table for her experiments, I shrug on my red wool cloak and slip outside.

Twilight in Paris is my favorite time of day. Work is done. Clouds of bilious gray wipe away the last vermilion streaks of the sunset. The moon peeks out. Either a sliver or the entire orb. Stars, when the sky is clear.

But no matter what, every night at this precise moment, a battalion of nearly eight hundred allumeurs spills into Paris's main streets, hefting long poles with swinging lamps at the tips. The uniformed men open the gas pipe inside each shiny black lamppost and light its corresponding lamp.

In little more than half an hour, the City of Light is completely illuminated.

It's enchanting. I'd live in Paris for this spectacle alone.

As the streetlamps bloom around me, the allumeurs in their smart blue-and-black uniforms scurry back to wherever they came from. I imagine them living in little burrows beneath the city, like a colony of rats, swarming en masse at nightfall. I too have a mission to accomplish.

By now, Domingo is at home, though I cannot head there. Not with Marguerite still on the loose. I have no notion where she lives, but I do know how to find the shop belonging to her father, the taxidermist who stuffed the dead songbird attached to her bonnet.

In fact, when I reach Rue des Capucines, I see that the taxidermy shop is right next to a milliner's. In one window display, a crowded menagerie of dead woodland creatures. In the sparkling window next to it, row after row of extravagant ladies' hats. Most of which indeed boast a variety of feathers, if not an entire exotic bird.

This must be the place.

My reticule dangles heavily from my wrist. I didn't know what I might need, so I packed a little of everything: Laudanum, for a sleeping draught. White powdered arsenic, mixed with sugar. A length of twine that can easily be tied about wrists—or a neck. A straight-edged razor recently sharpened. A pincushion, bursting with my best needles.

And my sketchbook. You never know when inspiration might strike.

I pass the hat display and peer through the window of posed dead animals. The interior of the taxidermist's is wallpapered with marble-eyed facsimiles of life. Birds, marmots, minks, shrews, dormice, rabbits . . . even two silvery seals, and a spotted brown-and-white fawn.

In the center of all of that death sits Marguerite. At a fancy table. With tea. And cookies.

I swing open the door and step inside.

Marguerite is about to serve herself a steaming cup. She pauses in the act of pouring to glance up and nearly spills scalding water on herself at the sight of me.

"Angélique! Ugh, what are you doing here?"

"My bedchamber doesn't have enough dead seals?" I walk around the cluttered shop, trying to take everything in. "How does one catch a baby seal, anyway? Do you wade into the water? Stand by with a club on land? Do they wander up to the Arc de Triomphe until you show up and stuff them into canvas sacks?"

Marguerite is not amused.

"Our specimens come from the Baie de Somme on the Normandy coast," she tells me haughtily. "And we shoot them. A small bullet hole is no trouble at all for a skilled seamstress. Not that I'd expect someone like *you* to have acquired such a talent."

I stare at her in surprise. "You work all day for Madame Violette and then stuff wild animals at night?"

She shakes her head and finishes pouring her tea. "I stopped helping Papa when I started with Madame Violette."

"Then why are you here? Is this really your favorite spot for tea?"

She shrugs. "Death doesn't bother me. I'm used to it. I don't mind keeping an eye out for last-minute customers while Papa visits Maman next door."

"Your mother is the milliner?"

"The very best." Marguerite gestures at the dead-songbird hat lying on the chair next to her. "My parents made that for me together when I turned sixteen. What are you doing here? Did you get lost on your way to work at the brothel?"

"I was out for a stroll and thought I saw you through the window. What's all that stuff over there?" I point at a worktable filled with lumpy bags and stoppered jars of strange substances.

"Taxidermists preserve animals by skinning them and treating the hides with arsenic and mercury. Papa prefers arsenic soap, but the powder is cheaper. Maman uses the chemicals too, for her felt hats. Anyway, once the skin is cured, we only keep the skull and the most delicate bones. The rest is wire and stuffing."

Arsenic . . . soap?

I didn't hear a single word of the explanation after that. I had no idea arsenic soap existed. If it's good enough to embalm baby seals, it's good enough for the likes of factory owner Monsieur Fournier. I wonder if there's any way to easily swap whatever they currently use with this lovely new variety. I could even scent it with one of Elodie's pretty perfumes. I edge closer to inspect the workstation.

"Are you ready for the contest?" Marguerite asks. "Of course not. The day after tomorrow, when Madame Violette picks a winner, it'll be me. You can't imagine what a marvelous design I've come up with."

"Something fur-lined," I say automatically. "Predictable."

Her face turns red. She glares at me. "Better than whatever you decorated yours with. Spiderwebs? Dust balls? Tears of despair?"

I pick up a heavy, stoppered glass bottle. I'd think it was a decanter for wine, except the liquid inside is metallic and shiny, like melted silver. I start to uncork the bottle to smell whatever is inside.

"Leave the stopper on," Marguerite commands. "That's mercury. Breathing too much is intoxicating, and I don't care for another headache."

"It would affect you all the way over there?" I say in surprise.

"It's cold out. When the windows are closed, the smell gets into your brain. We can never tell whether Mother has drunk too much brandy or made too many felt hats in a row."

I place the bottle back on the table. Very interesting. Might mercury be as poisonous as arsenic? This shop has plenty of both. Two hefty sacks of arsenic. I wish they had one of the soaps on display instead. I'm eager to see what those might look like.

"Ma fille!" trills a distant female voice. "Did you take *all* of my cookies?"

Marguerite doesn't answer. Unless you count popping another cookie into her mouth as answering.

"Tout de suite!" calls a sharp, deep voice. Presumably her father.

Marguerite lets out an aggrieved sigh and forces herself to her feet with a muttered curse. At least the ungrateful wretch still has her parents. If mine were alive, I wouldn't waste a single moment before running into their arms.

"I said I'm coming!" she yells, then grumbles, "Salaud! I haven't even had a chance to add milk and sugar to my tea." She slaps half of the cookies into the palm of her hand, then jabs a finger at me. "Don't touch anything while I'm gone. If a customer comes, tell them I'll be right back. And leave the cookies for me."

With that, she disappears through a rear door.

I waste no time dumping a sachet of poisoned sugar into her tea. I'm not sure that's enough arsenic to take effect right away. I can't make it *too* sugary, or she might suspect something is wrong. I wish there was something I could do to the milk.

Glancing around, I catch sight of the stoppered mercury bottle. Perfect. I run to fetch it, then hold my breath as I spill a good portion into the tiny silver milk pitcher. I restopper the mercury and place it back where I found it, then give the milk a few energetic swirls before setting it back down and closing the silver lid.

I've barely snatched my hands away when Marguerite sweeps into the room. I expect her to eye me with suspicion, but I'm standing exactly where she left me. Marguerite has never viewed me as a competitor or a colleague, much less as a threat.

She settles back into her seat, dumps sugar and mercury-milk into her arsenic tea, then takes a long sip.

Once again, I hold my breath.

Her forehead lines briefly, and she gives the cup a funny

glance. Is the mixture sweeter than she expected? Or does mercury have a metallic taste? My heart starts to beat faster. I hope I won't have to club her to death with a baby seal and mount her on the wall.

She smiles and takes another long drink, then picks up a cookie, apparently unconcerned about whatever unusual element she noticed in her tea. Cheeks full as a chipmunk's, she leans forward to whisper, "Did you hear about Henrietta?"

I have no idea how to answer this. Of course I heard about Henrietta. I was there when she died. Even if I hadn't been, her corpse was discovered within the hour and the tragic accident referenced in the morning papers. She was buried yesterday afternoon.

I'm done with Henrietta.

"What about her?" I ask carefully.

Marguerite reaches for another cookie, then puts it back and presses her palm to her stomach instead. She takes another long drink of tea before responding. "They found her still wearing her mother's fur muff . . . which her mother then took off the corpse and wore to the funeral!"

I'm not sure whether poor dead Henrietta would be offended or delighted by this. "How do you know it was the same fur muff?"

Marguerite doubles over slightly, then gestures around her. "I recognized it."

Her voice is strained, as though it hurts to talk. Maybe even to breathe.

"Are you all right?" I ask softly.

Marguerite appears confused. "Maybe I did eat too many cookies. I'm no better than Jacqueline."

Oh, chérie. This time, the cookies are not the problem.

"Here, love," I say solicitously. "Let me pour you another cup of tea."

She's not even watching as I add plenty of mercury-milk and the rest of the poisoned sugar from my pocket. Her eyes are closed as she winces in pain.

I push the warm cup and saucer into her hands. "Drink this. It'll fix everything."

She nods and gulps it down without question. I imagine the toxic liquid pooling there in her stomach, the mercury traveling through her veins while the arsenic rots her from the inside out.

"I don't feel well," she whispers.

"Come with me." I take her by the hand. "We'll go outside for some fresh air."

It might take an hour or two for the poison to finish its job. We can't have her parents stumbling across their dying daughter in time to summon a doctor.

Before we leave, I uncork the bottle of mercury and place it beside her teacup. Ah, Marguerite. Her parents know she's been working herself to death, sewing night and day, covering for colleagues, forgoing sleep in favor of work—only to come home to even more demands from her own family. Mind the shop, coddle the customers, no rest for you. The poor, overworked pet can't even eat a cookie without being reprimanded and sent to handle more tasks.

Untenable. Constant work is no kind of life at all. Little wonder our Marguerite might wish to escape her circumstances by any means necessary. A little mercury in her tea, along with a forbidden biscuit, and farewell to all her troubles.

As well as to the protégée position.

Marguerite stumbles along at my side like a drunkard, allowing me to lead her down the street and around the corner to a dark alley. I nestle her onto the hard stones next to a grimy brick wall. She doesn't notice. Her eyes are closed. She's no longer grimacing. She doesn't move.

Good. She'll seem as peaceful when they find her in the morning.

"Thank you, Angélique," she murmurs, before slipping from consciousness altogether.

I touch her cheek with my scarred hand. "It was truly my pleasure."

CHAPTER 24

That night, I cannot sleep. I wake up a bundle of nerves. It's Sunday—the day of rest—but not for me. I've dispatched my competition, which means tomorrow morning Madame Violette should have no choice but to name me her protégée.

But of course, she has choices.

If she thinks my entry wouldn't have ranked highest on its own merit, she might decide I'm still too much of a neophyte for the position. She could hire someone else. Anyone else. *Everyone* else. Paris is awash with out-of-work seamstresses with far more experience than an eighteen-year-old former dye girl with a crooked finger.

Someone else might correctly suspect that my being the lone survivor of our cutthroat competition means that I took matters into my own hands rather than leave the judgment to my employer. In which case, even if my design summons harps and trumpets from the heavens as angels sing, Madame

Violette won't just sack me from my post—she'll report me to the police.

My involvement in my coworkers' maladies would be impossible to prove. No one saw me do anything incriminating, nor could recognize my name. I've scoured the newspapers and lingered as close as I dare to the officer or two assigned to the scenes of the crimes to ensure no eyebrows are rising. In all cases but Marguerite's supposed suicide so far, the deaths were deemed accidental. None are being investigated. With all the death and crime in a city this sprawling, most of these aren't even worthy of a mention in the newspaper, much less a headline. The sole exception:

SOLD-OUT COMEDY MARRED BY TRAGIC FALL

The article stirred up more public outcry about whether safety concerns would affect future scheduled performances at the Odéon this season than any condolences for Henrietta specifically. Apparently, her uncle—the important industrialist—intends to maintain his presence in his luxury theater box despite his supposed grief.

How can the police draw any conclusions when they take only the most perfunctory of glances? This is Paris. Nearly a million people live in the metropolitan area. Our numbers rise by the day, though the opportunities for lodging and employment do not. Crime is rampant. Deaths are common. The police do not have enough time or interest to waste resources attending to the middle or lower classes, particularly if a simple, logical explanation is right there in front of them. They are relieved that no great detective work is required of them, so that they can turn their attention to the people who really matter.

Nonetheless, I *am* the last employee standing, if anyone bothers to look beyond the obvious. Madame Violette is the only one who knows of these coincidences. She is too afraid she's been cursed to share her theories with the police—who would laugh off her provincial superstitions if she tried.

Although I'm as safe from criminal prosecution as I could possibly be, my nerves will not settle until the position is mine and Elodie and I can breathe free at last.

When Domingo knocks on our door, I throw myself into his arms with enough force to knock him backward a few steps. He catches me.

"What's this?" he says, laughing. "I thought it would be impossible to tear you away from your work, and that I would be forced to be the human pig for Elodie's colognes yet again."

Horrors. I arch my chest into him, nestling further into his embrace. He smells positively delectable as he is, without any perfumes to mask his perfect scent.

I place the back of my damaged hand against my forehead and dramatically command, "Take me away from here, O gallant knight. I implore thee to rescue this poor maiden without delay."

The corners of his hazel eyes crinkle. He holds me a little closer. "It would be an honor and a privilege, my lady."

"Let us be gone, then," I beg.

He swings me in a circle, then hooks my hand about his elbow. "Where to, mi tesoro?"

"Anywhere but the darkness of my own mind."

"Ah. You seek a distraction. Let me see what I can provide." And then we're off, ambling at a lazy comfortable pace. South, in the general direction of the Seine.

I try to guess where he's taking me. "La Place des Victoires? Le Palais-Royal, where we might spy upon President Louis-Napoléon? The stock exchange, where we could . . . do nothing at all since it's closed on Sundays and neither of us is well-to-do enough to own stock in anything?"

Domingo shakes his head, his smile never faltering, so sure is he that wherever he's leading me is more marvelous than all of those wonders combined.

"Come, now. You're making me mimic Elodie."

We pass a string of theaters: le Théâtre des Variétés, la Michodière, les Bouffes Parisiens. Le Boulevard du Crime again? No. Domingo has a surprise in store.

When we reach the heart of the second arrondissement, Domingo pauses before a stunning, high-ceilinged covered passage lined with glass.

It is the Galerie Colbert, and it is spectacular.

A few years before I was born, this gorgeous enclave was built to compete with the neighboring Galerie Vivienne. Several facades line the sunlit walkway: bookstores, gunsmiths, belt makers, hairdressers, an herbal pharmacy.

The largest facade belongs to a shop called Au Grand Colbert, with stunning glass windows stretching from the pavement to the ceiling of the main floor. The windows are new, installed this summer. No other store boasts anything like it.

We gawp through the pristine glass. On the other side is

a wide selection of everything you can imagine: buttons, ribbons, lace, umbrellas, chairs, tables, mattresses.

"Can we go inside?" I ask hesitantly.

Domingo grins at me. "Of course."

As soon as we enter, I'm dizzy. The walls are six meters high and decorated with sculpted pilasters. There's a glass rotunda and a glass ceiling. Paintings dot the walls, as though we've wandered into the Louvre. The entire floor is crafted as a vast mosaic, featuring countless tiny perfect tiles in shades of gold and blue and onyx.

In the center of the building is an enormous bronze candelabrum, half a meter taller than Domingo. Its wide arms cradle seven crystal globes, lit expensively with gas, even before the sun has fully set.

"It's called the Cocotier Lumineux," he tells me. *Illuminated coconut tree.*

An absolutely mad idea, and utterly perfect. I've never seen any place more romantic in my life. My heart feels like singing. "Oh, Domingo, I love it."

"Me too." His intense gaze is directed at my marveling face, rather than toward our remarkable surroundings.

I blush, grateful that the light brown hue of my skin will hide the flush. Mostly.

The roguish sparkle in Domingo's eyes indicates that he sees right through me.

I make it a point not to meet his gaze as we stroll the aisles, perusing and exclaiming and touching all the wonders we pass.

Not long ago, my presence in a store as fine as this would

have raised brows and wrinkled noses. Thanks to Madame Violette's generosity with her remnants, however, my blue-and-lavender gown rivals any other. The furtive glances darted my way today are appreciative.

Especially those from Domingo. Despite my protests, he buys me a dozen pearlescent buttons, four scarlet ribbons for me and my sister, a bowl of lemon ice, and a book featuring the most important French fashion designers of the past century.

"They're all men," Domingo admits as he hands me the leather volume. "For now. In a year or two, the biographers will be writing about *you*."

I smack his chest with the book, but secretly I'm pleased. I want that future to come to pass as badly as Elodie wants to be a parfumeur.

"My biography will be shelved between the one about my sister and the one featuring a certain talented and devastatingly handsome Spanish immigrant whose shoes can be found on all the best feet."

Domingo grins at me. "Paris has no idea what's coming."

It really doesn't.

When we return to my front step at last, I don't want to wave goodbye and send him home like every other day. Today was magical, and precisely what I needed. Because of him, I feel human again. Alive.

Impulsively, I throw my arms around his neck and press my lips to his.

He freezes for a second before wrapping his arms around me, his warmth enveloping me. When the tip of his tongue touches mine, I nearly swoon.

The unfamiliar sensations uncoiling ravenously inside me knock me back to my senses. Before I pull back entirely, I give him a peck on his cheek, then slip inside the apartment and lock the door securely behind me.

I listen for his footsteps. He doesn't move an inch for several minutes. Then he is gone.

The taste of his kiss stays on my lips all night long.

CHAPTER 25

On Monday morning, I present myself at the dress shop before the first hint of dawn, my competition entry draped over my arm beneath a protective cloth.

Shaking with hope and anxiety, I'm waiting outside the door when Madame Violette descends from a hackney carriage.

She glances at me quizzically. "Qu'est-ce que c'est là? You know you're not supposed to take commissioned pieces home. We cannot risk letting anything happen to the merchandise."

"No . . . It's not a . . . This is my contest piece," I blurt out.

She stares at me as if this is the first she's heard of such a thing. "Your what?"

Madame Violette cannot possibly have *forgotten*.

Can she?

"The protégée competition," I babble. "You said whoever created the design that impressed you the most—"

"Oh, that." She unlocks the door and strides inside.

I hurry after her. "For my piece, I decided on a combination of—"

She sighs. "Angélique, can we discuss such matters later? Next month, perhaps. We have far too much work at present, and not nearly enough fingers to—"

Something in my face indicates that I'm going to dissolve into a quivering mass of jelly and tears if she doesn't look at my damn dress here and now.

"All right, all right. No need for hysterics. Show me."

I hand it over in silence. My carefully planned speech vanishes, along with the last flutter of my confidence. Discuss it *later*? Next *month*? When I am already the only seamstress left? Was I never even a contender for the role?

Madame Violette holds the gown up to the sunlight streaming through the store window, turning my seams this way and that. Brow furrowed. Lips pursed. As silent as I am.

It's enough to make me scream.

"Full, bell-shaped skirts," she says at last.

I nod. "Yes. They'd be supported by three crinoline hoops."

"White lace flounces, with a deep jade underskirt and matching decorative ribbons."

I nod again. I'm now a marionette. Nod, nod, nod.

"Much tighter bodice than currently fashionable," she muses. "A bold choice, tempered by the high neckline and demurely buttoned front. Your signature shade of green, as you know, is awe-inspiring. You're letting the color talk as much as the cut."

I can't stop nodding. My head is bound to roll off my neck.

"White lace collar and cuffs to match the white lace overskirt. Low, sloping shoulders and flared sleeves with an imaginative flourish give a touch of fairy godmother."

Did I mention I'm nodding to everything she says? Nod. Nod. Nod.

"Dans l'ensemble . . ." She holds it up again and tilts her head, frowning.

I hold my breath. I've *been* holding my breath. I'm about to pass out.

She turns to me and smiles. "I think we could make this *the* debut dress of the season. Every mother who loves her daughter will want her to be wearing this confection when she makes her first public curtsey."

For a moment, I cannot process her words. Then relief washes over me like a tidal wave, nearly drowning me.

She likes it. *I did it.*

"A-and . . . ," I stammer, "as for the related assistant position . . ."

"It's yours, Angélique. You've been quite efficiently taking the lead since I proposed the contest. Marguerite will be disappointed, as she was your only true competition. In any case, félicitations. You are officially my protégée. Now go put that exquisite dress somewhere safe, because our first customers will arrive at any moment."

Marguerite's days of disappointment are over. I race to drape my dress over Henrietta's empty worktable. A pang of guilt gives me pause, but I push it away as best I can. With my sister's safety—and my career—now secure, I shall concentrate solely on the people who wield their positions of power like swords, cutting short the lives of the destitute and desperate.

Soon I rejoin Madame Violette in the reception area.

"I'd like you to give some thought to how we can make this season our best yet," she tells me.

"Have you considered my idea about the lower classes?"

"Angélique," she says with a sigh, "the lower classes are lower because they don't have any money. This is a business. It runs on money. We need to raise as much of it as we can."

"Yes, but isn't fashion also about feeling and looking one's best? Shouldn't everyone have that opportunity?" I've said this before. My argument is not going to work.

"Does every human deserve to look and feel marvelous? Bien sûr. But if they cannot afford to make that happen—"

"They can't afford to copy the elite, but that doesn't mean we should count them out entirely." I continue stubbornly, "Think cheap but pretty frocks. One design. One pattern. We could make dozens in a single week. Profit would be lower per gown, yes, but we'd make up the difference in volume—or at least, we wouldn't lose our investment. And we'd be doing good in the world at the same time."

She gazes at me for a long moment. "I see you're passionate about this."

"It's what made me want to be a designer," I admit. "I've never dreamed of becoming a duchesse. I want fashion like this available to people like me." I gesture at the simple but beautiful dress I made for myself.

"That's sweet and honorable, chérie. I simply don't have

enough employees to handle a sudden increase in volume. Particularly since we don't know that this idea will work. Yes, you explained the math, but we don't know for certain that the lower classes will show up in droves to purchase an inferior product. And we risk alienating our wealthiest clients by diluting their sense of exclusivity."

"But . . . if we *had* more employees," I babble desperately. "And if I could promise we wouldn't lose a single wife of importance by also providing for common folk—"

"Oui. If you could promise that, I would agree to a trial."

Victory rushes through me. It wasn't an unqualified yes, and we cannot start today, but it is more hope than working-class girls like me had yesterday. I will do whatever I can to lift them up.

Before I can shower Madame Violette with even more unconventional ideas, she motions for me to stand next to her at the far side of the window.

"We'll talk later. Here comes the next duo to impress," she says. "Ultrawealthy Madame Fournier and her daughter, Blanche. They own a series of wretched but highly profitable textile factories across town. Their green dye is nothing like ours, though."

"Wh-what?"

Rather than slide effortlessly into my usual role of apathy, my heart shivers in staccato and the usual script vanishes from my brain.

This is the moment I've been waiting for. The next puzzle piece in my master plan will soon come through the door. The other customers' purchases were merely laying a trap to catch these two. Honey for flies.

"This pair are the flashiest and most blatant social climbers of all the nouveaux riches," Madame Violette whispers as we watch the duo approach. "They spend money like they're trying to rid themselves of it. I am happy to take as much gold from them as they'd like to get off their hands."

Before I can respond, the bell above the door tinkles in welcome, and Madame Fournier and her daughter sweep into the dress shop.

CHAPTER 26

I freeze. No longer a bouncing marionette but a marble statue.

The Fournier ladies have shopped here before. But that was when Jacqueline was the one helping up front.

The last time Madame Fournier and Mademoiselle Blanche saw my face . . . was in their death trap of a factory, scant minutes before their weaving machine stole the lives of my sister and mother.

In fact, the last words I spoke to them were *Have you thought of sharing even a fraction of your wealth with the workers face down in your factory?*

Their instant and unapologetic response was *But then there would be less for me!*

You could say we didn't part on the best of terms.

"Well?" Mademoiselle Blanche huffs at me with impatience. "Are you going to stand there all day, or are you going to check for our names in your little book? It's *F-o-u-r-n-i-e-r*, if you know how to read."

Her equally self-important mother exhales a dramatic *Is this what passes for good help these days?* world-weary sigh. "Is your employee listening?"

They don't recognize me.

They don't recognize me.

Because I'm in the wrong place. They expect someone of my birth to be on the streets or in one of their squalid factories. I also don't look the same as I did that dreadful night. I am decked out head to toe in one of my new creations, draped in finery the old me would never have been able to afford. They *wish* they looked like me. There could be no better disguise.

At my extended silence, Madame Violette shoots me an alarmed glance and clears her throat loudly.

Showtime.

I shake myself and launch into my usual patter. "Oh, are *you* the ladies in question? In those colors, I assumed you were the maids, and we were waiting for your mistresses to arrive. Let me see . . . ah, here we are. Fournier, spelled correctly. I do see you've arrived six and a half minutes late. That time cannot be made up and will result in a nominal charge. Now, if you'll come this way . . ."

The Fournier women gape at me as I spin on my heel, turning my back on them, and stride to the farthest dressing room without bothering to check whether they're keeping up.

"What's wrong with these colors?" stammers Blanche behind me. "Papa dyed this silk himself in his factory."

Her papa has never once set foot in the dye room. He leaves the dangerous activities and actual physical work to desperate people with no other options.

"It's putting me to sleep, for one," I say without glancing up from my blank sketchbook, as if bored. "I've already forgotten what you look like. A lady's dress should do more than make a statement. It should make a *memory*. If you can't wear something unforgettable . . . Why bother with such rags at all?"

Madame Fournier sputters incoherently.

I ignore her and motion Blanche up onto the wooden stool. "Go on, then. Let us hope there's something that can be done with you."

Blanche climbs onto the stool with alacrity and stares at me with terror and hope in her eyes.

For the first time in our two families' long and tortured history, it is *I* who hold the power.

"Hmm." I frown, circling the stool to eye her critically. I turn to a fresh page in my sketchbook and grimace. "You don't make it easy, do you."

A tiny, strangled gasp of pique escapes Madame Fournier's throat. She snatches the notebook and flips through the pages. "But—this is empty! Every page is blank!"

"And it will stay that way," I inform her coldly as I pluck my newest notebook back out of her hands. "Unless this creature you've spawned can inspire me."

Madame Fournier's jaw drops. "You . . . I didn't . . . *You're* the designer? I heard it was a young, prickly genius, but I never . . . Can't you do *something* with Blanche? We'll be hosting the fête of the year, and my daughter must unequivocally be named the belle of the ball."

I narrow my eyes at Blanche and tap the end of my pencil

against my cheek. "What kind of gown are you in the market for?"

"Green," she blurts out.

Madame Fournier explains, "We've seen the designs from this shop that incorporate touches of a jade even deeper than we can produce in our factory."

"I told Papa to make them try harder," Blanche murmurs. "My brother says—"

"Allow your father to worry about Odin," Madame Fournier snaps, then turns to me. "Obviously, our silk is the highest quality on the market. And with Madame Violette being the most sought-after modiste . . . my daughter cannot have less than the best of the best for our masquerade ball."

"Head-to-toe green silk," Blanche reiterates, nearly begging. "A costume in an exclusive pattern, available only to me. I must be, as you said, unforgettable."

Drape her in arsenic from head to toe by her own request? If she insists. It will certainly be a day I won't forget.

"I'll take one too," Madame Fournier adds.

Blanche shoots her a sulky pout.

"In a different design, of course," I break in smoothly. "Though I must warn you, our custom designs do not come cheap. Nor does our signature dye, which is why other customers have only been given small swatches of it."

Also, because I'm the only one who can dye the material perfectly, and who knows how to ensure only the worst of the elite receive the high-arsenic version. While women like these deserve a taste of the strife they blithely inflict upon others,

I have no interest in giving more problems to the lower and middle classes. For them I wish only health and beauty.

"Money is no object," Madame Fournier assures me. "Profits at our factory have never been higher, and expenses are minimal. We haven't given workers a raise in wages since we opened our doors. Whatever you're offering, we can afford it."

Oh, I know they can. And they deserve my very worst. I'm tired of injury and illness wiping out the poor. I believe it's past time a bit of misfortune struck the untouchable rich and powerful—if only as a temporary malaise. Madame Fournier has no idea what's coming.

"In that case, what I propose," I begin, keeping my voice low, as if imparting a life-or-death secret, "is that you host not the masquerade of the season but rather the event of a lifetime. It's not enough for Blanche to gad about in the finest gown money can buy."

Incredibly rude of me to use her daughter's name without the honorific "Mademoiselle," as if Blanche were the impoverished orphan and I the fine lady.

Madame Fournier doesn't even notice. "It won't be enough? What else should I do?"

"You must require *all* your guests' costumes to incorporate our designs in this specific color, men and women. Everyone will wish to attend your party, but only the richest and most fashionable will be able to afford to do so. And everyone will know it."

As for the guests who have trampled on the poor to achieve their riches . . . I'm happy to provide an extra dose of my special ingredient to their costumes.

I add conspiratorially, "Showing up on your doorstep dressed all in jade, mask in hand, will be a social coup for anyone who manages to achieve it."

"Don't you mean 'mask on face'?" asks Blanche.

"Of course not, darling," I say with a little laugh. "It's a masquerade in spirit, not in practice. Everyone will want everyone else to know that they made the cut. That the best modiste in Paris and her protégée accepted their business, that you then welcomed them across your threshold."

"Ohh." Madame Fournier clasps the square of green cloth to her décolletage, her eyes glittering with avarice. "Blanche will be wearing the finest costume of them all, and everyone will see!"

"Precisely. The names of your guests will be listed in every newspaper, their faces sketched by every caricaturist. . . . They'll talk of your fête for months, all the way to Rome and London. I won't be surprised if Queen Victoria herself begs to attend your next soirée."

Madame Fournier is practically drooling at the idea. "Yes. It shall be as you say. Whatever you need to make it happen."

"When is the ball scheduled to take place?" I inquire.

"Christmas Eve," Blanche answers. "We'll have fireworks at midnight. The merrymakers in attendance could officially remove masks then, too."

Beside me, Madame Violette nearly swoons in panic. The masquerade is a month away, and I just promised we'd create custom-tailored costumes for all the most exacting socialites and aristocrats in France.

I shoot her a quick *Don't you dare ruin this for me* glare.

My limbs are shaking with anticipation. The chessboard is mine. I'm so close to winning. Once the capitalists are twirling in my special green finery, slowly being weakened by it, I will have avenged not only my dead parents and sister but also the fallen family members of the other poor souls who lost their loved ones to the careless whims of the upper class.

"Prices will be commensurate with the occasion," I say aloud, not so much for the Fournier ladies' benefit but to remind Madame Violette of the stakes.

This Christmas party will not only make her career, like she's always dreamed, but will also gild her bank account to such a degree that she will never need to work again if she doesn't wish to.

And as for the rest of *these* ladies' carefree lives . . .

The clock is ticking.

CHAPTER 27

The next day, Charlotte fails to show up to work. No one is left but me.

Madame Violette loses her mind.

She's crouched in the middle of the floor in an empty dressing room, with me hovering over her, stroking her shoulder, like a mother hawk attempting to coax her newborn chick to taste a clump of freshly regurgitated worm.

She picked the right protégée. I'll prove it to her.

"It will be fine," I assure my mentor. "You'll see."

"How will anything be fine?" she bursts out, her black eyes round and panicked. "I'm cursed, I tell you. Jacqueline ran away; Béatrice got hurt; Pauline, Henrietta, and Marguerite suffered tragic accidents and died; and Charlotte is too sick to leave her bed. Meanwhile, we have more work to do now than ever before!"

"And more coin to do it with," I remind her. "What we're charging the Fournier ladies alone is more than you'd normally earn in a month. Multiply that by hundreds of guests, all of whom we can charge a premium for rushed delivery, and you have more than enough funds to hire any help we need."

With the added bonus that these new hires will not be eligible to steal my new protégée position.

"If I put up a sign, I'll have a thousand applicants by morning," Madame Violette wails.

"Is that such a bad thing?"

"Of course it is. Too many candidates is as awful as too few. How can I possibly determine which have the skill and speed to produce two hundred unique costumes at the highest level of quality?"

"Madame, I'll help you," I promise. "I'll oversee every one of the applicants myself."

"I can't spare you," she reminds me. "I need you here with the clients, and in the back with the dye, and in the sewing room.... It's impossible! We cannot manage on our own."

"We don't have to. I know someone who has a deft hand with a needle. Do you trust me?"

She nods. "Implicitly."

"May I hire—"

"Anyone half as capable as you are," she says with feeling.

"I can do better than that. Please give me until tomorrow."

While Madame Violette collects herself, I check on the batch of silks in the dye room, then return to the sewing room. As I settle into my station, I select pencil and paper—but not to draft a Now Hiring announcement for the newspaper.

I already know who should fill these seats.

My pencil flies over the sheet of paper as I name my former colleagues' replacements.

Zaidée
Coralie
Séraphine
Mme Aubert
Mme Tremblay

The five women and girls who helped me at Fournier's textile factory when my mother and sister were torn apart before my eyes. I was too panicked and grief-stricken to remember how to breathe, but they summoned the right people and helped me make funeral arrangements.

It gives me no small amount of pleasure to poach Monsieur Fournier's best workers out from under his nose. These ladies' talents are being wasted there, and here they'll be safe, better paid, and respected by Madame Violette.

The only problem is that I've been banned from the factory, and I don't know where they live. It may take some investigation before I manage to contact them all and extend an invitation they won't hesitate to accept.

Next to each name, I jot where I think they might reside and any acquaintances we have in common. I realize with frustration that my data is sparse. It might take several days until I am able to successfully rescue these women as they once rescued me.

. . .

By the time I finally stumble from the dress shop, hands swollen and back aching, night has fallen. Lonely gaslights line the streets, which contain only the occasional pedestrian or carriage.

All the shops have long since closed.

Including Domingo's.

He's waiting for me anyway. Seated on an upside-down wooden crate beneath the Closed, Come Back Tomorrow sign. Lost in a book. I didn't even know he liked to read. I realize how little attention I've been paying him recently, despite how wonderful he's been to Elodie and me.

As soon as I hire new seamstresses, I'll have much more time to—

Oh. No, I won't. Now there's a masquerade to design gowns and costumes for.

But after *that*, I vow silently. New year, new Angélique. After the masquerade, my world will be nothing but Domingo and Elodie, and creating affordable fashions for people like us.

At the sound of my footsteps, Domingo peers up from his book. His entire face lights brighter than a gas lamp at midnight. He marks his spot with a scrap of leather, shoves the book in his pocket, and reaches for my hands.

"I thought you'd never leave work," he says as he dances me in a joyful circle.

I wish I felt like dancing. I'm dead on my feet.

"I have to go straight home," I tell him as he shines my shoes. "Elodie must be worried sick."

As we walk, he chatters animatedly about his successful implementation of my suggestion: A lavish, swirly *D* now decorates the heel of every shoe designed by Domingo.

"They think it stands for *divin*," he confesses.

"You are divine, mi torero," I assure him. "Congratulations!" It's not enough, but it's a start. He deserves so much more.

Domingo wiggles his eyebrows. "Did I earn your undying love?"

Laughing, I push him away. "Try again tomorrow."

For the rest of the journey, his steps are noticeably jauntier than usual.

"Go home," I tell him when we reach my door. "My sister needs me. This is the latest I've ever arrived home. For all I know, she's rocking on the floor in a panic, thinking something happened to me the way it did to our mother and sister."

Domingo's face turns serious, and he gives my hand the briefest of squeezes. "Be kind to her. I'll see you tomorrow."

I take a deep breath and open the door.

Elodie launches herself into my arms as though she's been shot from a cannon.

"Angélique!" she squeals. "I did it! I'm doing it!"

All right, I'll admit it: She doesn't seem particularly anxious about my well-being.

"You did what, exactly?" I say sourly, peeling her from my tired, sweaty flesh.

"I couldn't find an apprentice position, but with the tools Domingo acquired for me, I've learned ever so much. He bought me a dozen roses, like he promised—for you, too, though I don't think you glanced at yours—and I turned all twelve of mine into rose water. I've been selling it by the bottle all day!"

I stare at her. "You . . . what?"

"I'm a street vendor!" She chortles and spins a pirouette. "The bottles are small, and the buyers are wary, so my income thus far won't cover much more than a bit of cheese to go with our crusts of bread for breakfast. But it's a start! My career has begun! I'm finally on my way!"

My heart clenches. She is not going to like what I have to say next.

"Elodie." I reach for her. "Listen to me."

"It's *working*." She shoves her hand into her pocket and pulls out a fistful of dirty sous. "That's real money. By next week, I'll be able to buy *you* a plum at the market."

"Elodie," I say again. "That's wonderful. I'm very proud of you. But you have to put your hobby aside for now."

"It's not a hobby!" She shakes the coins in her hand. "I earned real—"

"I need you at the dress shop. Madame Violette needs you. We've lost our employees and are desperate for someone clever with a needle. That's you, cabbage. With a little practice, you'll be as good as I am."

"No!" She backs up, eyes wild. "It is *not* me." She points at her makeshift laboratory on the dining table, next to what I presume is my vase of twelve wilting roses. "*That* is me. A parfumeur. A real one. I can't stop now, Angélique. Not when I've finally—"

"Cabbage, you have to. I'm not asking. We need you, and you're going to help. It's only until I can hire and train enough seamstresses. You'll earn more your first month there than you would after an entire year of selling rose water."

"A month!" She stares at me as if I've suggested she volunteer to be stretched on the rack, followed by some light drawing and quartering. "You can't be serious, Angélique. Look at the hours you keep! I won't have time to continue learning, much less sell my creations."

"With you there helping, perhaps I won't need to work such long hours," I tell her.

A lie. If anything, I'll get less sleep than ever trying to keep everything on track for what will be an infamously unforgettable masquerade.

"I won't do it," Elodie says stubbornly.

"You have to," I snap. "You have no choice and must do as I say. I'm doing this for you, cabbage. For us. And it's not every moment of your time. Don't forget, a year and a half ago, the government ruled to reduce working shifts from eleven hours a day to ten."

She scoffs. "Monsieur Fournier keeps his factory workers busy for fourteen or fifteen hours at a stretch."

"The worst industrialists ignore the law," I admit. "But not Madame Violette. She's wonderful. She reminds me of Maman. You'll love her. It's nothing like the textile factory. It's comfortable and safe. We'll go in together. Madame Violette will adore you."

"I hate her already," Elodie spits. Tears run down her face. "And I hate you!"

She runs into our bedchamber and slams the door.

I start after her, then change my mind. She'll do as I say, but she needs a chance to cool down. I turn to the table instead. Ninety-five percent of the surface bears beakers and bottles and oils and infusions and a contraption I assume is the famous Faraday burner.

The only other item is the vase.

I stare at it, my chest hollow. How did I miss my own flowers? I guess I haven't been eating breakfast. Or supper. There hasn't been time. Every day, I rush from my bed to work and back without so much as glancing around.

I'm looking now.

This isn't our old, chipped vase. It's a new one. Delicate blown glass, in the pink and gold colors of dawn. Brand-new. Beautiful. Marred only by its collection of wilting roses. They must have been here a week or more. My stomach twists. I didn't even say merci.

When I pick up the vase, most of the limp, wrinkled petals dislodge. The dry red discs sink out of sight into the dirty water, leaving me holding nothing more than a collection of dead stems with sharp thorns.

CHAPTER 28

Elodie is with me as we near La Croix & Sons. We are not enjoying each other's company. My sister hasn't spoken to me since I dragged her to Madame Violette's that first morning at dawn and plopped her down in Henrietta's old chair.

Not that I would have had the time for yet another argument. Between helping attend to clients, teaching Elodie what to do, and managing my own work—which now includes taking over the projects previously belonging to all my other colleagues—I barely have time to breathe, much less to battle.

The new hires have arrived. It took some time, but I tracked down the five women by waking up early to surveil the factory entrance from a safe distance. Then I was able to intercept Zaidée on her way to work, and she gratefully passed the message to the others.

My five allies and I greeted each other today with fierce hugs and watery smiles, tears streaming down our grinning cheeks.

Elodie didn't lift her gaze from her needle, pointedly ignoring us with every fiber of her being, but nothing could dampen my high spirits. Work, however, always beckons, and I was forced to abandon the sewing room often to attend to customers with Madame Violette or toil in the dye room.

Now, as my sister and I reach the front of the shoe shop, Domingo sweeps a courtly bow. "Buenas tardes, señoritas."

Elodie can muster a pretty smile for *him*, I see. She doesn't speak Spanish, but—

"Buenas tardes, señor," she responds, giving a perfect curtsey.

I blink. Apparently, my sister has spent more time with my beau than I realized.

A shiver dances across my skin. Night has fallen, and the temperature borders on frigid. Autumn has descended with a vengeance, and winter will be here soon. As soon as I get a spare moment—and the upcoming increase in salary at month's end—I'll have to reinforce my sister's threadbare winter cloak and procure a warmer pair of gloves for her.

Domingo rushes over, shoe polish in hand. He kneels before me and begins to work his magic on my boots.

I would rather have a foot massage. Or a bowl of hot soup in a comfortable chair before a crackling fire. Although the other workers have shorter shifts, mine was a fourteen-hour day, and I am exhausted. My legs can barely keep me upright, and my stomach is caving in on itself.

"We don't have long to tarry," I interrupt Domingo. "Elodie

is tired and hungry, and it'll still be an hour before I've finished cooking supper."

For the briefest of seconds, the hurt is plain on his face. This is our special ritual. A romantic shared moment he savors every single day. Providing for me, caring for me, being with me. And now I'm telling him to hurry it along. I feel like a monster.

"Forgive me," I blurt out. "I didn't mean—"

"Forget it. I'm almost done." He half-heartedly swipes his brush against the other shoe, then rises to his feet. "Let me put this away, and I'll walk you ladies home."

"I want my boots done, too!" Elodie pleads, lifting her skirts to her ankles.

Of course she does. I should have thought of it myself. My shoes get shined every day, thanks to Domingo, but hers have never been buffed in her life. There are even holes forming at the tips of her big toes because she's worn these old half boots for too long and her feet are still growing.

Domingo kneels before her as though she is a princess. He carefully shines the worn leather as if these boots were the most precious thing in all the kingdom.

Elodie beams with pleasure. She's so radiantly happy with the novel experience of being pampered that she even accidentally smiles at *me*.

I feel worse than ever. I'll tell her I'm not hungry tonight and let her have the entire supper for herself.

This time, when Domingo returns the shoe polish to the store, he needn't hang the I'll Return Soon sign. It's late, and La Croix & Sons is closed. Elodie and I are the ones keeping Domingo from *his* supper.

I wish I could invite him to join us, but then no one's belly would receive enough sustenance to get full.

He offers each of us an elbow, and we set out on our way.

"How was your day?" he asks Elodie.

"Terrible," she replies without hesitation. "My fingers hurt from gripping a sewing needle for hours, and no matter what I do, Angélique yells at me."

I grimace, keeping my face straight ahead so that she doesn't see it.

"I hate sewing," she says emphatically. "I'm a parfumeur. And I'm not going back."

"You *are* going back," I snap, then realize I've done exactly what she accused me of. I gentle my voice. "Cabbage, I expect good work out of you because I know what you're capable of. I know you'd rather be doing literally anything else, and I want you to have the freedom to do so. This post isn't for the rest of your life, I promise. Just until the masquerade."

Domingo's dark eyebrows shoot up with interest. "Masquerade?"

Have I not told him? Good heavens, my mind is foggy. I squeeze his arm a little tighter and give him a small smile.

"Some rich family is hosting a Christmas Eve ball, and we're providing the costumes," I explain.

A little frown mars Domingo's brow. "A rich family? Which one?"

I shake my head as though I cannot quite recall, though of course the name of the evil Fournier family is etched into my soul. Domingo may or may not recognize the cursed name, but my sister does. Elodie wouldn't understand why I'm bending over backward to help our mortal enemies host the most unforgettable party of all the season.

And I can't tell anyone what my real goals are.

"Angélique is designing all the costumes," says Elodie with pride. "Fine ladies line up like dominoes, hoping for her attention."

And they shall fall like dominoes too.

"You should do the same thing," I tell Domingo.

He makes a comical face. "Attract a queue of women by tempting them with my irresistible attentions?"

I elbow him in the ribs. "Become an exclusive provider for the masquerade, of course. A special line of dancing slippers. One style for men and another for women, each bearing the distinctive mark of the best high-fashion shoe designer in Paris."

He seems intrigued. "Do you think it would work?"

"I'll send the customers to you myself," I promise. "They have more money than they know how to spend. I'll tell the ladies that if they and their husbands want to appear remotely presentable at the fête of the season, there can be no substitute for the very best, which is Domingo Salazar of La Croix and Sons."

He grins at me as though I've handed him all the stars in the sky.

"Charge five times the cost of the current highest-priced shoe," I instruct him. "They'll pay it happily. And be sure to point out that swirling *D* of quality so they can lord it over their friends. They think they are divinity, but it is *your* work that is divine. When you open your own shoe shop in le Passage des Panoramas someday soon, they'll recognize your mark and flock to give you their money."

"Eres una diosa," he tells me. "If you can make this happen, I vow to spend the rest of my life spoiling you."

As I smile up at him, the late-November wind rushes between us, blowing my skirts away from him and bathing us with icy air. Gooseflesh ripples over my skin. My tightly coiled entrails let out an audible gurgle of hunger.

At the sound, Domingo trips over a crack in the pavement. He nearly sends all three of us face-first into the street, cracking our skulls open on the unforgiving concrete.

I hope this is not a harbinger of disaster to come.

CHAPTER 29

The next morning, Elodie still will not speak to me any more than she has to, but she trudges mutinously by my side and takes her seat without comment.

As the other women arrive, their eyes light up at the sight of me, and every single one of them bounds over to give me yet another hug for having rescued them from Fournier's textile factory.

"You're friends?" Elodie finally asks, her voice hesitant.

"Friends? We fought side by side." Zaidée lifts her left hand to show that her middle finger is missing up to the first knuckle. The physical scars have healed, but as for the long-term effects of years of living in constant fear that the wrong move could cost a finger, or an arm, or your life . . .

Coralie, Séraphine, Madame Aubert, and Madame Tremblay join in with war stories of their own.

I actually wish they wouldn't—my family and I kept Elodie as sheltered as possible from the horrors of Parisian factories—

but I will not stifle the others' words now that they have the freedom to speak without fearing the loss of their jobs.

Elodie asks why any of us would choose to subject ourselves to such hell on earth and receives a rude awakening.

"Most women don't get to choose anything at all," says Coralie.

"Most people," adds Madame Aubert, likely thinking of her late brother.

"Not in this economy," Séraphine agrees. "We count ourselves lucky to find employment that might not kill us for a few years, when the alternative would see us dead on the streets in a matter of months."

"Your sister is the most amazing woman I know," says Zaidée. "She walked away on her own two feet, not carried out on a makeshift stretcher."

"Though I was almost fired for attending to my dying father," I remind her. "And banned from the property a few months later when my worst nightmare repeated itself."

"You came *here*," Coralie insists, her eyes shining and glossy. "And you brought us here with you. I can never thank you enough."

"Then get to work," I scold her gruffly, half joyful and half embarrassed. "Or else I will say very mean things about your éclairs."

Protests and cackles fill the room as the ladies chatter happily while attending diligently to the soft, safe fabrics on their laps.

Elodie sends me covert glances beneath her eyelashes as

she sews, a begrudging respect in her eyes replacing some of her earlier ire.

I wish I could stay and chat, but I cannot. Every detail of these costumes must be perfect, and I cannot give Elodie or the other seamstresses elements soaked in lethal levels of arsenic. After a quick round of instructions, I must hurry from the room.

Perhaps you'd think now that the sewing room is crowded again, my days might get a little easier. You would be wrong.

I have more responsibilities than ever. Assistant, taskmistress, dye girl, seamstress, customer service, custom design work. Listing all my tasks takes half the day. But this is what I worked so hard for—this is the life of a fashion protégée.

At lunchtime, the new hires smile and put down their tools. Compared to the hell of Monsieur Fournier's factory, Madame Violette's shop is heaven. We can take breaks and eat a full meal without fear. In a flash, the sewing room empties, save for Elodie and me. I offer my sister both halves of the sandwich I brought for us to share.

Elodie pokes at the cold hunk of baguette as if its thin ham and cheese innards have congealed before her eyes.

I don't have time to talk her into consuming sustenance. I want to lay my forehead against the hard, flat wood of my worktable and sleep for the next twenty-nine minutes.

I dare not. If I let myself close my eyes, I may never open them again.

"I hate this," I hear Elodie say.

I clench my teeth. "Just eat it."

"Not the sandwich. Working here. I would rather be—"

"Elodie—"

"I was *happy*," she chokes out wretchedly. "I liked listening to my governess, even though I knew she wasn't really mine. I liked hunting for wildflowers to brighten the darkness of our home. And now that I finally have the equipment to practice making real perfumes, you won't let me—"

"You have all day on Sundays."

"I'll be too tired on Sundays! You don't even sleep. I don't know how you're still awake. Or alive. This isn't good, Angélique. Not for me, and not for you."

"It's temporary," I remind her.

"Is it?" she says scathingly. "That's what you said before. Like when you said I could have a tutor of my own. Or that we would finally take a holiday to the beach and see the ocean. 'Wait until I earn the assistant position, Elodie. Once I become Madame Violette's official protégée, everything will be different.' Well, you're right. It's different, and it's awful. I hate it."

At least this time, she didn't say she hates me, too.

"Please," Elodie begs. "Let me quit. You've got other workers now. You don't need me."

"I do need you," I tell her. "I'll always need you. You're my sister. And you're right, I've been unspeakably busy. This is the only time I get to see you. I promise, cabbage, as soon as the costumes are delivered, you can go back to your perfumes with my blessing."

Elodie lets out a huff and takes a vicious bite of her sandwich, her brown eyes swimming with tears.

"And I'll do even better than that." I scoot my chair closer to hers. "After the masquerade, I'll personally champion your perfumes all over Paris."

She glances up at me over the sandwich, not chewing, desperate to believe this could happen.

"I *promise*," I tell her staunchly. "I'll do everything in my power to ensure that this time next year, you have a laboratory the size of this sewing room, and four annoying assistants of your own eager for you to train them in how to do things your way."

The corner of her mouth curves up, and she swallows her bite. Her big eyes are hopeful again.

"I would like that," she says softly.

"You'll have it, cabbage. You'll have everything you've ever wanted. And then we *will* take that holiday to the sea, like we've always dreamed. Two sisters, with our bare toes in the sand, enjoying the wet kiss of ocean waves on our legs as the sun warms our skin."

Her eyes sparkle. "I want that so much. A true holiday, just me and you. And maybe Domingo. Do you think we—"

"Angélique!" calls Madame Violette. "Come at once!"

Aargh.

"Forgive me, mon petit chou. When Madame needs me, I must attend her call." I reach out to stroke my sister's cheek, but her face is closed off to me already. A waxen mask of rage and hurt and resignation.

I let my hand fall back to my side without making contact.

Out front, Madame Violette is welcoming in a mother and daughter excited to have their first fitting for the upcoming Fournier masquerade ball.

There's no need to launch into the old patter that turned our little snowball into an avalanche. Our reputation has taken on a life of its own. Our new clients would sacrifice their firstborn child on an altar if it moved them a few names higher on the waiting list.

As I measure the women and detail my findings in my notebook, they chatter on about the ball, and the expected music, and the rumored guests.

A spark of an idea occurs to me.

"Might you have your invitation on hand?" I ask, keeping my tone as casual as possible. "Madame Violette and I would be charmed to see it."

I hold my breath with anticipation. I'm a seamstress, not a forger, but if it is at all humanly possible to re-create an existing invitation with my name instead . . .

Both ladies recoil from me as though I farted in their champagne.

"No, we do not," the daughter bites out with a haughty toss of her head. "And no one else will show you theirs, either."

Well then.

I press my lips together and resume taking measurements as though her response doesn't bother me in the least. I keep my head down so as not to make eye contact with our clients *or* Madame Violette—who no doubt knows exactly what I'm thinking.

C'est moi, the most sought-after designer protégée of the moment. Recipient of endless compliments and countless pots of gold for the glamorous contents of my exalted imagination.

And still not good enough to sully their precious invitation by glancing in its direction with my guttersnipe eyes.

"Thank you, Angélique," Madame Violette says gently. "You might want to go and prepare a bit more silk."

I nod and stalk back to the dye room with my head held high. To the devil with those fine ladies! Soon I'm swirling a new batch of expensive silk in my special dye.

The recipe has changed slightly. After settling my old colleague Marguerite for her final nap in that darkened alley, I strolled back to the taxidermist's shop and walked away with both sacks of arsenic hidden beneath my coat. I'm glad I did. I'm going to need them.

CHAPTER 30

The next Sunday is special. Thanks to my protégée wages—and some sacrificed meals—I've finally saved up enough money to afford proper gravestones for my mother and sister.

This won't be one of those giant marble angels almost as tall as la Colonne de Juillet, the monumental column in the center of la Place de la Bastille. Even if I had the funds, my private grief is not for the world to see. It is the weight of infinite emptiness carried forever in my heart.

These headstones are small, flat, simple. Exactly like the one that marks my father's grave. The cheapest stone the mortician could offer was the most my mother could afford. The new plaques will match perfectly.

The cold harsh sun shines over three of the dead—Maman, Papa, and Anne—and three of the living—me, Elodie, and Domingo. Rather than let him slink up behind us as an interloper, this time Elodie and I invited him as part of the family. We may not have much, but we have each other.

Domingo pulls the new gravestones in a wagon. He claimed he could carry them, and possibly he could, but the risk of tripping over the uneven terrain is too high. He would survive, but the stones would not. And my mother and sister have waited long enough to be honored in this way.

The old markers sit crookedly in the chilly breeze. It has only been a couple of months, but already the wood is weather-beaten, the names I painstakingly carved now worn and blurred by the relentless wind.

Overhead, the sun shines with merciless ferocity, but down below, sliding on the muddy earth surrounded by thousands of graves, Elodie and I clutch our threadbare coats to our too-thin frames and shiver against an insidious cold that seeps into our bones.

The lonely stems of what were once bouquets of flowers protrude from the greasy soil next to each grave. A sign that Elodie visits here as often as I do. And that nothing beautiful ever stays that way forever.

I brought a spade, but I do not need it. The wooden markers pop out of the black earth like rotten teeth falling from rancid gums.

Elodie bites her lip. "What do we do with those?"

I don't know. Our empty fireplace is in want of fuel, but I'm not sure I can bear to use my family's grave markers as tinder, even if the wood was only temporary.

"We'll decide later," is all I say now. "Domingo, would you help me—"

"I'll do it. They're heavy." He reaches for the first stone, then pauses and turns around. "Unless you'd rather help?"

Elodie and I exchange searching glances. *Do* we want to be the ones to press permanent slabs of stone atop our mother's and sister's graves?

She takes a small step back, and the question is answered.

"We wouldn't be the ones to carry the stones in a big royal funeral either," I assure her, my voice low. "Carrying our grief is burden enough."

Elodie takes my hand and holds on tight, like she used to do when she was a child.

She is still a child. And an orphan now. I am her mother, her father, her sister. I must keep her safe.

Domingo places the stones where the wood once stood and brushes them free of dirt. Brittle leaves still cling to the trees overhead. Their dust will soon fill the crevices of the names and dates atop these stones.

I will come every Sunday to clean up. To tell my family how much I miss them. To promise on their very souls that their cruel and unnecessary deaths are being avenged.

"Anything you want to say?" Domingo asks.

Nothing I want him or Elodie to hear. I shake my head, then turn to her. "How about you, cabbage?"

She stares for a long moment, then whispers, "They cannot hear anymore."

"Not their bodies," I agree. "But their souls are around us. You're not alone, Elodie."

Her eyes are huge, mournful, and they seem far older than the eyes of any child ought to be. She does not appear to believe me.

I wonder if I should be taking her to church on Sundays. Perhaps then she'd believe in angels.

Or perhaps she's seen too much in twelve short years to have faith in anything anymore.

"Thank you," I murmur to Domingo, then return my gaze to my sister. "Shall we go home?"

She glances over her shoulder. "Is your coworker in this cemetery?"

For a moment, I am too surprised to speak.

Domingo frowns. "Is she attending a funeral today?"

"No," Elodie says. "She's dead."

He turns to me in question.

Merde. I should not have told her. I don't even remember telling her. That is how anxious and exhausted I have been.

"Marguerite," Elodie prompts. Perhaps she heard this name from Madame Violette.

"No." My voice is low. "Her grave lies in Père Lachaise."

"Oh," Elodie says softly.

No further explanation is necessary. The poor are not allowed to bury their dead in the holy ground of Père Lachaise. Even certain rectangles of dirt are only for our betters.

"I hope nothing happens to you," Elodie says in a rush, her eyes shiny.

I grab her hands. "I'm not leaving you, cabbage."

She thinks this over, then adds, "Or Madame Violette. If you were to lose your job..."

"I won't," I promise. "You're safe."

"Is Madame Violette?" Domingo teases, unaware of the

237

lengths I will go to in order to protect my family. "Should she worry about you taking over her dress shop?"

"She has absolutely nothing to fear," I say with feeling. "Operating a storefront is more work than I ever imagined, without any of the fun. I'd happily sign a contract to be the resident designer at someone else's shop, if it meant I wouldn't have to deal with any administration myself."

He clutches his hands to his chest and lifts his face to the sky as though praying to the shoe gods. "Wouldn't that be heaven?"

I loop one arm with his and the other with Elodie's. "Someday our genius will be recognized."

But as I stare at my family's graves, my heart still yearns for one thing:

Revenge.

CHAPTER 31

Late the next week, I try to send Elodie home from the dress shop at a reasonable hour, but she insists on waiting for me.

"If you work, I work," she says with a sigh. "With both of us doing our best, maybe you'll even have supper tonight."

It's been so long since I had time for a decent meal, my stomach doesn't even bother to growl its discontent anymore. Nonetheless, I make certain we leave Madame Violette's with enough time for Elodie to eat and get a good night's rest.

As we near La Croix & Sons, she skips ahead of me to where Domingo awaits us. I expect her to shove her foot atop his for a shining, but instead she retrieves a small bottle from her pocket and presses it into his large palm.

"What's this?" he asks with interest.

"A masterpiece," she replies grandly, then mumbles beneath her breath, "I hope."

He unstoppers the little vial and gives a tentative sniff. His eyes widen and a smile curves his lips. "A new cologne? This is the best one yet! May I try it on?"

Elodie squeals and jumps up and down, clapping her hands. "Oui, s'il te plaît!"

He places a drop on his wrist, then thrusts his arm out to me for final approval. "What do you think, Angélique?"

"You smell delicious no matter what you do," I tell him.

Elodie's lip wobbles, and I wish I hadn't spoken. This is her moment.

"I'm sure it's wonderful. Here I go. Watch me." I dutifully raise Domingo's muscular arm to my waiting face and lower my nose to the pulse point at his wrist.

As I inhale, I breathe in his scent as well as an entire other universe. Musk and sandalwood and bergamot. He smells like a strapping man, and deep forest, and expensive spices shared by candlelight in the turrets of tall castles.

"Good God, Elodie." I turn to my baby sister in awe. "*You* made this?"

She bursts out crying.

"Cabbage, what is it?" I drop Domingo's wrist in alarm and rush to pull my disconsolate sister into my arms. "Is everything all right? What happened?"

"I didn't think you'd like it," she sobs into my woolen cloak. "I thought you'd say it was a nice effort . . . for a child. If you had time to smell my perfume at all."

"Oh, Elodie." I squeeze her tight, like I used to do when she was a plump-cheeked baby. "It's more than a good effort. It's bloody phenomenal. World-famous parfumeur Pierre-

François-Pascal Guerlain *wishes* he could make a cologne like this one. He should be an apprentice to *you*."

"She peels her face from my bodice and peers up at me with wide, red-rimmed eyes. "Really?"

"Really. This isn't some merely 'acceptable' perfume, cabbage. You perfectly captured Domingo's essence in a tiny little bottle."

A smile blooms across her face. "You really like it?"

"I love it."

"So do I," adds Domingo.

"I knew *you* would," Elodie says dismissively.

Domingo and I burst out laughing.

"Am I so predictable?" he asks.

She shakes her head. "Not in the least. I've been making this cologne for you for weeks."

His lips part. "So . . . every time I said 'a little too sharp' or 'not so cloying' . . . "

She nods with pride. "I was determining your tastes and calibrating the ingredients accordingly."

Calibrating extract balances! My baby sister!

I stare at her in wonder. She *is* almost thirteen. Not a child, but almost a young woman. And she's always been a genius. If I can custom-design clothing, why shouldn't Elodie be able to handcraft proprietary perfume blends, unique to each client's body chemistry and taste preferences?

"How about your shoes?" asks Elodie. "Did any of the people Angélique sent over buy a pair of dancing slippers?"

"Did any of those deep pockets dance off with my creations?

We don't have a single pair left in stock, thanks to your sister. We're so far away from keeping up with demand that we've had to raise prices three times in a week." He shoots me a disbelieving look. "As you predicted, the inherent difficulty in obtaining my footwear has made it more popular than ever."

"And they all carry your mark?" I prompt him. "This is your future we're shaping."

"Nothing to worry about there," Domingo replies, a roguish glint in his eyes. "Old man La Croix accidentally let slip that I am the one who designed the most popular items, and I've become something of a celebrity right here in the store. I'm not even allowed to sell anymore, much less dirty my knees by fitting shoes on feet. We've hired two young lads to handle menial labor. *French* garçons. Taking orders from *me!*"

"Domingo, that's marvelous!" I wrap my arms around his neck and kiss his cheek.

He shakes his head as though he can't quite grasp his change in fortune. "People who previously looked down their noses at me, as though I belonged on the bottom of their shoe, now gaze upon me with respect. I don't know what to do with myself. And I owe it all to you, Angélique."

"No, you don't," I tell him sternly. "You owe it to your own talent and your skill, like Mademoiselle Elodie. You two were always going to be extraordinary, with or without me. I'm simply pleased to have been able to play my small part."

He holds out his elbows. "Come on, then, fellow prodigies. Allow me to walk you brilliant ladies home."

We're halfway there before I realize he didn't shine my shoes today . . . or even offer.

Was it because yesterday and the day before, I was so dead-on-my-feet exhausted that I couldn't keep my attention on his earnest ministrations and accidentally started walking off before he was even done?

Or is it because Domingo is becoming so successful, he no longer has time for *me*?

Acid burbles in my belly at the unwelcome suspicion that we've crossed an important line. Something precious has irrevocably changed between us. Gone for good.

I hope I do not lose him altogether.

CHAPTER 32

In the rear pantry of the dress shop, I shove a sweaty hunk of lank black curls out of my face and give my wooden oar another spirited swirl through the dye vat. My muscles no longer ache at night after I do this. My body is once again used to hard labor. As well as long hours spent hunched over a sewing needle.

It will be worth it. Christmas is coming soon.

I dump in another healthy bowlful of arsenic and mix the powder into the vat of brilliant green soup. Never could I have imagined a better way to avenge the working-class citizens en masse.

Every last one of the very worst people will be wearing my creations: entitled aristocrats, exploitative capitalists, misogynistic bankers, unscrupulous moneylenders, colonizers, factory owners who treat their workers like the cheap handkerchiefs they produce.

The entire evil Fournier family and all their guests.

Our oppressors will wear their deadly new finery for the

first time on Christmas Eve, which means I am free to load up the poisonous jade dye with as much arsenic as I please.

No one will have any reason to suspect anything is amiss. Their symptoms will be gradual, like Charlotte's. The delay will make it impossible to draw a direct line between cause and effect. Especially for those who also purchased everyday items like stockings and nightwear. They'll never cease suffering and won't know why.

But I'll know. Our "betters" will reap what they've sown.

And after the success of the ball, Madame Violette will see the wisdom of turning our efforts to clothing the masses. People of working class may not have tall piles of gold like nobles do, but we far outnumber the aristocrats and bourgeoisie. Selling elegant couture at reasonable prices to a vast new audience hungry to be catered to will enrich everyone's lives, designers and customers alike.

It will be my honor to usher in the new wave of beautiful, accessible fashion soon to take over Paris and beyond.

"What are you doing?"

I glance up. It's Elodie. I motion for her to stay out of the pantry. "I'm dyeing the fabric we need for the costumes. It's smelly and sticky and dangerous. Stay in the corridor. You shouldn't come in here."

She shifts her weight. "When you left the factory, you said you would never be a dye girl again."

"This is different." I give the oar another push through the vat.

Elodie doesn't appear convinced. "Different how?"

I'm not bowing and scraping in service to my betters. I'm

making them suffer, the way they've made so many others suffer. It's not just revenge. It's justice.

"I have a plan, cabbage. You'll have to trust me."

Elodie wrinkles her nose. "Will the costumes stink this bad?"

"No," I say quickly, though I suppose that's only partially true.

Nothing smells as bad as this vat does right now, but even after the silks have been hung up to dry, a malodorous residue clings to each fold as the gloved seamstresses cut and sew. Even the small square of cloth we use as a sample contains a lingering touch of the decrepit.

"I could scent it for you," Elodie offers. "Something light, to counteract the stench."

"That's not a bad idea," I admit. "That crowd would kill for a brilliant new color *and* a matching bespoke perfume to complement it."

Elodie smiles and leans against the doorjamb. "I'll see what I can whip up."

"Do you even have time for whipping things?" I ask her. "I thought you said I was overworking you, like the wicked fairytale villain I am."

"Only Monday through Saturday," she assures me. "I still have Sundays to work on my own projects, remember? In between naps."

I pause in my stirring. "I am sorry, cabbage. As soon as the masquerade ball—"

"I understand," she interrupts, with a maturity beyond her years. "And it's not all hideous. I hate the sewing, of course, but

I love spending time with you, even if this is the only way I can do it. And I already know how I'm going to spend every franc of my first month's wages."

"Food and warm winter garments," I tell her firmly.

She grins. "More essential oils and new bottles for my creations. Fancier ones. The sort that make people think whatever's in them is worth any price I set."

I raise an eyebrow. "Does a junior seamstress's salary cover fancy bottles like that?"

"It will cover exactly one," she says, her eyes gleaming as though she's calculated the purchase to the precise sou. "With luck, that's all I need. I can show the prototype around as proof of quality and claim my product is delayed due to too much demand. Then I can place interested names on the waiting list for a fifty percent deposit."

"You scheming little wench," I breathe with respect. "I've taught you well."

Her face flushes with pride. "If you should have any other words of wisdom to impart, my ears are open."

I smile at her. "I'll see what I can whip up."

She hurries back to her station. It doesn't take me long to come up with the next obvious step. Because all the dresses we create are custom sewn, there are no shelves to display premade goods here. Domingo's shoe shop, on the other hand . . .

What goes better with a debutante's new dancing slippers than a seductive scent to reel in a dashing catch?

CHAPTER 33

Within a week, an early winter comes to snatch the last hours of autumn away from us. As Elodie, Domingo, and I walk our well-worn path home, we huddle close together to leech each other's warmth, rather than as a gesture of affection or chivalry.

Only a few rotten brown leaves remain on the ground, by now so dried out that each gust of icy wind is enough to shatter the brittle foliage into decaying confetti. We trample the rest beneath our feet. The wind kicks the resultant dust up into the mouths and eyes of the pedestrians behind us.

We keep our faces down to avoid the same fate, the low brims of our hats and bonnets flapping like the tails of dying fish forced from the safety of the water.

"Pot-au-feu?" asks Elodie, teeth chattering.

"Of course," I reply.

What was once a Sunday ritual is now a daily one. We'll hunch over steaming bowls of stew every night until spring. The better off can afford to add meat to theirs. My sister and

I now number among them, thanks to my new salary. Growing up, she used to hate the weekly cauldron of watery carrot broth. Now she can't wait for supper.

They are small changes, but tangible ones. We are moving in the right direction. Next year will be even better, I can feel it.

"I have good news, Mademoiselle Elodie," says Domingo.

She rubs her hands to warm them. "Better than hot pot-au-feu?"

"Much better. You, mi querida, sold your first high-class perfume today."

Elodie screams and spins around in wild circles, flinging her arms out wide.

Domingo and I are forced to jump back to avoid a beheading. We laugh and cheer her success.

"Half in advance?" she asks when she catches her breath.

Domingo places a pile of coins in her palm.

The screaming and twirling commence anew. At last, she collapses into me and gives a dramatic kiss to her closed fist. "This is enough to purchase an ornate bottle *and* the best ingredients. Which means the money I'll receive on delivery is all for *me*!"

I kiss the top of her head. The practical side of me is thinking it would be wiser to spend profits on coal for our fireplace or provisions for our larder, but the sisterly side of me wants her to treat herself to whatever she wants. Spend it all on chemistry beakers and pots of ice cream if she wishes.

"How much do we owe you?" I ask Domingo.

He tilts his head in confusion. "Me?"

"Isn't that how it usually works when one sells something on consignment? A percentage goes to the store that provides the display space."

"Bah." He waves his hand. "Elodie's arrangement is with me, not the store. And I say the money's hers."

"Monsieur La Croix won't complain about giving up precious shelf space?"

"Not if he wants me to keep working for him. No fewer than *two* shoe shops have tried to poach me from his store, right in front of him. Monsieur La Croix raised my salary on the spot to keep me from considering their offers."

I clap my hands and let out a little squeal of excitement. "But, mon cœur, that's marvelous! Why aren't you spinning around and screaming like Elodie? This is cause for celebration!"

He gives me a crooked grin. "I was hoping you'd say that. I'd like to celebrate by spending a day with my best girl. Tomorrow is Sunday. I thought you and I could take the train to Versailles, have lunch in the little café overlooking the gardens, then take a tour of the—"

"Domingo, you know I can't," I say gently. "I barely get a few hours of sleep as it is, and I haven't truly taken a Sunday off in weeks in order to work on the masquerade costumes. After the party—"

His jaw hardens and the sparkle disappears from his eyes. "Sí, sí. After the party."

Elodie glares at me accusingly. "Two *weeks* from now."

"See?" I tell them both. "It'll be here and gone before you know it. After the masquerade, I'll have Sundays free again, and shorter hours. By then the new seamstresses won't need me hovering over them. Plus, come spring, Madame Violette wants to find a bigger shop to rent. We'll be able to hire twice as many workers. I'll have so much free time, you'll be sick of seeing me everywhere you turn."

"I doubt that would happen," he says without meeting my eye.

I'm not certain if he means he'll never be sick of my presence . . . or if he doubts that any of my promises will actually come to pass. My stomach clenches at his obvious disappointment. The last thing I want is for him to feel unimportant or unwanted.

"I know I'm not spending as much time with you as you deserve," I admit. "I haven't enjoyed being this busy for so many months either. But it's for a good cause. Do you know how long my parents worked to make half the money I do now? This stress is almost behind us now. The worst is already over."

We walk in silence for several long moments.

"*I'll* go to Versailles with you," Elodie chirps at last. "I've always wanted to see the royal gardens. Even if this late in the year all the flowers are dead and the fountains are empty. I can imagine what it would be like in spring. And I've never been on a train."

"Then it's a deal," Domingo says. "Eight o'clock?"

She grins up at him. "Eight o'clock."

I grind my teeth and try not to be jealous. All this sacrifice is going to be worth it.

They'll see.

CHAPTER 34

A week has passed, and Elodie will not shut up about her visit to Versailles with Domingo.

"And there's an orangery south of the château," she bubbles to the other seamstresses, "where trees can stay warm even in the winter—"

I don't have to turn off my ears. I'm only in the sewing room for brief moments at a time. Long enough to hand off the latest pieces I've cut and instruct the others on how to piece my designs together.

If the women have more questions of late, it is because I am doing an increasingly worse job of explaining my vision. How can I explain, when I am so fatigued I can barely see straight? Lack of sleep—lack of everything—makes me impatient and irritable. When I *am* around, I am poor company for everyone.

Not that I'm ever anywhere for long. I must perform four different posts, all at the same time. Dye girl, personal assistant, designer, manager of the new hires. Not so new anymore,

Dieu merci. I don't have time to correct their mistakes, so their growing self-reliance is a welcome relief. I'm working longer hours than I ever did at the factory.

"Angélique!" Madame Violette calls.

I hurry to the front of the dress shop.

These days, the reception area stays as crowded as a fish market. The air is equally ripe, with so many bodies clustered close together. I hand out three-centimeter-square scraps of cloth with a drop of Elodie's perfume on each one and recommend the ladies stop by La Croix when they finish here to buy their own if they'd like to smell at all tolerable.

They're used to my brusque manner and have utter and complete faith in my fashion sensibilities. In half an hour, they'll descend upon Domingo like a flock of crows and swoop away with every bottle on the shelves.

Elodie will be happy. She works here half days now, in order to handle perfume requests. I miss her when she's gone. Not only because she's my sister but because I trust her to keep watch on the other seamstresses. She's my eyes and my voice while I'm in the fitting area or swirling liquid in the dye pantry.

"How exclusive are you?" a woman I've never seen before asks Madame Violette. "Do you only take a certain number of appointments per year?"

The bejeweled stranger is as gaudy as a chandelier. Which can only mean she isn't nobility, but wishes she were. A rich industrialist's wife, like Madame Fournier. A socially ambitious spendthrift with more money than heart. The perfect client.

"Oh, chérie," says Madame Violette with a chuckle. "My

girls and I could take on every fine lady in Europe if we wished. But given the price of true luxury, very few souls can afford *us.* Most inquiries aren't worthy of my time. You, my dear . . ."

The client positively glows at the implication that *she* is the exception.

My mentor and I lock gazes, smiling with our eyes instead of our mouths. Madame Violette doesn't need me anymore, not for these fishing expeditions. She can hook the upper class's painted lips and reel in their flapping bodies on her own.

CHAPTER 35

Between Elodie's half days in her kitchen laboratory and me staying at the dress shop past midnight to work on costumes or to dye yet another batch of silk, morning has broken by the time I see my sister again.

She skips up to me with unusually good cheer and throws her arms around my neck. "Today is the day—"

"No time. Let's go." I grab my cloak and toss Elodie hers. "We're late for work."

Her smile disappears, and then she gives me the silent treatment the entire way there. The next time she speaks is when we pass La Croix & Sons.

It's not quite dawn, so the shoe store won't open for another few hours. Domingo isn't here yet. We can see the shelf of perfumes through the front display window. Two more orders are hanging there.

Elodie gasps and points. "Do you see that? I took your advice and doubled the price, and they're *still* buying them up.

I can't believe it. We should ask Madame Violette to put up a shelf in the reception area so that we can sell perfumes with the dresses."

Oh, God. One more thing I'd have to deal with. I cannot handle anything else right now.

Nonetheless, I make a mental note to bring this option up with Madame Violette after the masquerade, once we've begun the search for a bigger dress shop. There Elodie can have an entire dedicated glass case. But I don't want to promise anything until I've spoken with Madame Violette.

"This is good enough for now," I tell Elodie.

She stares at me in disbelief. "But the women who shop at your modiste—"

"I said *no*. Madame Violette's customers are there to buy costumes, not cologne. Focus on the goal."

Her brown eyes well with hurt.

"The only important goals are *yours*," she mutters. "And never anyone else's."

"That's not true," I protest. "You're too young to understand. Maybe once you're a teenager—"

She sends me a look filled with such venom, it's a wonder I don't curdle on the spot.

I ignore her childish mood swings and keep walking.

When we get to the sewing room, Elodie heads straight to her seat and starts in on her work without sparing me another glance. The women file in soon after.

I open my mouth to give them their instructions for the day, but Elodie beats me to it.

She's probably trying to vex me by speaking pleasantly to our coworkers and not to me, but it's honestly a weight off my shoulders to know she can handle herself as well as the other seamstresses.

Without excusing myself, I duck away to start a new round in the dye pantry before heading up front to assist Madame Violette.

The reception area is swamped already, and an hour flies by before I have a spare moment to check on Elodie and the others back in the sewing room.

As I walk in the door, she glances up at me with an eager, expectant expression. Exasperation flares along my veins. What does she want, a medal for doing her literal job? It's not even a full one. She works half days. Where's *my* recognition for being four people at once while at work, then acting as both sister and parent while at home? For bringing attention to Madame Violette's, Domingo's, and Elodie's work while putting more coins in their pockets? For seeking retribution for the deaths and suffering of the lower classes?

I shoot her an irritated look—if she's trying to be annoying, she's succeeding—and her face falls. She jerks her gaze back to the work in her hands and barks orders to the other women.

Some of the seamstresses turn to me. I'm not certain how to read what I find in their expressions. A few appear angry or offended. Perhaps it stings to take orders from a twelve-year-old child.

If Elodie were wrong, I would have corrected her, but she knows what she's talking about. So I simply give the others a "Well? You heard your instructions!" and stride out of the room to take care of my other duties.

It happens three more times. A bizarrely hopeful expression from Elodie, followed by a mulish pout. I cannot handle her mood swings right now. I'm barely hanging on to my own rope.

"Stop making that face!" I finally burst out in frustration. "Don't worry about me. Pay attention to what you're supposed to be doing."

She looks like she's going to cry. I don't have time for this.

I stalk off to the dye pantry and don my protective layers. I've barely started to work there when I hear Madame Violette calling me from the other side of the dress shop. I stop stirring and hurry toward the reception area, glancing through the open door of the sewing room as I pass.

Elodie isn't in her chair.

I stop walking and poke my head into the room. Elodie isn't in it at all.

"Where is my sister?" I demand.

The women stare at me blankly.

"For God's sake, it hasn't even been five minutes!" I explode. "Where did she go?"

My supposed friends glance at each other, then return their eyes to their tasks, except the eldest, Madame Tremblay.

"Perhaps you should not have yelled at her, my dear."

I groan in frustration and hurry off to help Madame Violette. Elodie's probably sulking over a chamber pot in the water closet. I'll check there as soon as I finish whatever the modiste needs me to do.

But Elodie isn't in the water closet. Or anywhere in the dress shop, for that matter.

I peer into the sewing room every twenty minutes, every ten, every five. Wherever she went, Elodie isn't coming back. She's gone.

"Angélique!" Madame Violette shouts. "Come quick, I need you."

"I can't. You'll have to take care of it," I call back. "Something's wrong. I need to find my sister."

I run all the way home, narrowly dodging pedestrians and bits of rubbish. By the time I burst through our front door, my lungs are on fire.

"Elodie?" I croak, panting. "What's gotten into you?"

She's not here. The house is empty.

Where has she gone?

It's not noon yet, but perhaps she cut her half day short to go work on her perfumes. I race all the way back to Rue de la Paix, heart pounding, lungs screaming for air.

When I reach La Croix & Sons, the two new perfume orders are still dangling from the shelf, waiting for Elodie.

My sister hasn't been here, either.

Did she run away? Lord, help me. As I catch my breath, I berate myself for not checking her room for missing clothing. Now I'll have to run back to where I just came from. Again.

"Can you get Domingo for me, please?" I ask the young salesman Monsieur La Croix hired to help with customers.

He shakes his head, too busy attending to clients to pay me much attention. "Sorry, miss. Domingo isn't here today. He's home sick."

Well, merde. That means Domingo won't have the least idea what happened to my sister.

"Thanks anyway," I mutter, and set out once again for home.

"Elodie?" I call hopefully as I unlock the door.

Nothing. The house is silent as a tomb, and every bit as dark and foreboding.

My legs are jelly after having sprinted across Paris three times. Or maybe my limbs are unsteady because of a terrifying suspicion that I might never see my sister alive again.

I limp into our bedchamber and throw open the crooked door to our little wardrobe.

The canvas traveling bag is gone, as are Elodie's nightgown and her prettiest dress. I gasp and crumple to my knees.

She really has run away. My baby sister *left* me.

And there's no way she can survive on the streets alone.

I begin to hyperventilate and grab the closest thing I can find to cover my face. It's an old pinafore of hers. It still smells like my sister. And proves how very young and inexperienced she is.

Running away from home is dreadful enough, but to leave half of her clothing behind, right when winter is worsening? Elodie is brilliant with perfumes but doesn't have the head for strategy. She has a long, bright future as a parfumeur ahead of her. Safe work. Happy life. Nothing like the wretched short lives of the girls on the streets, who succumb far too young to disease or tragedy.

I can't permit that. I will walk every boulevard and back alley in Paris until my feet bleed through the holes in my shoes if I must. I will *not* let anything happen to Elodie.

My heart flutters like a wounded hummingbird. I'm dizzy with fear and leaking a steady stream of hot tears as I stumble through the streets. I won't be able to survive the loss of my remaining sister. Especially knowing that I'm the one who drove her away.

I have to find her, before it's too late.

CHAPTER 36

By nightfall, I still haven't found Elodie. My blood pulses in my veins, and my chest constricts. I've visited every café and ice cream parlor in the city and knocked on every boardinghouse door. I've peeked under every broken wooden crate in every rancid alley and visited every park and private garden, in case she's curled up in a barren flower bed or huddled beneath the empty branches of a leafless tree.

I'm nowhere near giving up, but I *am* desperate for reinforcements. The shoe salesman said that Domingo is sick, but maybe he's healthy enough to help me search for my sister.

Or at least to give me a hug and assure me everything will definitely turn out all right.

I haven't paused to eat, and I'm growing woozy from lack of food. I long for one of the many street vendors' hot, fresh crêpes filled with sweet fruit, but I duck into a boulangerie instead for a day-old croissant. It's cheaper and will be easier to shove into my mouth as I walk.

As I approach Domingo's apartment, I see a candle burning at his window. This is excellent news. Not only is he at home, but he might also be feeling well enough to help me.

Or possibly he fell asleep at his dining table and forgot about the candle in the window.

I approach with caution, deciding to peek inside before knocking on the front door. If he's asleep, I don't want to wake him. He can panic with me tomorrow if I still haven't found Elodie.

But before I'm halfway across what's left of the brittle brown grass, I can hear voices through the thin glass of his window.

It's Elodie. She's alive. *Safe.*

Relief washes over me with such force, I nearly throw up. I was so scared. So certain something horrible had happened to her, and that being a bad sister had driven her to it. When all along, she was . . . All along . . .

Frowning, I take a step toward the window. What the devil is she doing here with Domingo? Bringing him soup? How did she even know he was sick?

As I draw closer to the brick wall, the voices become clearer. They're not talking about Domingo's unexpected illness. They're talking about how lovely it's been to eat cake for lunch and play lively hands of mouche all day.

Cake. And not any boring cake. A tall, fresh gâteau d'anniversaire au chocolat.

Now I really *will* throw up. Have I spent the whole day worried I was a horrible sister? I've never been more right in my life.

Today is Elodie's thirteenth birthday . . .

And I forgot.

"Another round?" her sunny voice sings from the other side of the wall.

"So you can beat me again?" comes Domingo's amused reply. "Why don't we play piquet?"

"Because you're too good at piquet, and it's my birthday," Elodie answers with a laugh. "We can play piquet all day on January first, when it's *your* birthday."

"All right, then," he says. "Go ahead and deal."

As I listen to the teasing banter, I lean on the dirty brick wall and slide down until my derrière lands on the frozen soil beneath the window.

This must be how Elodie felt when she eavesdropped on children lucky enough to have a governess.

It is a special torture to listen to a happy family on the other side of the glass. To wish with all your heart that you were one of them, and to know that proof of your presence would only ruin their good time.

At least when you watch a play, you have the satisfaction of knowing it's not real. But crouching outside someone else's window very much puts you in your place.

"More cake?" asks Domingo.

Elodie groans. "I don't know if I can."

"You said you could eat the whole thing by yourself," he teases her. "And I've helped you with a quarter of it."

"Well, I *could've* eaten the whole thing by myself, if we hadn't stopped for ice cream on the way to the bakery. You should've stopped me after the second scoop."

Domingo gasps in mock horror. "Come between a girl and her ice cream on her thirteenth birthday? Never!"

I flash back to the morning's arguments with Elodie. How she'd started to say today was the day . . . only for me to tell her she was still a child. That when she was a teenager, maybe things would be different.

No wonder she doesn't believe a word I say.

"Ha! I win again!" she chortles, her words oddly garbled. "Your turn to deal."

She's probably talking with her mouth full. If I were in there, I would probably reflexively scold her for her poor manners and ruin the moment. Instead, she's enjoying cake and ice cream while spending the day with someone who cares about her. Someone who's taken her in as a little sister, not to impress me but because he's a good man.

"Unless . . ." Elodie's voice turns wheedling. "Are you ready to play? Please?"

I frown. Aren't they already playing cards? What does this mean?

It's Domingo's turn to groan. "Play? I'd honestly hoped you'd forgotten."

"Not a chance, señor. I ate the most ice cream, so I won the bet fair and square. I'm ready when you are."

A chair scrapes across a wooden floor. And then . . . the sound of a musician tuning his strings?

Elodie claps. "Do it, do it!"

"Don't rush me," Domingo grumbles. "I'm still learning this."

But then violin music fills the air, and it is glorious.

I recognize the tune at once: "Au Clair de la Lune," a classic French folk song. What I didn't know was that Domingo is learning to play the violin.

How long has this been going on? Is it new, and I haven't been around lately for him to tell me? Or did he start before we even met, and I've simply never shown enough interest in his personal life and hobbies to learn about this side of him?

When the song ends, Elodie shouts for another.

He plays "Frère Jacques," then "Sur le Pont d'Avignon," then "Vive la Rose" before setting down his violin. I'm not sure if the last is in honor of my sister's love of roses . . . or as a nod to me, since the lyrics are about a boy who gets tired of his girlfriend and dumps her for another.

I wouldn't blame him if he thinks I'm more trouble than I'm worth. I've 100 percent meant every promise about starting over after the Christmas Eve masquerade, but I'm not certain he'll stick around that long.

Not when even my baby sister has apparently moved on.

"That was incredible," she says now. "You could perform for money."

He laughs. "You're only saying that to be kind."

"Can we play écarté next?" Elodie asks. A yawn interrupts her words, and "écarté" sounds like she's blowing bubbles underwater.

"You look tired."

"I *am* tired. I want to play cards until I fall asleep. I'll go home in the morning when your neighbors leave."

"Are you *sure* your sister doesn't mind you spending the night?"

My eyes fly open. Is that why Elodie packed a bag with a single change of clothes? She wanted to spend her birthday with someone who cared enough to give her a little bit of attention and doesn't want to spoil the good feelings by going home?

"Angélique doesn't mind," Elodie says with confidence. "She won't even miss me."

"She's working until late again?" Domingo asks with sympathy.

"After midnight every night, then she's off again before dawn. I never see her unless I go to the dress shop, and even then, she only glances in the door as she's dashing from one side of the store to the other. I'm not sure she notices me."

"Do you want me to talk to her for you?"

"No," Elodie answers in the softest, smallest voice I've ever heard in my life. "It wouldn't help. Angélique is very busy. She has more important things to worry about than me."

My throat tightens, and I press the back of my head into the rough brick of the wall.

"You know what else is important?" Domingo says with false cheer. "Birthday gifts!"

Elodie gasps. "I thought the cake and the ice cream *were* my gifts!"

Liar. My sweet Elodie probably thought a human person voluntarily giving up a few hours of his time in order to spend the day with her *was* the gift. All the ice cream and chocolate cake in Paris cannot compare to Domingo leaving work to take her under his wing.

Whereas I couldn't even manage to say *happy birthday*

this morning, when my baby sister threw her arms around my neck and gave me every clue in the world.

"Here," Domingo says. "Open it."

A long moment of silence. And then . . . wild squealing.

"These are the prettiest perfume bottles I've ever seen in my life! I love them! You are the very best! I can't wait to use them!"

"Oof" is all Domingo manages, which means Elodie has tackled him in one of her infamous hugs.

The sort I used to get, back when I still deserved them.

I notice neither one of them has said *I wish Angélique were here with us.* Why would they? I make myself even smaller, huddling against the brick with my arms wrapped tightly around my bent knees. I wish I could shut off my ears, but instead I torture myself by straining to hear every last sound.

"Thank you so much for everything," Elodie tells Domingo fervently. "You're like the elder brother I never had. Until now, I never understood what I was missing."

"The pleasure is mine, little sister."

"I miss having a real family. Why don't you marry Angélique so you can be my real brother?"

Domingo sighs. "If only it were that easy. Angélique won't let me truly court her. Sometimes I'm not sure she remembers I'm still here."

Another knife to my chest. I grimace in self-loathing. In placing all my focus on revenge and protection, I'm belatedly realizing how dreadful I've been to both of them. Domingo and Elodie are the two people I love most, and they're better to each other than I've been to either one of them.

As I listen to their happy chatter, my heart breaks tenfold. My sister didn't run away to punish me.

She didn't even think I'd realize she was gone.

CHAPTER 37

After another spirited game, Domingo's neighbors stop by. They turn out to be a teenage girl maybe a year or two younger than me, and her little sister. As thrilled as I am for Elodie to make a friend her own age, I am less delighted that, while those two play, Domingo and his pretty neighbor have nothing to do but pass the evening together.

At least, I'm assuming she's pretty. I can't see through the walls, but why wouldn't she be gorgeous? Nothing else has gone my way today. And tonight won't be any better. Not with Beautiful Neighbor spending hours with my beau.

I don't have the right to be angry, though logic doesn't stop me. It's nobody's fault but mine that I forgot my sister's birthday. Domingo inviting his neighbors over was a stroke of genius. A way to kill three birds with one stone. A party atmosphere, built-in chaperones, and a new companion for Elodie.

That doesn't mean I have to like it. I can sit here on my numb derrière, my back against the scratchy brick, hating all the ways I failed my sister in my attempt to do the opposite. I drove her away. I hope I haven't done the same to Domingo.

I hold my position beneath the window until my legs are as frozen as my toes. My teeth chatter. Although the conversation on the other side of the wall never turns flirtatious—if anything, Domingo mentions my name far more often than I would have guessed—I viscerally wish I were burrowed up next to him.

I try my best to hate the nameless, faceless Neighbor Girl on the other side of the wall, but Elodie is having the time of her life. And the truth is, under any other circumstances, I too would be eager to have fun.

When my sister grows drowsy enough, Domingo insists she and the other girls take the bed, and he'll sleep on the sofa. I cannot imagine his long, lanky form fitting on the two-seat sofa, but I am not surprised that he'd prioritize others' comfort.

One of us ought to.

If I'm going to interrupt their peaceful evening, this is the moment. Yet I cannot bring myself to do so. My presence is neither missed nor welcome, and I cannot blame them.

"Hé! Vous là!" A passing woman jabs the point of her umbrella in my direction. No, not a passerby—she's heading up the walk as though she lives in this building. "What are you doing lurking over there?"

I scramble up from the frozen soil in the most awkward way possible—hunching my spine so I am well out of view from the open window, lest Elodie and Domingo catch sight of me peeping in like a beggar.

"Sorry," I murmur to the woman as I scurry past, keeping my head down and my voice low. "I was just leaving."

Removing myself is the right choice anyway, rather than ruin Elodie's birthday by saying or doing the wrong thing—or making her think for even a second that I've arrived to do just that. Shoulders heavy, I trudge back in the direction I came from.

It's late. I should go straight home.

I head to the dress shop instead.

Work is all I know. The only thing I'm good at. I've helped grow Madame Violette's career, Domingo's, Elodie's. Not to mention my own. My designs are deadly but breathtakingly beautiful. Each delighted client tosses out words like *astonishing* and *exquisite*.

"Angélique, *there* you are!"

I glance up from my leaden feet. I've arrived at the dress shop. Madame Violette is locking up.

"I didn't mean to be gone for so long," I say. "Something important came up with my family, and I—"

"Here, take this." She presses a cold brass key into my hand. "I had one made for you. There are several more orders for the debutante dress you designed, so be sure to dye another batch of silk, and two of satin before you leave tonight."

"I had actually hoped—"

"Oh, and I left the measurements for a group of bankers' wives at your workstation. Christmas is coming, and they'd like to surprise their husbands with lacy lingerie. I know that doesn't give much time to design and sew the pieces, but they paid a premium. Plus you work so quickly."

"There's already an entire stack of—"

"I'd love to chat, chérie, but I'm running late. My husband will return from his trip abroad tonight, and I ought to take a bath before he arrives. I'll probably be in late tomorrow morning, should everything go to plan." She gives me a wink, then rolls her eyes. "I pray our sons let us have a moment's privacy."

Of course.

Madame Violette has a husband. And a family.

I do not.

"Well, I think that's all, but if not, you'll figure out what else needs doing. Have a productive night, Angélique. I'll see you in the morning!" And she's off like a whirlwind.

I unlock the door and step inside.

It's dark, but I welcome the shadows. I am one of them. We move together like raindrops sliding back into the ocean.

I could light a candle or a lantern, but I know every inch of this shop by heart. I learned to navigate in the dark long ago, in the years when my family couldn't afford candles.

A dancing orange glow from the gas lamp outside glitters like broken glass against the front store window, providing more than enough light to see that coming here was a terrible mistake. I want to go home. No, I want to go to *Domingo's* home and crawl into bed with my sister.

But she hates me. And there's nothing at home but the ghosts of those I have loved and lost.

Shoulders bent, I make my way to the sewing room. There is indeed a new stack of requisitions piled atop my workstation. Jacqueline's old table. Mine now. Just like I wanted.

I turn my back on the infinite orders awaiting me and make

my way to Elodie's clean, neat sewing station. I sit down on her chair. It's not warm from her narrow bottom but hard and cold. The sewing needles sparkle in her pincushion like spears of diamonds. A moonbeam catches the edge of the shears, glinting in invitation.

I don't touch any of it. Elodie shouldn't have had to, either. Good God, I'm a terrible sister. Not to mention the prior colleagues I hurt far worse than I intended.

Bleh. I wish I could run away from me, too.

Suddenly, fiercely, I miss my mother so badly, tears stream from my eyes. My spine crumples, no longer able to keep me upright. My wet cheek sticks to the buffed wooden surface of the worktable. Smooth and slippery. Can't risk catching expensive fabric on a stray splinter.

If only I knew how to mend things with Elodie.

Maman would know what to do. She would give me a big hug and pull Elodie in too, and the next thing you know, the entire family would be piling together like puppies, laughing and wiggling in each other's warm, safe embrace.

But I don't have a mother anymore. Or a father. Or a middle sister. And if I don't mind my steps, I'll lose Elodie and Domingo, too. My breath hitches.

The loss of Anne and my parents wasn't my fault. That honor goes to Monsieur Fournier, who physically held me back as his machines destroyed two more disposable humans.

But Elodie running away? Oui. C'est à cause de moi.

She didn't think I'd *notice*. She didn't think I'd *care*. I've made my baby sister believe with her whole heart that she matters less to me than a vat of dye or a strip of measuring tape. I've made her think she is not a person, not an individual with her own needs and wants but a tool in my work belt. A pawn, placed wherever I choose to put her. A peon existing solely to feed the machine of fine fashion for the upper classes. No better than Monsieur Fournier.

Bile rises in my throat, and I push myself upright to wipe my cheeks. In my quest for vengeance over my sister's and parents' deaths, I didn't mean to become my enemy's mirror image. I meant to destroy him. Instead, I have destroyed the precious bond I once shared with my sister.

Something has to change. And that something is me.

CHAPTER 38

The next Monday, before leaving for work—which means rising half an hour after dawn—I leave a note on the kitchen table for Elodie:

Mon petit chou,

You do not have to work at the dress shop today. Please spend your free hours doing whatever it is that pleases you.

Bisous,
Angélique

I've also left her fresh flowers in the vase, and her favorite pain au chocolate from the bakery on a small plate next to the note so she'll be certain to see it.

Despite sleeping two hours later than usual, I am the first to arrive at the modiste's shop. I unlock the door, prepare the first vat of dye Madame Violette asked me for last week, and then settle into my chair to review the measurements for the lingerie order.

I'm finishing the first sketches when the other seamstresses stream in. Now that they've settled in here, they know exactly what I need without me having to walk them through every nuance.

I hand the new designs to Zaidée. She has displayed the most raw talent. "Here. See if you can cut the pieces to the right measurements. Make reusable patterns, and arrange each section efficiently, so as to waste the least amount of material possible. Any questions?"

Her eyes widen with a mix of panic and excitement. "Me? But you always cut the pieces. We just sew them."

"If you don't think you have what it takes to be a protégée yourself one day, I can—"

"I'll do it!" She presses my sketches to her chest, her cheeks flushing and her eyes sparkling. "It'll be exactly like you've shown us. You'll see."

"I'm counting on it."

"Angélique!" calls Madame Violette from the front of the store. "I'm here!"

Excellent timing.

I leave the ladies to their work and stride out to the reception area to greet my mentor. Madame Violette is hanging up her cloak and bonnet.

"Did you get everything completed that I asked for?" she asks as she stuffs her gloves into her reticule.

"No," I reply evenly. "I did not."

She spins around in surprise. "You didn't? Well, I suppose it isn't the end of the world. I'm sure you're almost done now. By the way, I have a few other things you could help me with. I've received an order alteration request from the vicomtesse—"

"No," I repeat. Quietly but resolutely.

Madame Violette gurgles as though her silk scarf is choking her. "What did you say?"

"What I should have said weeks ago. Madame Violette, I appreciate this post. I adore *you*. Being your protégée is an honor and a privilege that I wouldn't trade for the world. But we both seem to have lost sight of the fact that I am only one person. You can't expect anyone to perform the duties of four full-time people without at least paying them for as much."

Her lips work silently for a moment; then she pulls the leather gloves back out of her reticule and dumps a pile of coins into the palm of her hand. "Done."

She holds the money out for me like a master offering a treat to his puppy.

I don't take the bait.

"No," I say again, gentler this time. "I'm not asking for your money. I'm asking for time to spend with my family. I'm asking you to honor the terms of our original agreement. I won't be staying past nightfall or working on Sundays anymore."

"But . . . who will . . ."

"An excellent question. The good news is, the masquerade is almost here. The costumes will be delivered later today. Nothing else is truly a priority. If you insist on meeting additional unreasonable deadlines, then there is no reason to wait until spring to hire more girls."

"There are only six workstations—"

"Which means employees could work in shifts, if necessary. The law limits adult workers to ten hours per day. Curtailing that time slightly would give each team much-needed rest and double your capacity. At the prices you're currently advertising, along with the myriad fees you're charging for prioritized delivery and other premium advantages—"

"You're right." Madame Violette gives me a rueful expression. "You're simply so *capable*, it's easy to forget you're also human. Of course you have other things you'd like to do with your time. And you're absolutely right that I can now afford to double the employment roster so two teams can work in shifts. It's a clever idea. *All* your ideas are brilliant."

I'm not too certain my beau and my sister would agree with her assessment, but I'm working on it.

My mentor forces the pile of coins into my hand. "No more staying late or coming in early, and no more Sundays. But you're still getting that raise. At the end of the month, I'll calculate numbers properly and reimburse you for all these weeks taking on the roles of four separate employees with such aplomb. Starting the first of January, I'll even give you ten percent of profits for each item you personally design. How does that sound?"

It sounds like a miracle. I want to hug her. Or maybe it's me who still needs a hug.

"Thank you." I add the mountain of new francs to my reticule. It has never been so heavy. "The ladies are already hard at work on the lingerie. Might I have an hour free?"

Madame Violette smiles at me. "Take the rest of the day. You deserve it."

I'm glad she gave me so much time, because it takes hours longer than expected to complete my next mission. By the time I arrive at La Croix & Sons, it's already midafternoon.

Elodie and Domingo have their backs to the street and so do not see me approach. When I enter the store, they are absorbed in an animated conversation before the display case of jade silk stockings and fancy bottles of perfume.

"May I interrupt?" I ask.

They both whirl around.

Domingo's hazel eyes warm at the sight of me, but my sister's gaze is hooded and cautious, as though she has been kicked too many times to come near me now.

I try to smile anyway. "Is there somewhere we can talk?"

There really isn't. Not inside the store. Customers browsing with flashy walking sticks or padded bustles bump about everywhere, like a school of piranhas dumped into a small fishbowl.

"Outside?" Domingo suggests.

"Sure."

Soon we are all standing in the sunshine, off to the side and out of the view of customers and passersby. Elodie immediately shades her face with her hand. Or maybe she simply doesn't wish to look at me.

"What are you doing here?" she asks, sullen. "Shouldn't you be at the dress shop?"

"I had something more important to attend to," I tell her. "That something is you. Happy late birthday, baby sister. I'm sorry I didn't tell you when I should have."

She doesn't respond. Just watches me warily.

I hold out a small folded rectangle.

She accepts it between two outstretched fingers, as though I've handed her the shed skin of a snake.

"That's your birthday present," I tell her. "But before you open it, there are a few things I ought to say. Things you both need to hear."

Elodie folds her arms over her chest defensively.

Domingo tilts his head, reserving judgment but open and interested.

"First, Elodie, close your eyes."

"What—"

I kiss Domingo with so much sincerity he lifts me off the ground with happiness.

After I return to my feet and my senses, I take a deep breath. The words pour out of me. "I've been beastly to both of you. I'm terribly sorry. You don't deserve it. Not only will I strive to be more aware and more sympathetic, I'll also be working fewer hours at the dress shop, starting today."

Elodie's eyes widen, and her hands drop down to her sides. "You *will?*"

I nod. "I informed Madame Violette this morning. My evenings and Sundays are once again free to spend with both of you. We can even take leisurely breakfasts together like we used to, Elodie."

Her mouth falls open. "*I* don't have to go in early either?"

"Non. You needn't go in at all, cabbage. You never wanted to work there to begin with. And now you don't have to." I motion to the folded piece of white cardstock in her hand. "Open that paper. It's your birthday gift."

She's still staring at me like I've sprouted three heads, but she unfolds the small stiff rectangle obediently. It's a calling card. "Monsieur . . . Charles . . . Navarre? Who is that?"

"Your new tutor," I tell her with a grin. "He'll be spending Christmas with his family, of course, but he's all yours starting the eighth of January. You get him two hours a day, five mornings a week."

Her brown eyes shimmer. "A real tutor? For me?"

"All for you. He's not your world-famous Pierre-François-Pascal Guerlain, but Monsieur Navarre is a respected retired parfumeur from Marseille, with decades of experience. It's a start, at least. I hope he's a boon in whatever you—"

Elodie throws her arms around me with a choking sound somewhere between a laugh and a sob. "This is my dream come true! You're the best sister ever."

Not quite yet.

There are still a few more surprises in store.

CHAPTER 39

The rest of the week passes in a blur. Suddenly, it's almost Christmas. The dress shop closes on Christmas Eve—the day of the Fourniers' masquerade ball—and won't reopen until the week after New Year's Day, giving me an entire luxurious fortnight to spend with Elodie and Domingo.

We're in his apartment now, sitting around a circular dining table piled high with gifts.

"Me first," says Domingo.

"No, me first!" shouts Elodie.

They're not arguing over who gets to unwrap their own surprises, but rather which of us gets to be the first to gift the others the presents we bought.

And why wouldn't we be in the spirit to share with each other? Our bellies are full of chestnut-stuffed goose—the best meal Elodie and I have tasted in our lives—and we're spending the day with the people we love most in the world.

"Me first," I say, knowing I will be vetoed immediately.

"I'm the oldest," says Domingo. "And you're in my house."

Elodie starts to protest, but I shake my finger. "That was a very good argument. Eldest first, then the baby, then me."

"I'm not a baby," she huffs in great offense. "I'm thirteen years old, and I—"

"Well, if you don't *want* to be second, I don't mind going in your place."

"I'm the baby," she says quickly. "Second is me."

Domingo hands each of us two lumpy, awkward packages wrapped in colorful paper. All four are tied with white ribbon and decorated with an extravagant bow. The larger pair of packages is blue-and-white, and the other two parcels are red. Elodie and I start with the blue ones.

"Boots!" she yells, immediately bending to try them on her feet. Her previous pair, with its battered old leather and embarrassing holes at the toes, lies discarded on the mat by the front door.

"These are gorgeous," I tell Domingo as I slide my stocking feet into my own new pair. "Very warm and sturdy and practical. You really *are* the oldest, aren't you?" I tease.

He grins at me and leans back in his chair, interlacing his fingers behind his neck to watch us.

Elodie and I hook arms and clomp around the parlor, a pair of little lost reindeer gamboling in a glen.

"All right, all right," says Domingo with a laugh. "Don't wear out the soles before you even get a chance to try your new boots outside. You've got another present to unwrap."

My sister and I remove our boots with care and place them carefully beside the door before retaking our seats. We open the red packages next.

Elodie squeals. "Dancing slippers!"

"With your swirly *D* right there on the heel!" I sound like my sister, high-pitched and vibrating out of my skin with excitement. "You designed these?"

Domingo rises from his chair and takes a dramatic bow.

The beautiful slippers slide immediately onto Elodie's and my feet. We waltz around the parlor—or would, if we had any idea how to waltz. It's all we can do not to step on each other as we spin in ungainly circles before the fire.

Domingo makes a terrifying sound like he's suffocating on his own snot in the heroic effort not to guffaw in laughter at us. "Good God, have you *no* sense of rhythm?"

"It's not like there's music playing!" I rub my chin as if lost in thought. "If only we knew a violinist who could provide a pretty melody."

"And dance lessons," Domingo adds. "It's embarrassing to have you two squirrels loose in my parlor."

"Dance lessons!" Elodie claps with delight, then hauls Domingo to the center of the room. "Start right now. What do we do first?"

"I'll be the orchestra," I tell them, and hum a traditional song.

It isn't until we've mastered the waltz, the quadrille, and the minuet that Elodie and I realize hours have passed and our gifts still haven't been given. We remove our slippers with regret, promising them we'll be back soon for more dancing.

Elodie hands Domingo and me each a small parcel wrapped in simple brown paper and tied with twine.

"They're signature scents," she blurts out before we've even unknotted the twine. "No one else in the world has the exact scent you hold in your hands. Custom tuned uniquely to each of you."

Domingo and I immediately apply a few drops of bespoke cologne to our wrists, then make a production of smelling each other and becoming hopelessly intoxicated. I swoon into his arms with a dramatic sweep of my wrist to my forehead.

He steals a kiss as we crumple to the floor.

Elodie chortles in delight.

"Now me," I tell them once Domingo and I have managed to haul ourselves back into our chairs. My gifts are the largest and lumpiest of all, wrapped not in paper but in tiny scraps from Madame Violette's remnant closet sewn together into a quilted mosaic of bright colors.

They open their presents eagerly. Inside are warm winter cloaks, and woolen scarves to match. I've embroidered Elodie's set with her favorite flowers. Domingo's is lined with jaunty musical notes. An embroidered violin nestles in one corner of the scarf.

I accept my hugs, then squeeze back harder, setting off a hugging contest that leaves us all breathless and merry.

As the spirit of Christmas fills us, I can hardly believe how far we've come. From wounded, indigent orphans to respected creators, craftsmen, and entrepreneurs with a bright future ahead of us. This is what happens when hard work and good fortune collide.

For perhaps the first time in my life, I truly feel blessed.

"Can you please play your violin now?" Elodie asks Domingo. "Angélique and I will dance to your music."

"I'm not sure that's the best way to tempt him," I stage-whisper.

He grins at us and retrieves the violin case from beside the sofa. "Maybe with enough practice and dedication, one day, you two might become slightly less embarrassing."

I stick my tongue out at him and sweep my sister into a comically inept waltz.

As we dance, I cannot help but think about the green dye again. Though there are heavy amounts of arsenic added to most of tonight's masquerade costumes, much of that clothing may be worn for only one night.

What if it *isn't* enough to weaken the industrialists and prove they aren't as powerful as they think? What if those who enrich themselves through the blood of the less fortunate merely contract little tummy aches and wake up tomorrow morning believing themselves slightly hungover from too much champagne, only to slide back into their old habits of greed and exploitation?

What if the man who killed three members of our family suffers no consequences at all?

Untenable. I'll have to come up with a contingency plan. Something drastic.

Domingo puts down his violin. "Good God, Angélique. What are you thinking about so furiously? There's bad dancing, and then there's whatever it is you're attempting to stumble through."

I wince. "Sorry. You're right. I wasn't fully attending. Tonight is the masquerade—"

"Why do you care so much about rich people? They don't

care about us. You and I might be the names du jour, but come tomorrow some other bauble might catch their eye, and we'll be forgotten. Or discarded altogether."

I *don't* care about the ruling class. Not in the way Domingo means. I am ridding the streets of devils like the Fournier family, one poisoned petticoat at a time. Restoring balance to the world. Making Paris a safer place for little girls like my sisters, and for hard workers like my parents.

It's not just a green silk stocking. It's well-deserved payback.

But to Domingo, I murmur, "I'll try to keep my mind here with you."

He raises his brows. "Better yet, both of you had better promise to come back tomorrow to celebrate Christmas Day. I'll buy breakfast."

Elodie shouts, "Pain au chocolat!"

Domingo and I exchange grins. He dances me around the room, and this time, I am 1,000 percent present. I love the way he feels, the way he smells, the way he holds me to him possessively as we waltz through the parlor.

"What are you doing on New Year's Day, birthday boy?"

His eyebrows rise. "Turning another year older?"

"How about taking a train ride with Elodie and me?" I ask.

"The sea?" Elodie squeals. "Are we really going to the sea?"

"It's Domingo's birthday, not yours," I tell her with a laugh. "We'll go wherever he wants."

"And of course I want to go to the sea with my two best girls." His eyes glint wickedly. "The water will be frigid. You'll have to tell me all about it after I throw you in."

Elodie shrieks.

I shake my finger at his chest. "I'll show you frigid—"

"Is that right?" He leans in for a kiss, and I close the distance. Elodie wrinkles her nose dramatically but smiles when she thinks we can't see her. She's as content in this moment as we are.

I vow to keep the three of us this safe and happy for the rest of our lives.

CHAPTER 40

It is late by the time I get Elodie home and tucked into bed. Later still when her chest finally rises and falls in the slow rhythm of deep sleep.

I slip out of the house and follow the flickering gas flames deeper into the city.

Tonight is the Fourniers' masquerade ball. I don't have an invitation to enter their home, but no one can stop me from lurking across the street in the shadows.

Attending the party would be meaningless anyway. I want to dance on their graves, not on their parquet. The arsenic seeping from most of the costumes will undoubtedly have ill effect, but not before my eyes. If it can take days to die of a direct overdose, I can't expect superficial reactions to appear much faster.

I try to remember how long it took for Charlotte to start staring vacantly while she scratched the new sores on her arms and legs. Her nightgown contained only a fraction of the poison I used in these costumes. With luck, boils will erupt on the Fourniers' flesh as they swirl through their ballroom.

Partygoers spill out of fancy carriages like weevils tumbling from spoiled bread.

They look stunning, these enemies of mine in their emerald-green costumes. Starting with the Fournier Twelve: Monsieur Fournier and his son, Odin the Odious, plus five other cruel, exploitative men who control the most dangerous factories in France, along with their five equally heartless male heirs, trailing behind.

Everyone can hear them talking. Their loud voices carry as though they've arrived at the party already drunk.

Perhaps that's exactly the case.

Apparently, these twelve are attending tonight's Christmas party against their will, as a favor to their wives and fiancées. The *real* party will be one week hence, when the men gather at their elite gentleman's club on New Year's Eve to drink and scheme.

They intend to put their brains—and resources—together to figure out how to squeeze even more speed and efficiency from their overworked employees in the coming years. Injuries and deaths be damned.

I hope they choke to death on their absinthe.

Other guests follow. There are the bankers who derive their wealth from predatory loans, knowing the interest will never be repaid and that the desperate souls who rely on them will be destined to remain poor.

Idle heirs and heiresses whose family money comes from

plantations in the Caribbean that profit from the labor of enslaved people. Not to mention aristocrats who do nothing but spend the fortune of their forebears without ever asking themselves how so much money was amassed in the first place.

These people in positions of great power could choose to make society better. Provide living wages and better working conditions for employees. Push for laws ensuring safety. Implement legal repercussions for any business owner who endangers a fellow human in order to line their own pockets.

Alas, they do not consider others. And so they will dance the night away, rubbing poison into their pampered skin until dawn.

I wish there was more I could do besides make the worst of them scratch a few open sores and spend a week or two squatting over a chamber pot. It is satisfying to know that these inconveniences will not end with the masquerade. Every time they don one of my special corsets or stockings or dresses or waistcoats, the symptoms will start again—with just enough of a delay not to link cause and effect. With luck, they'll suffer all year—or longer.

But it is not enough. The working people need permanent change. Not masters who itch but employers who give a damn. The lower class has suffered long enough. It is past time for commoners to win.

And I have an idea that could spark a revolution.

CHAPTER 41

Eleven o'clock at night on New Year's Eve. I expected to be nervous. Instead, every nerve in my body is wired with electricity. I feel like I could leap over the Arc de Triomphe and land on my toes like a ballerina. My muscles are itching to *start*, to *do*, to *finish*.

To settle the score.

"Soon," I whisper beneath my breath. The murmur feels as loud as a battle cry. A belligerent bugle rising above the cacophony of the night.

I am not the only one on the prowl. The streets are as crowded as the grand Fête Nationale celebration every July. The year will end in less than an hour. Fireworks at midnight. Drunken kisses, laughter, music. Tomorrow we rise with the perennial hope that *this* year, we will be our best selves, and the world will reward our righteousness with health and happiness, good food and great moments with family and friends.

That is, *most* of us hope. The elite scheme.

Over on the opposite side of the Champs-Elysées is Les

Chanceux, the exclusive gentleman's club only open to the richest of the rich. Countless barons and vicomtes have been turned away at the door, to their eternal public humiliation.

Les Chanceux is not for the lesser aristocracy. The nobility hasn't ruled Paris for years. Les Chanceux caters to the real gods of France: filthy rich industrialists like Monsieur Fournier and his confederates. Arrogant, entitled tyrants whose soft, unblemished white hands scoop up desperate, hungry citizens and wring us dry until not a single drop of usefulness—or life—remains.

The cursed Fournier Twelve are nestled inside their hive. From the shadows across the street, I watched them arrive two by two. Genteel pairs of monster and heir. Sowers of destruction and continued misery cloaked in tailcoats and top hats.

They think they have it all, yet they want even more.

I am here to give them exactly what they deserve.

A trio of drunken revelers jostles against me, causing the contents of my satchel to clink noisily against the empty wooden tray dangling at my side.

I expect a slurred "Excusez-moi," but it never comes. The swarming, stumbling crowd is blind to everyone but themselves, each merrymaker too tipsy to remember their own name, much less my ordinary face in a city of well over half a million inhabitants, most of whom are out here with us in the streets, holding torches and liquor bottles—an explosive combination—while singing at the top of their lungs. I have never been more invisible.

It is time.

I slink across the teeming street, threading my way between throngs of men and women and adolescents with the practiced ease of a mouse skittering beneath horses' hooves and carriage wheels.

Rather than approach the impenetrable front door of Les Chanceux, I circle around a fetid alleyway to the servants' entrance at the rear. The roar of the crowd is only marginally dulled by the tall stone buildings.

Although the alley's inhabitants are sparser, they pay me even less attention than I received on the public street. No one glances my way as I balance my wooden tray on a broken barrel and arrange the contents of my satchel on top: twelve delicate glass containers the size and shape of small pears, each with a fancy blown-glass stopper and a handwritten tag, tied with an emerald silk ribbon the same shade as the liquid inside.

I tilt my cap lower, to hide my face in its shadow. And *there* is the hint of the nervousness I expected. My costume is impeccable. I resemble every other harried, hardworking errand boy scrambling to deliver champagne here and chocolates there. All to pamper our betters, who will not even grunt to us in thanks for spending our holidays in service to them. We are no more noticeable than flies, and just as quickly swatted away.

Nonetheless, I run my lines through my head as I hook my empty satchel over my narrow shoulders and lift the wooden tray with great care. I have an ironclad story to explain my presence and my parcel.

My curly black hair is hidden under my hat, braided tight to my scalp. My breasts are bound with a long strip of linen beneath my loose servant-boy overcoat. I rehearsed a story to explain my appearance in case my disguise is not enough to hide my gender and I am barred at the door.

I knock with my foot. Twice. Three times.

At last, the door swings outward. I open my mouth to announce my unscheduled special delivery, but no one is on the other side to hear it. The overworked staff of Les Chanceux scurry hither and yon with their own responsibilities, too focused on the next task on their endless list to have time for curiosity about anyone else's. I hurry inside the building and manage to close the door behind me.

Here I falter, just for a moment. I sewed and plotted my way into Monsieur Fournier's lair, but now that I've breached the entrance, I've no idea how to find him.

Neither I nor anyone I've ever known has set foot inside Les Chanceux, so I have no helpful map pointing me in the direction of the dozen men single-handedly responsible for most of the working class's misery. But I cannot stand at the threshold, gaping at the crystal chandeliers and gold-filigreed wallpaper all night long.

I stride off down the first corridor I find, shoulders back, chin high, gait confident. I've no idea where I'm going, but no one else needs to know that.

What few doors exist are open wide. The purpose of this club is to see and be seen. As though to say, *We are the rulers of this city. A pantheon of our own making. All-powerful and untouchable!*

Their hubris makes my search easy. Unhindered, I stroll through parlor after parlor, each outfitted in crystal and gold and royal purple, until I find the ostentatious den of the Fournier Twelve.

The door to this room is half open. I close it with the heel of my boot as I enter. The click of the latch engaging is lost beneath the thunder of the grandiloquent voices of twelve self-important men, each absolutely certain that whatever they're saying deserves far more attention than anything anyone else is blathering about. Volume rises, and glasses clink.

Several of the men have tossed their tailcoats over the backs of their chairs and rolled their sleeves up to their elbows. Perhaps this public deshabille is proof that the wealthy needn't conform to the same strictures as the rest of society . . . or perhaps it is to relieve the pain of prominent boils on the arms of those who came in contact with my special costumes.

I am pleased to see that it worked—and that it hurts.

With a sudden movement, the owner of a railway struggles out of his tailcoat and flings it over his chair, as the others have done. The white sleeves underneath are dotted with splotches of wet crimson. He shoves the material up as far as it can go to scratch at a scab.

The largest processor of iron ore leans back in his chair with a wry expression. "Itches like the devil, doesn't it?"

"You too?" asks the rail magnate without pausing his scratching.

"Some kind of measles," Monsieur Fournier informs them with confident authority. "A third of our guests came down with the same thing. We caught it from one of them."

"You should see my wife," the kingpin of a cotton-spinning

empire says with a grimace. "Scabs from head to toe, and vomiting without cease."

"None of us wanted to see your wife *before* she took ill," jibes one of the heirs, and then the men are off with insults and ribald jests, all concern about their ailing women forgotten.

"I'm dry," the heir to one of the worst coal mines in Nord-Pas-de-Calais interrupts as he wiggles his empty glass.

"Where the devil is the next round of champagne I ordered?" Monsieur Fournier scowls toward the door—and finds me.

I freeze, no longer a harried delivery boy but rather once again a terrified little girl, standing in a spreading pool of her family's blood while screaming hysterically for help that never comes.

"That's the wrong order," Monsieur Fournier barks, furious. "I asked for six more bottles of champagne, not . . ." His eyes widen, turn avaricious. He licks his thin lips. "Is that a tray of absinthe?"

The rest of the men tease him, claiming Monsieur Fournier never did order the champagne. Everyone knows he prefers absinthe. Is this a special treat, just for them?

That is my cue.

I step forward, a capricious genie escaped from a bottle. Unlike these men, I shall play fair—a concession Monsieur Fournier never afforded me or the others.

What happens next is up to him.

"These are complimentary samples from an anonymous supplier." I lower my voice and my tray, so that the twelve beautiful stoppered bottles pass in front of Monsieur Fournier's nose. "They're to be given as gifts to the twelve most valuable employees among all your factories."

Indeed, from this angle, Monsieur Fournier cannot miss the four words printed on each heart-shaped tag: *MOST VALUABLE* across the top, with an elegant cursive *Thank You* beneath.

"You're saying they're not for *me*?" he bellows in disbelief, his face twisted into comical incredulity.

"Now, now," protests one of his cronies. "Even a glutton like you cannot drink twelve shots of absinthe in one sitting."

"And live," mutters another, to the merriment of all.

"I'm a glutton too!" shouts one of the monsters' drunken heirs. "Does that mean *I* get a shot of absinthe?"

The entire table erupts into a riot of drunken laughter and pointy elbows and greedy hands.

"I'm sorry, sir," I murmur to Monsieur Fournier. "My donor's instructions clearly state that these gifts are to go to the employees whose hard work is the reason for you and your friends' success—"

"Bah." Monsieur Fournier snatches a bottle from the tray and holds it high. "Since when have men like us cared about other people's precious rules?"

"Or about the thousands of workers responsible for our wealth?" sneers Odin the Odious, to the delight of the others.

"Hear, hear!" laughs the table of monsters.

"I don't see any employees in this room," says Monsieur Fournier. "Just the twelve of us, and twelve servings of absinthe. What do you say, gentlemen? Aren't we the most valuable of all?"

His fellow snakes cheer and puff up their chests.

"In fact," Monsieur Fournier continues, "our workers should be thanking *us*. We're the ones putting food in their mouths. It's only fair that they put a fine treat into ours!"

"Yes," I murmur. "This is only fair."

"Go on, then," he orders me. "One flask of absinthe for each of my colleagues and their sons."

It is not plain absinthe.

It is equal parts absinthe and arsenic, with a drop of green dye.

It is death in a bottle.

"As you wish, sir." I give a deferential bow, then make my way clockwise around the table. Just to needle Odin, I leave him for last rather than serving him first.

These powerful men do not thank me as their greedy hands close around their bottles. I do not exist for them in any meaningful way.

Soon these monsters will no longer exist for me either.

The heir next to Monsieur Fournier pinches his fingers against the blown-glass stopper of his flask.

Monsieur Fournier grabs the heir's silk-covered wrist as if it were his own son's and squeezes violently until the heir's spasming fingers are forced to relinquish their tenuous hold of the glass stopper, leaving the bottle corked.

"No one drinks until I drink," Monsieur Fournier says coldly. His eyes are chips of ice, and his twisted face is no longer a mask—it is a true reflection of the blackness of his soul.

"No one drinks until Fournier gives the word," the heir calls out in a shaky voice.

"Or at least until I get *my* flask," says one of the other industrialists. "Hurry it up."

The others laugh. No one is looking askance at Monsieur Fournier. They're looking at *me* with impatience. It is not so much that the tense moment is now over, but rather that greed and violence were never out of the ordinary for them to begin with.

"The lad said the bottles aren't *for* us." Odin's voice rings out clearly. "We're to choose twelve deserving workers amongst everyone's holdings—"

"For Christ's sake," snaps Monsieur Fournier. "You'd give a drop of absinthe to every peon in Paris in your never-ending quest for 'fairness.' I've had it. Unless you want me to disinherit you this very night, shove your sanctimoniousness for once and drink your damn shot with the rest of us!"

My mouth drops open. Luckily, no one pays me any mind. They are all looking at Odin. Not in shock, as I am, but with expressions of exasperation and annoyance. As if this were the last straw in a mountain of unwelcome appeals for kindness and empathy.

Monsieur Fournier and his son are famously often at odds with one another, but I never would have guessed the reason was *this*. That a monster like Fournier has accidentally spawned a creature capable of staring evil in the eyes and pleading mercy. The rumors of Odin's cruelty were likely fabricated by his father.

Odin's is the final flask, sitting alone on my outstretched tray, inches from him.

"Take the absinthe," his father growls between clenched teeth. "Or else, when we get home, so help me God—"

I pretend to shove the tray toward Odin too hard and too fast, so that I am forced to jerk the tray back in haste, lest it smash into my elegant client's neck.

The pear-shaped glass bottle makes no such stop. It sails off the edge of the tray, shooting over Odin's shoulder faster than anyone can reach for it.

In a blink, the delicate glass lies shattered on the marble floor, shards of transparent beauty in a spreading pool of viscous green poison.

"You imbecile!" Monsieur Fournier spits out, raising a clawed hand at me as though barely holding himself back from wringing my neck. "Abruti, couillon, crétin . . . Clean up your mess!"

I kneel but do not touch the broken glass. Beneath my lowered lashes, my watchful eyes are on the men. They have forgotten me already.

"And now, a toast!" Monsieur Fournier calls out merrily, as if he has not just berated someone else's employee after threatening to disown his own child. "We'll drain our bottles together in unity on the count of three, but first . . ." He lifts his flask of poison into the air like a gladiator holding high the severed head of his enemy.

The others do the same. *Almost* all the others. Odin sits with his arms crossed, openly glaring at the other eleven, as if hoping their glasses of absinthe will magically turn into poison.

I am about to make his dreams come true.

"The men at this table," Monsieur Fournier continues, "are the crème de la crème of Paris. We are the new ruling class of this great nation. And we will not relinquish that power to anyone for any reason."

The others cheer.

Monsieur Fournier casts a snide sidelong glance at his son. "Fairness is for fools. We take what we want!"

The cheers get louder.

"If someone is beneath us . . . we shall step on them to raise ourselves higher!" Monsieur Fournier bounds to his feet.

Everyone but Odin does the same.

Monsieur Fournier climbs atop his expensive leather chair. "May this year bring even more wealth and power than we've amassed thus far. We are unstoppable! The world is ours for the taking."

"I'll drink to that!" calls out one of the heirs.

The other men whoop in agreement.

Monsieur Fournier grins. "In that case . . . un, deux, trois!"

They unstopper their bottles and toss the gorgeous hand-crafted tops to the floor, where they shatter on the marble.

As one, all eleven tilt back their heads and pour liquid green arsenic straight down their gullets.

Only one of them frowns. "That wasn't as good as . . ."

His complaint is lost in a clatter of breaking glass as the men fling their empty bottles to the floor, making an even bigger mess for me to clean.

And destroying all evidence of any crime in the process.

"Of course it was terrible absinthe," Monsieur Fournier

says in disgust. "It was meant for our workers, not for us. The next time I see—"

The door swings open and a pair of sweaty, flustered serving lads rush in, both carrying two bottles of champagne in each hand.

"Pardon the delay, messieurs," gushes the first, his head bent reverently. "We've brought you eight bottles instead of six, as a courtesy on the house."

Just like that, the low-quality absinthe is as forgotten as the well-being of their factory workers. Each man clamors to be the first whose empty champagne glass is refilled. In no time, they are chattering and drinking as if there has been no interruption at all.

Before they back away, the two serving lads spy me on the floor in a sea of broken glass and hurry to help me. While they sweep the glass, I wipe away any trace of momentary imperfection. By the time we are through, a bloodhound would not be able to find fault in the sterility of this marble floor.

No one questions why I'm on the ground. The empathy in their eyes and their quickness to help tells me all I need to know.

I follow the boys out the parlor door without a backward glance for Monsieur Fournier and the other monsters. They don't deserve another second of my time. And they ought to be counting down their own.

Direct ingestion of arsenic might normally take up to four days to kill, but by morning, hangovers will strike with a few new sensations. A tummy ache. Vomiting. Diarrhea. Common symptoms of too much drink, if a bit more dramatic than usual. Shortness of breath. Irregular heartbeat. Red, puffy skin. Could be too much alcohol, could be influenza. Who's to say? Then numbness and tingling. Pins and needles. Muscle cramps and spasms, as though they've toiled all day at one of their own machines. A bloodier discharge from their various orifices as their organs begin to fail, one by one. Pain. So much pain. Inside and out. Final days filled with unending agony, before the sweet release of sudden death.

Odin, as sole survivor, will be the only witness alive with enough clues to piece together that perhaps the anonymous gift wasn't the boon it appeared to be. If Monsieur Fournier and the others had listened—had they cared a single iota about anyone besides themselves—they would still be alive.

The thought of a potential witness should make me nervous, but it does not. Odin might suspect the purity of the delivery lad's motives, but he cannot prove anything. Perhaps the cause of death was nothing more nefarious than an unhygienic batch of poor-quality absinthe. Or the ungodly amount of alcohol drunk by eleven men in one night.

Besides, even if Odin suspects, he'll never tell. By his own admission, Odin understands fairness. He's had to put up with his father for longer than I have. For years, he's been yearning for freedom. I'm eager to see what he'll do with it.

Especially now that he knows someone's watching.

I lean my empty tray against a wall, then step outside into the alleyway. For a brief second, the sky is black. And then the night erupts into bright streaks of color.

Fireworks, everywhere. Cheers and whoops, all throughout Paris.

Joy fills me. I break into a jog, racing home to where Elodie and Domingo await me. We have much to celebrate. It is now officially Domingo's birthday and the start of a wonderful new year for everyone. My heart thunders as though I've climbed a volcano, gazed into its deadly magma core, and lived to tell the tale.

I did it. I avenged my parents' and sister's deaths and took a stand for all the thousands of others like us. Those who died, those who were injured, and those who live in fear, knowing their turn could come at any moment.

Tomorrow may not bring health and safety for every citizen of Paris, but while I still have breath in my body, I will never stop fighting. My wounds do not diminish me. The past gives me the power to forge a better future.

I raise my fist and howl at the moon. It is indeed a happy new year.

CHAPTER 42

The sea stretches before me in waves of frothed blue splendor.

Without taking my wondering eyes from the sparkling water, I reach my arms east and west. Elodie clasps my unblemished hand in hers and pulls it to her chest. I cannot feel the rapid beat of her heart through so many layers of winter clothing and a wool coat, but the trembling vise grip on my fingers and the excited bounce of her body tell me everything.

Domingo takes my other hand and raises it to his lips. It is impossible to feel the warmth of his kiss through my new leather gloves, but I swear that I do. As he keeps my hand pressed to his mouth, the soft heat sinks through the leather, permeates even the toughest of my scars, and shoots a frisson of electricity into my blood. His kiss travels through my veins, warming every inch of me from the inside out, until I am tempted to fling my blood-red coat to the white sand of the beach and race into the ocean to cool my ardor.

But who am I to douse a flame?

I give Elodie's hand one last squeeze before gently extricating my fingers from hers. She doesn't even notice, so rapt is she by a childhood of fictional seasides come to life before her.

The North Sea is lovely. But there is a boy I love even more.

I throw myself into Domingo's arms. Suddenly, rashly, inelegantly. Rather than being knocked off balance by my abrupt attack, he hugs me tight, as though he's been waiting for this moment since we stepped off the train half an hour ago.

As though we've both been waiting for this moment our entire lives.

I press kisses to his cheeks, his jawline. "Happy birthday, mon amour."

He laughs as my puckered lips travel all over his face, his eyelids, his ears. "Happy new year, amorcito."

I let him catch me at last. The combined heat of our open mouths sends tiny spirals of fevered little breaths into the frigid salty air.

"This visit would be better in the summertime," he murmurs against my lips.

"It's perfect now," I reply.

Letting my knees go limp, I sink to the sand, bringing Domingo with me. As we fall, I grab the bright blue hem of Elodie's woolen coat so that she tumbles down with us. We land in a giggling heap, a trio of frolicking kittens curling into each other for warmth.

Elodie's bonnet slides from her head, the white silk ribbons catching it loosely at her throat.

I press a kiss to the soft black baby hairs curling at one

of her temples, sorrier than words can ever describe that we weren't able to make this trip with our whole family, like we had always fantasized.

My sister gazes up at me as if reading my mind. "The whole family *is* here."

She leans back into me and Domingo, clasping my right arm and his left around her tummy as though fastening a belt, and then gestures wide with both her hands as if to say Papa and Maman and Anne *are* the beach. Our loved ones are not lost. They are with us in every grain of sand. Every drop of water. Every speck of salt. Every ray of sun. Every kiss of the wind against our chapped cheeks.

As long as the gorgeous sea glitters beneath the sun, so too do we. In this life and the next.

"Will it be another late night tonight?" Domingo asks softly.

"Yes," I reply, snuggling into him. "With you."

He and my sister do not know the real reason why I rushed through the door to the final booms of midnight fireworks on New Year's Eve. They assume any late hours are spent at Madame Violette's dress shop, dyeing silk or cutting patterns for ball gowns.

That used to be correct. With the new year comes new changes at the shop. I have freed almost two dozen more women and girls from Monsieur Fournier's death trap—may he suffer in agony—and need no longer work myself raw.

With the new year also comes a new resolution: I shall be a good person from this day forth, and a worthy role model for Elodie. No more revenge, and certainly no more murder. I still wake at night from the guilt of it all, secure in the knowledge I've avenged my family, yet just as certain they would not approve of my methods.

From now on, I'm an ordinary seamstress and fashion designer. No, not ordinary—extraordinary. This is where my true talent lies, and what my contribution to the world around me ought to be. My career seems bright.

Madame Violette found a larger location for the dress shop just a few minutes up the road on fashionable Rue de la Paix. Not far from Elodie's master parfumeur, with whom she still hopes to apprentice one day. If any woman can, it's my Elodie.

As for what other changes the new year will bring . . . we'll have to wait and see.

I suspect the tide has turned.

EPILOGUE

Spring has come, and Paris is in full bloom. Bright flowers adorn wrought-iron balconies. Colorful petals sway on leafy, cheerful green trees. And at every fashionable throat is a drop of the sweetest scent: Elodie's latest floral cologne.

It is Monday, and I am on my lunch break. A full hour to do nothing, or anything I please. Usually, I spend the long sunny minutes with Domingo at Jardin des Tuileries, enjoying a light picnic and the warmth of each other's company amidst the beauty of nature and the rhythmic bubble of the center fountain. The water reminds us of the sea, and our upcoming two-week holiday with Elodie to visit the shore in summertime.

But today I am not perched on a stone bench with my back to lively Rue de Rivoli. Instead, I am approaching a place I swore I would never return to. A hellhole that still haunts my worst nightmares.

Fournier's textile factory.

Except, now there is a new Monsieur Fournier. Odin the

Odious, bane of his mother's and sister's existence, is now the head of the family—and master of the factory.

Under his oversight, unprecedented changes have flourished, including shorter working shifts, increased safety measures, and, most shockingly, the unmistakable sound of happy voices and spontaneous laughter spilling out the open doors.

I edge closer, drawn to the sound. At my approach, several workers catch sight of me. They pause what they are doing to smile and wave, secure in the knowledge that they will not lose their jobs for taking a brief second to interact with another human. I wave back in wonder.

It is like waving at a dream. A mirage that existed only in my mind, those dark years when I had to grit my teeth against the pain and the exhaustion to make it through one more hour, one more day, one more week.

I yearn for Maman and Papa and Anne. For them to see the changes my intervention has wrought. But then I feel the kiss of the spring breeze against my cheeks, and I know our lost loved ones are with us everywhere we go, because we carry the best pieces of them in our hearts. We all feel the same release and joy as the workers inside the factory. Instead of hollowness, I fill with warmth and pride and hope.

There is still much to do. For the first time, a better future actually seems possible.

The inglorious disbanding of the former Fournier Twelve dominated the newspapers for weeks. Over the course of a few short days, the tyrants took ill one at a time, then all at once. The eleven deaths were every bit as gruesome and elongated as their embattled workers could dream.

At first I feared Odin would be charged with their murders, as sole survivor—and outspoken dissident. Since the dawn of time, many an heir has killed to hasten his inheritance. And Odin's long history of strife with his father was no secret.

But Odin escaped scrutiny. In part because he gained no particular advantage with the death of the other ten men, and in part because the elite don't suspect poison. None of their servants would *dare* raise a hand to harm their betters. Besides, the men's symptoms were no surprise. Merely an exaggerated version of the same persistent affliction that has been affecting the wealthiest Parisians for the past six months. Many of those who attended the Fourniers' Christmas masquerade also contracted the same symptoms.

The gossip rags immediately called Madame Fournier's hygiene into question.

FOURNIER FÊTE WITH FATAL FLAW

JOYEUX NOËL: A PLAGUE FOR CHRISTMAS

MME FOURNIER GIVES THE GIFT OF MALADIE

Although she was able to deflect blame by pointing out that only some of her fashionable guests were affected, her reputation as a hostess is permanently damaged. She'll never host another soirée again.

After the Fournier Twelve took ill, the papers began calling the cholera-like symptoms the "plague of the upper class." A moniker the most self-important wear with pride as they scratch the fresh scabs of the lesions beneath their expensive green garments. To those convinced of their superiority, their mysterious illness has become as fashionable as tuberculosis, the wasting disease of the beautiful and the artistic. If ostentatious bloody lesions mark the ruling class as better than the peasants, dying of the malady is the ultimate mark of status.

I have never seen more smug mourners at any funeral. Dying to be next.

I'm happy to let them. Good riddance.

The sudden loss of the eleven cruelest industrialists sent their respective empires into turmoil.

Odin's swift changes were a welcome relief to his workers—many of whom still look around in disbelief, marveling at an attainable pace and tasks not designed to kill them in the name of profit.

The boards of directors for the other institutions scoffed at Odin's soft-hearted folly until the results of the changes became clear. Like Madame Violette, Odin instituted multiple shifts, thereby employing double the quantity of desperate citizens without working any one of them to the bone.

The cost was slightly higher and initial output was significantly lower, due to thousands of new workers in need of training, as well as the daily transition between first shift and second. Odin quickly became the laughingstock of the Parisian elite.

As it turns out, happy employees, well-rested employees, *safe* employees are far more productive and efficient than exhausted workers barely subsisting under constant fear for their lives.

The Fournier factory became more profitable than ever, sending a windfall of gold into Odin's bulging pockets—two-thirds of which he immediately shared with his employees by raising every single salary overnight. Gossip rags report that his mother and sister received not one sou.

His competitors immediately scrambled to replicate his successes, raising wages and standards of living all across Paris.

Unemployment is still high and poverty still rampant, but every day, the "lessers" have a little bit more. More income, more sleep, more time to spend with their families outside the cramped, sweltering factories.

Domingo and I have more freedom than ever, too. Though he always finds time to polish my shoes, we both work shorter days and spend most of that time designing our respective products. No more kneeling on the ground before wealthy aristocrats for him, shoving pampered feet into expensive shoes. Domingo provides the designs and oversees the production. He now owns 10 percent of La Croix & Sons. His iconic swirly *D* swings from a white wooden sign above the door. Clients ask for him by name.

No more cutting and sewing for me, either. I have a plethora of talented seamstresses I can trust to turn my designs into reality.

The only menial task I've kept for myself is my in-demand, signature secret-recipe green dye, reserved for our wealthiest patrons—and showing no sign of diminishing popularity. I'm certain Zaidée or Séraphine would eagerly lend a hand, now that it no longer contains lethal levels of arsenic, but for the moment I'm content to send the price of the limited-edition dye soaring and thus spend less of my precious time hunched over a vat, reminiscing about past persecutors.

Vengeance is behind me. Though my revenge worked out for the best, the lengths I went to were wrong. After walking away from Monsieur Fournier's club, I'd much rather spend my days with my family.

Elodie, Domingo, and I now live together in a comfortable apartment. Elodie has her own bedroom, wide enough to include a long table filled with her chemistry projects. Her tutor says she's the brightest student he's ever taught. He has no doubt Elodie will be able to apprentice the master parfumeur of her choice soon.

During the day, Domingo and I share a small, sunny parlor where we design our fashions. Sometimes in long, frenzied hours of companionable silence, and sometimes punctuated by exclamations of delight as we show each other the latest drawings in our sketchbooks.

This afternoon, he must present his latest creations at the shoe shop. I wish him luck and give him a kiss on his way out the door. When I turn back to the lunch table, Elodie has picked up Domingo's discarded newspaper and is gazing at the front page with an odd expression.

"Have lady parfumeurs been named the new royalty?" I tease.

At first she looks startled, as though I've caught her in the middle of a naughty prank. Her cheeks darken slightly, as if she is blushing. "Have you seen the headlines?"

I shake my head.

When no suspicion fell on me after the deaths of the Fournier Twelve, I stopped reading the papers altogether. Murdering a guilty party every time there's an injustice in the world would be a full-time job—and turn me into a monster little better than they are.

I have been revenge-free since that day, and much the better for it. My focus is on the new line of affordable dresses I've designed for the lower classes. Madame Violette was the first to showcase my ideas. The pieces are now being sold on consignment all over the city.

I wish the papers would write about *that*. Good news, for a change.

After relinquishing the clothing she modeled for me, Charlotte recovered from her mysterious illness. She is no longer competition and is much humbler as my right-hand woman in my quest to bring fashion to the masses.

"No," I admit. "I haven't checked the headlines for months. Did something happen?"

"Well," Elodie says, "something is still happening. The illness affecting the wealthy keeps spreading."

I frown. Now that I'm no longer adding extra arsenic to the clothes of those who deserve to do some penance, the effects of the poison certainly cannot worsen. If anything, with every washing, the fabric should become slightly less deadly.

Of course, journalists do love to be as alarming as possible. "Do you mean the symptoms have shown no sign of abating?"

This is equally unlikely, but it is an exaggeration I can easily imagine going to print.

"It's spreading," she repeats firmly, her eyes glittering.

A prickle dances down the back of my neck. Something isn't right. "Can I please see the article, cabbage?"

"It doesn't have all the information." Elodie smiles slyly and lowers her voice. "Can I tell you a secret?"

Why is she lowering her voice? We are alone in our own house.

Something is very wrong.

I scoot my chair next to hers and sit as still as I can to hide the shaking in my legs. "You can always tell me anything you wish, cabbage. I would never betray your confidence, no matter what. You know that."

Her eyes dart away as she gnaws her lip. Then she whispers, "I know what you did."

My flesh goes cold and clammy.

"Wh-what?" I manage hoarsely.

"Fragrances are chemistry." Her big brown eyes meet mine. "So is dye. Did you think I wouldn't notice the ingredients, when you mixed your special green at home for the contest?"

I stare at her, my brain lacking any coherent words.

"Or how the proportions changed when you volunteered to become dye girl for Madame Violette—after claiming you'd never do that job again?"

I cannot formulate a response. The only phrase my brain is capable of forming is *Elodie knows, Elodie knows, Elodie knows.*

She smiles and announces proudly, "It was easy to do the same to my perfume."

My mouth falls open. A wheezing gasp escapes my dry throat. "You did what?"

With a yawn, she loops her arm through mine and lays her head on my shoulder. "I've always wanted to be just like you, and now I am. We create works of art with a secret twist. Every rich person who buys my most outrageously expensive cologne or perfume sprays themselves a little closer to death."

This is not *just like me*. This is a nightmare.

Worse than having temporarily become a monster myself, I've created a much worse monster in the no-longer-innocent baby sister I did all this to protect.

My attacks were *targeted*. Not at every Parisian better off than we were, but at the specific capitalists who exploited the poor. And I'm done now. Revenge complete.

Elodie, my sweet little sheltered cabbage, on the other hand . . . is killing indiscriminately. Not simply the greedy industrialists who murdered our parents, but any random person who can afford a bottle of eau de toilette and has the misfortune of choosing hers.

With horror, I realize my baby sister fully knows this. Despite our poverty, Papa once managed to scrape together enough sous to purchase a perfume for Maman—and Elodie slept with the empty bottle beneath her pillow.

She's not killing out of vengeance, or a warped sense of social justice.

She's killing because she finds it fun.

"You're the best big sister in the world," my unintentional protégée says drowsily, snuggling into me as she's done since she was a small child. "And I promise, this is only the beginning."

AUTHOR'S NOTE

After several years writing primarily Regency romance, it was an absolute blast to leap into a different time, place, and genre! This setting is anti-historical. While a line early in this story implies that a recent revolution is to credit for the racial equality depicted, no miracle eliminating racism actually occurred. Although Black people have lived in Europe for centuries, it was not, with very few exceptions, as part of or in equal social rank to the upper classes, much less titled aristocracy.

However, other fantastical plot elements depicted in *The Protégée* absolutely did take place in the real world: namely, industrialists supplanting aristocrats as the ruling class of Paris during this time, and the widespread use of poisonous green dye.

Prior to the Industrial Revolution, aristocrats and royals were at the top of high society. Suddenly, it became possible to amass unimaginable wealth without having been born into a rich, titled family. Industries such as iron, textiles, and railways enabled a growing percentage of privileged men to create dynasties. These "capitalists" were viewed with envy and fear, and were understandably considered a threat due to their enormous power.

A modern comparison would be the billionaire founders and figureheads of massive corporations often infamous for the poor treatment of their workers or their willingness to abandon ethics in exchange for profit. In the same way that we recognize these names and faces today from seeing them splashed on TV, newspapers, magazines, and social media, the same thing was happening in nineteenth-century France with newspapers, magazines, pamphlets, caricaturists, and word of mouth. Over the course of this century, capitalists became the upper class.

There were actually multiple real-life versions of the dye Angélique uses in this story. One of the most famous is known as Scheele's green. Arsenic-based green dye was used in everything: clothing, wallpaper, candy, paint, books, toys, furniture, carpeting, and so on.

Although these versions did not contain quite as much arsenic as Angélique added to her revenge garments, fashionable women fainted in green dresses, children stayed sickly in green nurseries—and Napoleon Bonaparte's hair tested positive for arsenic poisoning, due to his having lived in a green-roomed house during his exile. There are even accounts of acute poisoning from green-dyed candles, and at least one diplomat made an official complaint to Queen Victoria that her green wallpaper made him ill.

The girls who worked in factories creating these dyes were very much in danger, often dying from repeated exposure. One such poor woman even vomited green before she died. Angélique's foggy thinking in parts of this story could have as much to do with breathing in toxic fumes as with her extended sleep deprivation.

Paris green—a pigment used by artists like Vincent van Gogh, Paul Gauguin, and Claude Monet, among others—not only regularly killed the factory workers manufacturing the color but also was later approved as both an insecticide and rodenticide due to its extreme toxicity.

Curiously, even after the adverse effects of arsenic in these green dyes became known, the bright emerald color did not immediately fall out of favor. It was beautiful, and for some, beauty outweighed all other concerns. History is full of the wild lengths people will go to in the name of fashion!

DISCUSSION QUESTIONS

1) A protégé (or protégée, in the feminine form) is someone who learns from a mentor. At the beginning of the book, who did you think was the titular protégée? At the end of the book, did you change your mind?

2) All through life, we learn just as much from observation as from structured lessons. What lessons did Angélique learn from the people in her life, like the factory owners, her boyfriend, her coworkers, and Madame Violette?

3) Angélique did not intend to kill Jacqueline and indeed vomits into a chamber pot once she realizes what she's done. Nonetheless, Angélique intended to cause temporary harm. At what point do her victims' fates stop being accidents, and why?

4) Angélique initially resents Jacqueline for being a self-important dictator who snaps at the working girls. Later, when Angélique has Jacqueline's position, she arranges employment for her friends from the factory—and then arguably treats them much the same. Do you think Jacqueline might also have changed over time? Is everyone inherently capable of changing?

5) Empathy is a major theme in this story. How does the presence or absence of it impact Angélique? Given all the lives she took, do you feel any empathy for her now?

6) When Angélique vows to do *anything* to protect and provide for her baby sister, she has no idea what lengths this promise will lead her to. Think of the statement "I would do anything for someone I care about." What other hyperbolic phrases could be twisted, and how? What, if any, are the ethical lines that should never be crossed, even for a noble cause?

7) In the novel's final act, when Angélique realizes she went too far, she vows to become a good person. Do you think she deserves forgiveness or punishment? Is Angélique a bad person or a good person who has done bad things?

8) Though this is a historical horror, there is also a romance. Angélique fears she doesn't deserve Domingo—or romantic love. Do you agree or disagree? Can Domingo truly love Angélique when he only knows certain parts of her?

9) Angélique believes that every sacrifice she makes is for her sister. Do you agree with her that sometimes we *have* to do things we don't want to do in order to ensure our own safety or quality of life?

10) At the end of the story, we learn that Elodie has not only been eavesdropping on a governess but also has been learning from watching her sister. Did Elodie's confession surprise you? Now that Angélique knows Elodie has followed in her footsteps, what do you think will happen?

ACKNOWLEDGMENTS

This book would not exist without the support of many wonderful people: My fabulous editor, Bria Ragin, whose delightful idea put everything into motion. My brilliant agent, Lauren Abramo, for your wisdom and support. The team at Random House Children's Books, including Wendy Loggia, Trisha Previte, Cathy Bobak, Colleen Fellingham, Tracy Heydweiller, Jenica Nasworthy, and Joey Ho, as well as the cover artist, Colin Verdi. As always, any mistakes are my own.

Much gratitude to Erica Monroe for invaluable feedback on an early draft. Enormous thanks to intrepid assistant Laura Stout for being my right hand in the United States, handling everything I cannot from Costa Rica. Huge thanks go to Amalie, Pintip, Alyssa, and Lacey for your unflagging encouragement and friendship.

Muchísimas gracias to Roy Prendas for being there every step of the way. Te adoro, mi poporico.

And my biggest, most heartfelt thanks go to all of you amazing, marvelous book lovers: readers, reviewers, educators, librarians, booksellers, and anyone who gushes about their latest read or gifts a book to someone else. You are the very, very best.

Thank you for everything!

ABOUT THE AUTHOR

ERICA RIDLEY is a *New York Times* and *USA Today* bestselling author of historical romance and horror novels. When not reading or writing, Erica can be found riding camels in Africa, getting hopelessly lost in the middle of Budapest, or ziplining through rain forests in Costa Rica, where she lives with her husband. *The Protégée* is her first novel for young adults.

ericaridley.com